Praise for
Killer of Enemies
by Joseph Bruchac

"This near future dystopia starring an Apache female superhero has the soul of a graphic novel. . . . Lozen's tactics and weaponry are detailed at length but within a cultural framework that fosters respect for the planet and its surviving natural inhabitants. **A good bet for fans of superhero fiction and graphic novels and readers in search of superpowered female warriors."**
—*Kirkus Reviews*

"What really makes the narrative vibrate is Lozen's sardonic voice, capturing both gallows humor and a very human vulnerability. **Admirers of kick-ass heroines such as Katniss Everdeen will definitely want to see more of Lozen**, and, since Bruchac ends with a pause rather than a period, a sequel is a tantalizing possibility."
—*The Horn Book Magazine*

"**From the moment I opened the cover, I was unable to put the book down.** With the soul of a graphic novel, eloquent and poetically written, this story is anything but just another post-apocalyptic telling. This book not only deserves to be read, but loved and shared by audiences of all ages." —**Patty Stein,** *Urban Native Magazine*

"**This unusual survival story brings a tight, emotionally spare narrative into the often overwrought dystopian genre.** . . . Readers who

prefer their warrior heroines with more battle-hardened sass and less self-reflection will find a lot to love here, as will fans of post-apocalyptic survival stories in less well-worn settings."
—*The Bulletin for the Center of Children's Books*

"A mind-bending fantasy that smashes across genre lines to tell a story about survival, courage, and lots of monsters. **Joseph Bruchac brings serious game. Highly recommended!**"
—**Jonathan Maberry,** *New York Times* **bestselling author of** *Fire & Ash* **and** *Extinction Machine*

"Abenaki author Joseph Bruchac is a masterful storyteller. His young adult speculative fiction novel *Killer of Enemies* affirms this with an imaginative saga set in the not-so-distant future. . . . [A] **novel that both honors Apache tradition and articulates how Native lifeways will always be indispensable.**"
—*Tribal College Journal of American Indian Higher Education*

"[N]ot just a gulp of fresh air, but a **hyperventilating-inducing adrenaline rush.**" —**Diana Pho,** *Beyond Victoriana*

$19.95 | Hardcover | Ages 12 and up | 978-1-62014-143-4
Also available as an e-book
For more resources for both **Killer of Enemies** and **Trail of the Dead**,
see leeandlow.com/books/2832

TRAIL OF THE DEAD

TRAIL OF THE DEAD

Joseph Bruchac

The Second Book of **KILLER OF ENEMIES**

Tu Books

AN IMPRINT OF
LEE & LOW BOOKS, INC.

New York

TU BOOKS, an imprint of LEE & LOW BOOKS Inc.
95 Madison Avenue, New York, NY 10016
leeandlow.com

Manufactured in the United States of America
by Worzalla Publishing Company, September 2015

Cover design by Ben Mautner
Book design by Isaac Stewart
Book production by The Kids at Our House
The text is set in Adobe Garamond Pro

10 9 8 7 6 5 4 3 2 1
First Edition

Cataloging-in-Publication Data is on file with the Library of Congress

This book is dedicated to my grandmothers,
Marion Dunham Bowman and Appolina Hrdlicka Bruchac,
and to all the women in my life who've taught
and continue to teach me the meaning of courage.

CHAPTER ONE
Wind of Breath

The hazy sun has just lifted a hand's width above the horizon. I start down the trail into the narrow canyon where a monster is waiting for me. I'd been warned of its presence an hour ago. The tingling in my palms woke me before dawn. Then I'd sensed its hunger. For us.

I'm about two miles away from the little cave where we sheltered for the night, a fairly safe place shown to me by my father a few months before he was murdered. Two hundred yards up in the rimrock, it's not visible from the trail below, the trail that leads to our destination—Valley Where First Light Paints the Cliffs. Unfortunately, that same route leads right past this valley entrance where that ravenous creature, whatever it is, is waiting.

It's not just the tingling I still can feel in my palms that tells me it's here. I can smell it now. It's a strange, musty odor and not a pleasant one. A little like that of the mega-snake I killed.

What I think of as my hunter's senses have been getting even stronger since we escaped from Haven. My olfactory nerve, in particular, seems to have kicked up a notch—or maybe a few dozen notches. Lately I am surrounded by smells wherever I go. It's like being in the middle of a river of odors always flowing around me. My nose may not yet be as sensitive as that of a dog or a wolf or a coyote, but it's way more than a normal human being.

At times it's a little scary being able to locate everyone I know and care about when they are within a quarter mile of me just by their body odors—which are not always totally pleasant. That has taken some getting used to. Luckily, their everyday scents are usually—not always—sort of pleasing.

Some more than others. Disturbingly so. Always being able to smell the people close to me makes me think about them that much more. My mother, my little brother Victor, my sister Ana, and my . . . ah, friend Hussein. And with those thoughts come the worries. How can I protect them? Can I even protect myself?

They all trust me and expect me to lead them. As if I know exactly what I am doing from one day to the next—aside from trying to get us all to Valley Where First Light Paints the Cliffs.

The thought of that valley brings a brief, bitter smile to my lips. That was where the small community of our people lived for a while until we were discovered. Will we find any of them still there—those who escaped into the hills when my father and uncle were killed and Mom and Ana and Victor and me were taken prisoner?

Valley Where First Light Paints the Cliffs. That was where, for a few brief years, we enjoyed as much peace as anyone could expect nowadays, in the dangerous new world our whole planet became after the Silver Cloud settled in. The Cloud burned or dampened out electricity everywhere on the globe, and the high-tech implants that had transformed the bodies of our highly enhanced overlords from homo sapiens to homo superiorus became unquenchable bonfires, turning the most powerful of our rulers into crispy corpses.

I shake my head.

Stop it, Lozen. Focus on what's now, not what was.

A small whirlwind comes whistling up the canyon, lifting red dust and dried leaves into it. I pull the aviator glasses down over my eyes as it gets closer, but instead of sweeping past, it pauses and begins to move back and forth in front of me. It bobs up and down, changing shape, dancing in a way that seems meant for me.

A real smile comes to my face as I watch it. Uncle Chatto told me that dust devils, as they're sometimes called, are small spirits of the wind, like little children. You sometimes see them chasing each other just like kids playing tag. You should never disrespect them or throw anything at one of them because it will bring you bad luck. But it's a good thing to see one. And it's good, too, to greet them.

The little whirlwind is still dancing back and forth a few yards ahead of me. Its clean aroma is as pleasant as the scent of the earth just before the rain—dried leaves and flower petals. I wait for it to move, but it just stays there. If it had eyes, they would be staring intently at me. It's as if it is waiting for something.

There's a bright yellow aspen leaf on the ground by my feet. It's about as perfect as any leaf can be, glowing golden in the diffused sunlight. I shift the strap of the scoped .308 Winchester on my shoulder, push back the holstered .357 magnum on my right hip so that it doesn't dig into my side, and squat down to pick up the leaf. Then I hold it out in front of me on my open left palm.

The whirlwind bobs back and forth like a top, then spins forward, so close that a bit of its breeze touches my face, almost like the caress of a small hand. Its breath explores my lips and I inhale a small part of it, exhale a bit of my breath back into it before it darts away, the leaf that was on the palm of my hand now a part of its column of circling, dancing air and dust.

"Aho. Thank you, little brother," I say in Chiricahua. "Thank you for the blessing."

And the warning.

It comes to me not with the whirlwind's touch, not with its breath joining my breath. Not in speech or in sound or in any sort of conscious thought that made use of words. It comes in what that whirlwind has just done—divided itself into two identical dust devils. As they whirr their way up the cliff, disappearing from my sight, they've told me something I needed to know.

What's waiting for me in that box canyon is not just one enemy, but two.

CHAPTER TWO

Into the Valley

I've dealt with more than one creature trying to kill me before. I should be able to handle this. First, though, I stand up and face back the way I came. I lift my goggles and scan the expanse of ground I've crossed. My eyesight has grown keener lately, and I can see much farther and much better. Not as well as an eagle or an enhanced One, pre-C, but I can now see distant things almost as well as if I was looking through a ten-power telescopic lens.

No sign of anyone following. The wind is at my back, so the current of scents is not flowing my way, but I am pretty sure I would still be able to smell anyone from our little group if they had followed me. Which is what both Hussein and my determined little sister Ana would have wanted to do. They still might do that if they have noticed I'm gone. That's why I have to take care of these two threats before we set out again on our journey.

Ana, of course, is still a bit too young to help. She can shoot a gun with great accuracy and has been learning how to use a knife. But she is still just a kid, not a grownup like Hussein.

Hussein.

I take a deep breath and let it slowly out. Perhaps if Hussein was fully recovered from the maiming of his hand, I would have let him come along. Or maybe not. My feelings for him are so confusing. I know he wants to be my partner, and I know he's a competent fighter. He keeps surprising me with how much he knows, so much that I sometimes wonder what his life was really like before, back in the pre-C days. I haven't asked yet. He'll tell me himself when he's ready. I trust him—pretty much. And maybe I think that my worrying about him getting hurt might slow me down or make me less effective. Maybe it would have been better if he hadn't joined us on our escape from Haven. Maybe it would be best if I just told him that we can never be more than friends.

I put my mind back on task—turn back to the canyon, hold my hands up in front of me, and use my power.

There, it tells me. *And there.*

Half a mile down into the canyon. On either side of the trail, just waiting. And my power allows me to touch their twin thoughts, thoughts so closely linked that the two are like one being, communicating with each other mind to mind. Not exactly in human words, but my brain can translate what they are thinking.

They know that I am coming and they are feeling smug and pleased about it.

No puny human hurt us.
Puny humans food.
First this one. Grab! Grab, tear apart, swallow.
Then other ones it left.
We leap there fast.
Grab! Grab, tear, swallow.
Good food.

A shiver runs down my spine. Their thoughts are cold, more or less reptilian. When my mind touches that of another creature I can sort of tell something about what it is like, sort of see what it sees. Warm-blooded creatures feel different from reptiles, and bird-things are sort of between the two. And none of the contents of their minds feel like the thought of human beings.

If they were within sight of each other I could even get some idea of what they looked like. But both of them are hidden, even from each other. All I can envision is their twin views of the narrow trail and the big grey boulders to either side.

I sigh and start trudging along. The first lines of this dumb old poem that my father used to recite comes into my mind. It sticks there like a mental burr I can't dislodge, its rhythm matching my steps:

Half a league, half a league,
Half a league onward
All in the valley of Death
Rode the six hundred . . .

And what the hell is a league? Is it longer than a mile or a kilometer? And why can't I think of something more pleasant, such as one of my heavy caliber rounds blowing out the nasty brains of those critters that want me for their brunch?

I need a plan. I don't have one, aside from my usual method of attracting the attention of whatever it is that wants to devour me and then taking it from there.

It's worked so far.

Half a league, half a league,
Half a league onward . . .

This box canyon is a big one, narrow though it may be. I can hear the sound of flowing water from the end of it, still half a mile ahead. Assuming I eliminate the two new enemies waiting eagerly to welcome me, this might make a good place for us to camp for a night or two before pressing onward.

Assuming . . .

The trail is still descending, but more gradually now. As it turns I view the place where I sensed the presence of those two patient predators. I'm close enough to take a shot from here. But all I can see is boulders. Some grey, some brown, some streaked red with iron and green with lichen. Nothing moving. Not even the glint of an eye keeping watch.

I keep watching, counting under my breath.

"One and one pony, two and one pony, three and one pony, four and one pony . . . "

I stop when I get to five hundred. Still no motion among the boulders two hundred yards or so ahead of me, even though my power keeps telling me—through the tingling in my palms—that whatever it is, it is still there.

Damn! Not good.

But I keep waiting. No need to hurry. Haste does not just make waste, it can get you wasted. Plus I am suddenly sensing something else. Not the presence of an enemy. But something or someone.

Hally? I think.

No responding thought. No trapdoor suddenly opening from the earth in front of me to disclose the gorilla-like head of the mysterious giant being that has for some reason taken a shine to me. But what did I expect? Hally has, thus far in my often-endangered life, never turned up when I've been looking for him. Why should that change now?

Still, the presence I'm sensing is not a danger to me, if my power is telling the truth as it always has before. I need to turn my mind to the matter ahead.

Which means playing the parts of both bait and trap.

CHAPTER THREE
Nothing, Nothing, Nothing

I t is not smart to simply dive in headlong. That's another of the things I was taught by my warwise elders, Uncle Chatto and my father. When danger lies ahead, take time to take stock, think about what you are bringing into battle with you, check your weapons.

I take a deep, deep breath and then let it out slowly. Even if I cannot see the enemies lying in wait, I have the advantage of knowing they are there, somewhere. I'm not going to be surprised, not just going along "la-la, la-la, la-laaah" like some innocent little bunny. Be calm, but also don't be clueless. Be ready.

I think about some of the stories Uncle Chatto told about men in his unit who got so amped up on their own nervousness, their blood so flooded with adrenalin that they would completely throw caution to the wind, charge into a hidden minefield and get blown up, or other men who would go through a whole battle and only realize at the end they'd never pumped in a round and had been pulling the trigger on an empty chamber all through a fight. Or who reached for their K-bar knife only to discover they'd forgotten to strap it to their belt.

So what do I have? I have my own knife to begin with, my Tennessee Toothpick. It's one of my favorite weapons. I unbutton the sheath and slide it out, hold it up so that the light is reflected from its carefully polished length, look at its lethal edge. The heft of it in my hand is comforting. It's sharp enough, heavy enough, well balanced enough to chop through a sapling with one swing.

Bueno!

I twirl it once in my hand, delighting in its balance, before sliding it back into the sheath.

Next I pull out my .357, the weapon that has saved my life so many times and terminated the existences of, at my last estimate, eighteen different gemods. I can't count the hours I've spent cleaning and oiling it. I haven't given it a name, like those corny old frontiersmen in the viddys used to do with their firearms. Like Davy Crockett, who called his rifle Betsy.

Anyway, good old un-Betsy, my no-name handgun, is ready to go. All the chambers loaded, I slip it back into its holster.

Then there is my rifle. I smile as I run my finger along the barrel. Perfectly balanced, even with that scope on top of it. Back when I was working for the Ones, the four overlords who ran Haven, especially when I was sent out by Diablita Loca—whose black soul, I am certain, does not rest in peace—it amused them to equip me as lightly as possible. Often I left the former prison with nothing more than my knife and a handgun. It troubled my friend Guy, the one-eyed weapons master at Haven, so much that he would sometimes throw in a little something extra to help me in my task.

But I was seldom given anything like this .308 sniper rifle, which could enable me to hit a target from a safer distance. It's one of the weapons we collected from the battlefield after the fight we survived a week ago, the one that saw the destruction of Diablita Loca and her little army of men, as well as a gemod that seemed to be half buffalo and half mountain.

I check my ammo in the two belts. .308 bullets in the one over my shoulder. The .357s in the belt around my waist, as always—that way there is no chance I might try to jam in a wrong-sized round. That was another thing that Uncle Chatto and my father had cautioned me about. There's no fun like jamming your own weapon that way.

I raise the rifle and scan the trail, look to the left, look to the right. Just as before, all I can see is nothing more threatening than big, rounded boulders. It'd be nice if the two hungry beasts were visible enough for me to shoot them from here. Close quarters hand-to-hand (or hand-to-talon, to be more accurate) combat is for suckers. One of my favorite scenes in the old viddys is the one where Indiana Jones, confronted by a sword-wielding foe challenging him to a duel, just says "Screw it," pulls out his gun, and shoots the dude.

I keep watching as a fly lands on my forehead and walks across my red headband from one side to the other before losing interest and buzzing off. The sun has moved two fingers high in the sky.

Nothing. Still nothing. Aside from that little awareness at the edge of my mind of someone else—not family, not enemy— somewhere not that far away. It's like an itch I can't scratch.

The only way to do it is to do it.

I sigh and stand up. Then, rifle held at the ready in front of me, I begin moving slowly, ever so slowly, down the trail toward the dual ambushers eagerly awaiting my arrival.

Half a league, half a league
Half a league onward . . .

The air has gone completely still. All I am hearing are the sounds of my careful steps and my own breath.

But two of my other senses are making shivers go down

my back. My nose is filled with that strange musty scent. It is warning me my enemies are much, much closer, almost too close. And my sixth sense is making my hands feel as if the rifle I'm holding is getting so hot it is about to burst into flames.

I stop walking. The two big boulders, each about twice the size of an elephant on either side of the trail, are no more than fifty feet away. I can't see what is behind them. And there's no way around them, the way the smooth, narrow walls of the canyon have closed in at this choke point. No way am I going any farther.

I stare at those two boulders.

And that is when one of them opens a gigantic eye and stares back at me.

CHAPTER FOUR

A Rock With Eyes

I t's funny how thought can move so much faster than anything else. Before I can even tighten my finger on the trigger a whole host of thoughts have whizzed through my mind, including these:

A rock with eyes?

Wait a minute, that is not a rock at all.

It's a monster, which means the other boulder is monster numero dos.

Lozen, you are so stupid. Muy estúpida!

Don't you remember what ambush predators do? They just sit still and wait for their prey to come to them.

Remember that buffalo gemod you killed with the rocket launchers just last week. Remember how it looked like a little hill until it finally moved.

Lozen, you are so stupid.

What if this thing gets you? What will happen to Mom and Victor and Anna? And Hussein. Hussein.

Do something, stupid!

Do something!

All those thoughts and way more are crowding my brain, but not slowing my reflexes. I'm bringing the rifle up, swinging it toward that one unblinking eye.

But fast as I am, the gemod is faster. Not that it moves its whole body. No, it doesn't have to. Instead, a huge mouth below that eye suddenly opens, almost too quickly to see, and something long and pink is spat out and comes shooting like a rocket toward me.

It's a frigging tongue!

It hits me with a sticky splat, wraps around my rifle, and jerks it back into its mouth, which closes again as quickly as it opened. I've almost been knocked off my feet, but I regain my balance and reach down, not for my .357, but with my left hand for my Bowie knife.

Shocked and surprised as I was at first, as the rifle was taken I moved into the zone where everything fast around me seems to have become slow. And that is why I can see the second creature, which I now know isn't a boulder but some sort of immense stone-skinned toad, open its mouth and shoot its forty-foot-long tongue, as thick as my thigh, toward me. And as I watch it come toward me in slow motion, I step aside, swing down the heavy sharp blade, and chop right through the creature's sticky appendage. Blood spurts from it as it falls, as flaccid as a deflated balloon.

"ROOWWWKKK!" An angry pained croak bursts out of its mouth as the second toad beast pushes itself up on legs that had been concealed beneath its body, both red-veined eyes open as it prepares to leap.

BLAM-BLAM!

BLAM-BLAM!

The four shots fired in double bursts from the .357 in my right hand all strike home, two in each of the second monster's eyes, and it thuds over on its side, its feet jerking in a death spasm. One enormous hind leg comes so close to me as it thrusts out that I have to dodge and roll to one side.

It's good that I've done that. Having all your bones broken by an immensely overgrown amphibian is never good for one's health. But there's a downside to my duck-and-dive maneuver. It means I have lost sight of the late Mr. Toad's equally malevolent mate. I come up to my feet with my back thudding against the side of the narrow canyon wall. Not hard enough to stun me or knock the wind out of me, but enough to give me a jolt that knocks my favorite pair of aviator glasses askew. It takes me half a second to straighten them, get my bearings, and turn to point my .357 toward the place where the first rock-like critter had been squatting when it stuck its tongue out at me in such an impolite way.

It's not there. Just an empty space in the piles of smaller stones that have been dislodged by its departure. The other expiring creature is still on its back, twitching, belly-up toward the silvered sky.

But where is its mate? Did it leap over me? I turn and look. Nope. Has it gone around the bend deeper into the box canyon?

I can hear the distant dripping of water in the ominous silence that has settled around me. Then I feel a familiar warmth in my hands, and as I hold up my left hand, my power directs me toward where my adversary has gone.

I look up, and there it is. Its feet must be like immense suction cups, because it has either leaped or climbed halfway up the sheer, smooth cliffside. It's a good hundred feet above me, stuck to the wall, head facing down.

But the way it is staring down at me with those cold, red-veined eyes, it is not trying to escape. The cold thought that suddenly enters my mind like an icy spear leaves no doubt about its intentions.

Crush! Crush puny human.
Then eat good food.

I seem to be as doomed as doomed can be.

CHAPTER FIVE

Duck, Lass

I'm attempting to take aim at one of its eyes, but that's not easy. The intractable amphibian has just turned its head slightly to the side. There's plenty else to aim at. It is way broader than the side of a barn. But if its skin is as tough as the rocks it resembles, my bullets might glance off or not penetrate enough to make any real impression on it.

I try to move my feet to get a better angle and suddenly realize that my left foot has become wedged between a couple of stones. It shouldn't be hard to work my foot free, but I can't do it with just one quick tug.

No time to waste. I have to try to take a shot and hope it'll result in something other than my own demise. As my finger begins to take up the slack on the trigger I sense that presence I'd felt before. Much nearer now.

"DUCK, LASS!" a voice shouts from somewhere back up the canyon behind me.

21

It's so familiar that I should know whose voice it is. No time to waste on vocal recognition, though. I drop into a low crouch.

WHOOOOSH!

I know that sound and I'm not surprised by what I see out of the corner of one eye at almost that same instant—a fiery arc that whizzes toward Toadus Giganticus Numero Uno. It's a rocket-propelled grenade.

WHOMP!

It doesn't just knock the monster off the wall of the cliff and kill it, it also blasts it forward just far enough so that most of its massive parts, now landing all along the trail, do not fall onto yours truly.

With the exception of an unpleasant mass of its far-from-empty intestines that come flopping down around me and on top of me like coils of odiferous rope.

SPLAT-SPLAT-SPLAT-SPLAT!

Ugghhh!

I've been knocked to my knees. Aside from my being alive, another positive result of the monster toad's being blown up real good is that the lubrication of what just engulfed me has made it possible for me to free my foot. But I am still trapped. I have to fight my way out, spitting stuff from my mouth, shaking it off my arms, waist deep in rubbery, disgusting viscera.

Why is it that monster killing ends up so often with me buried in guts or mud or bird doo-doo or whatever?

But I suppose that is an uncharitable thought, because right now I should just be feeling grateful toward the one who saved me. Who I am certain I will see after I wipe this final glop of toad poop from the lenses of my glasses.

There he is, coming down the trail, the just-fired AT-4 still on his shoulder, a grin on his scarred one-eyed face. It's my oldest friend and best ally from my years of servitude as the monster slayer for the Ones of Haven, the one who took the place of my father and my Uncle Chatto as much as any human being every could.

I'm still on my knees, the rocks around me so slippery with toad-guts that it's hard to stand. I holster my gun as he approaches, push my glasses back up onto my forehead, thinking I probably look like a raccoon with my face all covered with gunk apart from my eyes.

I want to say something, but my voice is failing me. There's a lump in my throat that has nothing to do with the toad offal I've just spat out. And my mind is overflowing with questions.

When did Guy leave Haven?

What's gone on back there since we escaped? How did he find me?

And how the heck did he show up at just the right minute to save me from being turned into an unfriendly amphibian's break-fast pancake?

"Good t' see you, lass," he says as he sets the single-shot

rocket launcher aside, hops nimbly over a boulder, and holds out a hand to help me up. Then he wipes the slime he's just picked up from my palm off on his khaki pants and grins. "Though I cannae say I approve of yer choice of body lotion."

I don't waste time trying to make an equally sardonic reply.

"Guy!" I say, my voice somewhere between a laugh and a sob.

I wrap both arms around him, press my cheek against his broad chest and squeeze him so hard it makes his ribs crack.

"I guess," he says, "we're both gonna be in need of a bath, little Lozen."

But there's a catch in his voice, too, as he says that. Then he wraps his own arms around me and we both just stand there for a while.

CHAPTER SIX

The Pool

finally take a deep breath and lean back to look up into Guy's scarred, strong face.

"Guy," I say.

" 'Tis me I am," he says, his voice dead serious.

I make a fist with my right hand and hammer him hard in the chest.

"Where?" I say.

I punch him again.

"How? How?"

Guy just looks at me, dead serious, as my blows—which would have knocked down most men—bound with a thud off his broad chest. After all, among other things, he used to be a middleweight boxer. Then he nods. He understands what I am asking.

It was often that way between him and me. No need to use

long sentences when so much was understood between us, an understanding that, perhaps, could only be shared between two people whose job it was to remove the gemod creatures that threatened all of our existence. That was my main task in life, it seemed, even after my escape from Haven. And it had been Guy's before he'd lost his eye and earned those scars taking out a beast that cost more than two dozen human lives before he terminated it.

Where have you been? That was the verbose version of my first question. How did you get here and how did you find me right now? Those were my second and third ones.

We have some serious catching up to do.

Guy grins. "Wash first," he says, pointing down the canyon. "Water, I hear."

Water. It's something we're always short of these days. Without electricity to power the pumps that used to bring it up from the deep aquifers, the dry land around has become even dryer. And it rains even less now since the Silver Cloud came. Most of the springs that my father told me used to flow along the trail through this dying land have disappeared. That's another reason we're heading for the valley that was our former home. The spring there flowed strong and steady. Just thinking of it reminds me how dry and parched I am feeling. Water.

The two of us follow the trail till we come to the canyon's end a few hundred yards farther. There, a small trickle coming out of the cliff has formed a pair of pools beneath it. The first little pool at the top is inviting, as clear as crystal. But the one below it is not. A pool some fifty feet wide, created by stones rolled together and then sealed with mud and twigs almost like a beaver's dam, its waters are rank.

"Oh my golly," I say as I looked down into its shallow, clouded water.

"Aye," Guy says. "Seems we got here just in time."

What we are looking at and shaking our heads about is proof once again of the falseness of the claims made by our old planetary overlords that the nightmare creatures they created for their amusement were incapable of reproduction. The pool, obviously created by the pair—a breeding pair—of giant toad beasts, is filled with gelatinous ropy strands. Each strand is loaded with eggs that are already developing into tadpoles that will grow to be copies of their parents. Black eyes look up at us, small mouths opening and closing as if the nascent monsters are already imagining the taste of our flesh. Even assuming only one in ten of them might survive, this pool is meant to be the launching point for hundreds of horrors like their parents.

I look at Guy and nod toward the dam of rocks. He nods back at me.

We fill our canteens from the first pool, drink until our throats are no longer so dry we can hardly talk. Then, after we fill our canteens again, we set to work. I block the slow trickle of water out of the first pool, and then help Guy remove enough stones from the barrier dam to drain the lower one. By the time the sun has lifted another two hands to the sky, we are done. The long, ropy masses are drying in the heat of the desert sun, the half-formed tadpoles within them no longer moving. The way the sun shines down, its light still bright, its heat unaffected by the silvered sky, seems to be an approval of our actions. After all, long ago, it was the Father Sun who finally agreed that the destruction of the ancient monsters by the Hero Twins was the right way to bring balance to the world.

Guy nods again at the first pool. After our sweaty work I can't think of anything better to do. I put my knife, my bandoliers, my goggles, and my holstered gun down on a flat rock, looking over at Guy.

"You first, lass. I'll stand by." He pats his own gun, a .44 magnum that hangs in a holster under his left arm.

I nod, grateful that I can wash off the grim, still smelly reminder of the battle I just survived with his help. Grateful, too, to have an ally by my side who is wise and careful to know that even after defeating enemies, one should never totally let down one's guard. He'll keep watch while I bathe, and then I'll do the same for him.

I slip off my boots. Then, still wearing my socks and the rest of my clothing that are as filthy as I am, I walk in up to my knees and let myself fall backward into the bathtub-sized pool of cool, healing water.

CHAPTER SEVEN

Explanations

We are making our way up the trail that leads out of the canyon on our way back to my family. The words from a mid-twenty-first century viddy that my father used to watch are going through my mind. It was a show called *Dolly Did It*, and it starred a silly Latina actress and her patient English husband.

"Dolly," her husband was always saying to her after she had gotten into the sort of trouble that Coyote does in our old tales, "you do have some explaining to do."

Explaining, for sure. I pause and rest my hand on one of the lichen-blotched black stones—a real stone and not some monstrous anthropophagus amphibian.

"Guy," I say.

"Lass?"

"How?" I swing my hand out in a gesture that takes on our

surroundings and ends with me tapping my chest.

He nods, understanding the question. *How did he find me here?*

Then he chuckles. It's a deep, reassuring sound, totally recognizable in that even when he chuckles, it seems to be with a Scottish accent. It's something, I realize, that I have missed hearing. It also brings a pang to my heart because it also makes me realize how much I miss my father. As much as anyone can in this life, Guy had become a surrogate father, someone I both trusted and cared for, gradually becoming certain he felt the same way about me.

Guy. My former supervisor and the supplier of the lethal tools that saved my life so many times. And now he's shown up to do just that in person.

"Long story?" Guy asks, holding his hands apart as wide as his broad shoulders and then bringing them close together. "Or short?"

"Short first."

" 'Twas obvious where ye might be heading. The valley where they first found you, eh?"

I nod. That makes sense.

But how did you locate me here in this valley right now? I think.

"Well, lass, it seems what ye got is contagious," he says in answer to my thought.

"Hunh?"

My reply is not exactly brilliant and it brings a twinkle to Guy's eye. He lifts his right hand and taps his forehead with one of his gnarled fingers, a finger broken more than once during his years of cage fighting.

"In here," he says.

I almost repeat my former clueless response when it comes to me. First my realization of what he means followed by absolute proof in the form of a wordless, silent voice that I sort of hear or feel—though it's actually neither sense—in my head.

Aye.

I shouldn't be that surprised. After all, Guy's not the first to intentionally send me a message from mind to mind. First was my highly hirsute overgrown ape-man buddy Hally. Then the Dreamer and then Hussein.

Jeez, who next? I think.

"Aye," Guy says aloud. "Who, indeed?"

I try to answer him, thought to thought.

Not who, I think. *What? What happened at Haven after we escaped?*

But it doesn't work this time. I don't reach him. Guy just looks at me, not replying in either spoken words or a transmission of thoughts. There is no pain, not even the small prickling sensation I'm more used to nowadays, now that I've been practicing this ability.

I'm not surprised. Thus far Hally is the only being with whom I've been able to carry on anything like a sustained conversation that way. With everyone else, it's only been a few words or a feeling. And I'm grateful for that. The thought of an ongoing head-to-head conversation with the Dreamer, even though I no longer think of him as evil, would be way too strange. And with Hussein it would be too intimate . . . or too embarrassing. I'm still trying to control—as least outwardly—my feelings about him. There's no room in my life for romance right now.

So I shift to the more conventional mode of interrogation.

"What happened?" I say to Guy, holding my hands palm up, spreading them to the side and then looking back over my shoulder.

"Chaos," he says. " 'Twas not just those wee explosions of yours—nicely done, by the by—but what came after among the Four. The Dreamer locked himself in and neither the Jester nor Lady Time seemed to know what to do. So Diablita took charge. Fewer of her men were hurt, and she pulled as many as she could from the ranks of our other two weakened overlords. Then she and her small army set out for you vowing to bring back your head. And not longer after she left, so did we."

We? I think. Somehow I suspect Guy is not using the royal pronoun. Who is with him? I'm about to ask that when Guy asks a question of his own.

"They found you?"

I nod.

"So?" he says, looking hard at me.

"It didn't go so well . . . for them."

"*All* of them?"

I feel myself blushing as I nod.

"But it wasn't just me," I say. "I had a lot of help."

Guy raises an eyebrow. He's not going to let me leave it at just that. So, as best I can, I recount what happened. It's an explanation that in any other world or time would seem too fantastic to believe. I mean, having Bigfoot as an ally. But I start with the part that is more logical, about the role that Hussein, despite his damaged hand, was able to play.

And realize I may be blushing even more as I talk about him. So I shut my yap.

"Fine lad, that one," Guy says. "But go on."

I take a breath and describe the ambush I'd set and how the unexpected presence of a giant gemod buffalo wiped out most of Diablita's men and almost cooked my own goose in the process before the rocket launchers I salvaged turned it into a giant barbecue.

"Buffalo?" Guy raises both eyebrows. "Fine meat, that."

It brings a smile to my face. For a moment the two of us are sharing the memories of the way most of my past missions to destroy monsters had ended—with me bringing back the gemod meat, which Guy and I would share.

"Would have been," I say, "but there wasn't anything to salvage after the fire."

"Too bad. But again, go on."

This is the hard part for me. Even though I'd come out the victor in both cases, it isn't pleasant for me to think back about the two human—real humans, evil though though they might have been—whose lives I have ended. But I tell Guy about my hand-to-hand combats with first Edwin and then Diablita and he listens quietly. Then, when I am done, he still says nothing. He just puts his hand on my shoulder as we sit there.

We are on a ledge of rock that faces west, away from the direction of Haven and in the direction of the valley where the scouts sent out by the Ones found me, killed my father and uncle, and brought my sister and brother and mother and me back as their prisoners. A cactus wren is singing from a clump of mesquite and a red-tailed hawk is circling overhead, the fan of its tail as red as the sun used to be. Except for the disused ribbon of highway below us, its crumbling pavement beginning to make its way back into the earth, and the silver sheen of the sky, it might be six hundred or six thousand years ago. No drones whistling through the air, no sounds of machines of any kind. Peaceful.

But it is not peaceful within me.

I need something. Well, not just one something. I need to find a place where we will all be as safe as any group of people might be these days, now that humans are as much the hunted as the hunters. But I need something else. I need some way to restore the balance within me so that I don't feel like I have some small animal trapped inside me trying to gnaw its way out of my guts.

I may appear outwardly calm, in control, strong, self-certain—and lethal to my enemies. And in a way I am. I'm still prepared to respond to any threat to my family. But I have this sick feeling within and I don't know what is causing it. I look over at Guy. His outward scars show how much he's gone through in his life. I don't have scars like his, not on the outside.

"Lass?" Guy says. It makes me realize I have just been sitting here, seemingly staring off into space but actually looking at the darkness I can feel inside me, for a long time. The sun has moved a hand's width across the sky.

"Okay," I say, as if nothing had just happened. "I guess we're all caught up."

Guy shakes his head. "Na."

"Na?" I echo.

"Not all of us," he says.

He is referring to the unanswered question my self-centered

musing took my mind away from. Exactly who was the *we* he had mentioned?

"You're not alone," I say.

"Far from alone," says a cultured voice from behind us.

It's a familiar voice and so, when I turn, I am not surprised at who I see standing there.

CHAPTER EIGHT

At Your Service

I might have jumped when that voice spoke up from behind us. But I had already been sensing a presence approaching us for the last minute or two, sensing it and recognizing it, but distracted enough by my thoughts that I hadn't paid it mind.

I look up at the unusually tall, elegant figure who executes a theatrically sardonic bow as soon as my eyes take him in. A half smile is visible on the exposed, unflawed part of his partially masked face.

"At your service, my efficient little assassin," the Dreamer says. "As are our ladies."

Our ladies?

Man, everybody wants to get into the act! Making me the involuntary ringmaster of an ever-expanding traveling circus.

The Dreamer raises his hand high above his head and beckons to the people he's just mentioned, their presence concealed till now by the curve in the trail.

Two women walk out into view. One of them, of course, is Lorelei. Rather than the blood-red sheath dress and high heels I've always seen her in before, she's wearing a loose-fitting military camouflage uniform and sensible hiking boots and her honey-blonde hair is tied back in a ponytail rather than piled high on her head. But it is unmistakably her. No one else has that tall willowy shape or that paper-white face, and I've never seen another woman who moves with that sort of grace. It's almost like watching the flow of smoke.

When she nods and smiles at me, though, there's nothing in her expression that is distant or superior—as there always was when she and the Dreamer were playing their roles back in Haven. Instead, her expression is almost wistful, like that of a teenage girl hoping to be accepted by a new group of possible friends.

"Lozen," she says in her musical voice, pressing her palms together in front of her. "I am so glad to see you."

I think she really means it. But I don't say anything in return. I just nod to her and turn my focus on the second woman.

I've seen her before, but where? Then it comes to me. In the armory! She was one of Guy's young apprentices, much younger than me, almost as young as Ana. She's the one who never talked and was always hanging back. Medium height, wide-shouldered and stocky, her face was often covered by a welding mask as she worked—nondescript, never in the foreground. Her raven-colored hair is hacked short, her arms and hands blackened from the work of repairing and readying weaponry. As soon as I recognize her I realize I've also heard her name before, spoken by Guy—who seemed to be the only one who ever spoke to her, now that I think of it. I've remembered her name because it seemed so unlikely for one who seemed to always hover in the darkness: Luz, Spanish for light.

She raises a hand, one with a palm stained with years of working with gun oil and explosives. Her broad, strong-looking fingers appear to each have been broken one time or another.

I like her already.

Hola, she mouths, then grins shyly, displaying teeth that are perfectly shaped and white as pearls.

Hola, I mouth back to her.

"So, my small and deadly friend. Might one assume that you are willing to accept us into your ranks?"

I look up at the Dreamer. I've seen the real person behind that mask, seen him to be a truly human being, a person with compassion who hid his heart in order to survive. To live and survive among monsters, one must seem to be a monster himself.

But that supercilious and superior tone of his does a good

job of hiding whatever sincerity there might be in the words he's just spoken. Continually playing a role, it seems, is as much a part of him as his height—a head taller than any other human I've ever met.

Then, as he did once before, he surprises me. He drops to one knee and holds out his hand. "Please," he says in a voice that is little more than a whisper. "We do need your help, Lozen."

And what other answer can I give?

"Yes," I say with as heavy sigh.

Guy chuckles as he steps forward and claps a hand on Luz's broad shoulder.

"We brought a few things with us, did we not, Luz."

"Si," she says, turning and pointing with her lips toward the base of the trail.

I step forward and look over her shoulder. No kidding!

"Go, lass, take a closer look."

I lope down the trail, the others who follow behind me momentarily forgotten. The things Guy mentioned are piled, quite carefully cushioned with blankets, in what used to be called a donkey cart, back when there were such four-footed beasts of burden. Although this particular donkey cart is about twice as long and wide and deep as the standard ones, more like something that should be pulled by a big horse. As a result it holds a whole lot of . . . useful things.

I reach out reverently to pick up one, and then another, to heft and look over its sights before putting it back down. I run my hands over the boxes upon boxes labeled with names of the manufacturers. I pick up one emblazoned with the words BLACK HILLS AMMUNITION.

"Fine source, that one, for obsolete calibers. 44.40, 38 Long Colt, .44 Russian," Guy says.

I step back and put my hands on my hips. It appears as if Guy has brought with him a major part of Haven's armory. Hand guns and long guns of all different sizes with their requisite ammunitions, as well as special treats such as that .84 caliber AT-4 Guy used to blast Mr. Toad.

"Thank you," I say, the grin on my face so wide that I feel as if my cheeks are about to split.

"Don't mention it," Guy replies.

With all that weight of ordinance, the cart must weigh a ton. Even on wheels it has to be no easy chore to pull it. I am about to ask who will do that, maybe two of us at a time taking turns. But before I can say another word, to my surprise, the Dreamer strides forward. He places himself between the twin shafts of the cart, grasps them, and lifts as if with no effort at all.

"Shall we proceed?" he asks.

Lorelei looks up at him with a smile as she reaches out to place a hand on his arm. Not pulling herself, but ready to walk

41

beside him as if the two of them were out for a stroll in some country garden out of an old viddy.

I look over at Guy.

"The man pulled it all the way here from Haven," Guy says, shaking his head. "Would nae let a one of us lend a hand."

The Dreamer tilts his head in my direction to look down at me through his mask with that one bright eye of his.

"If you would be so kind as to lead the way so that one might follow?" he says.

My, my. At my service indeed.

CHAPTER NINE
Little Wound

Jussst how many have you killed?"

Luther Little Wound thought of ignoring that question. He didn't like the haughty tone of her hissing voice. It annoyed him. He'd killed for less.

Instead, he lifted his chin to look up—though not that far up, for his own height was more than that of most men—at the masked face turned over an elegant shoulder to look back at him.

How many?

He mentally counted the numbers painted on that circular mask, a clock face hiding a scarred human countenance.

Then he added all up those numbers from one through twelve. One plus two is three. Three plus three is six, plus four is ten and so on all the way up to seventy-eight.

More than that, was his thought. But he didn't voice it.

"Enough," Luther said, his voice as devoid of emotion as the ticking of the clocks that filled the room. Clocks hung on every wall, other clocks resting on tables or standing on their own. In another fifteen minutes the room would be filled with not just their ticking but the sounds of their bells announcing the hour. He planned to be gone before then.

Lady Time turned the rest of her body toward him, raised her hands, and glided closer.

"Ah, and how many times have you died?"

"You know my name."

A thin, sibilant sound that might have been a laugh came from the mouth hidden behind the hole in the mask where full red lips had been painted.

"Yessss. Four Deaths, you are called. And each of those who killed you, who thought you were truly dead, you then returned to kill."

Slowly, he thought.

Slowly, painfully, and with the greatest satisfaction on his part as they looked at him imploringly and begged for death— while they still had eyes to see and tongues to speak. But, as before, he said nothing.

Instead, he cocked his head and held out his right hand in a gesture that conveyed a measure of politeness.

"Business?" he asked.

Another of those reptilian laughs issued from Lady Time's concealed and ravaged mouth. "Busssinesss, yesss. Of courssse.

I was told you were all busssiness, to the point. Come."

Luther followed as she glided—almost as if on wheels rather than the feet hidden by her long gown—toward the back of the room where the cacophony of clocks was even louder. As she moved, the servants who had been standing at attention behind her hurried to get out of her way.

One of them was a small hunched man whose sunken lips indicated a lack of teeth. No teeth—a strange thing indeed. In the decades before the Cloud, the new vaccines had made it possible that everyone—those who survived the necessary culling, including the lowest castes—had perfect teeth, free from all the agents of decay. It made no sense to lose an investment in a worker due to poor health. As soon as Luther noticed him, the toothless little man turned his head away—but not before Luther caught sight of a look on the man's face that was a strange blend of terror and hatred. A dangerous mix of emotions.

I'd kill that one if he was mine, Luther thought. But, as always, he kept his thoughts to himself.

Lady Time was speaking. He supposed he should be listening to her, half mad as she clearly was. Then again, all of those who used his services tended to be at least half insane. Part of it, he supposed, was a result of the maiming they'd experienced with the coming of the Cloud when their implants had melted away, taking bones and flesh with them. Once again he thought how fortunate he was that none of the changes that had made his own body so well suited to his profession had involved electronic adaptations of any kind, not even nanobots.

But just as much of their craziness was a result of their loss of another kind of power—that which had enabled them to rule with total impunity. Those who had survived the meltdown of their enhancements, at least. Luckily, ruling had never been one of Luther's goals. Simple power over life and death was quite enough for him, as long as there was enough death involved and his task of accomplishing such termination was challenging enough to make it interesting.

Which was why he was here.

He had travelled several hundred miles south from the site buried in a mountain where the Primaries, his usual overlords, had received a message delivered by a runner—the only surviving messenger of a dozen sent out from Haven—asking for assistance. It had amused Luther's Primaries and thus, more from that feeling of amusement than any real desire to strengthen an alliance, the decision had been made to send him.

It was a turn of events that greatly pleased him. The recent months had been unchallenging. The only thing that ever truly bothered Luther was boredom. Merely killing overmatched men in combats staged for the pleasure of his overlords was too easy, even when those men were given edged weapons and he used only his hands and feet—and teeth. He did appreciate the taste of warm, flowing blood.

He focused his attention back on his new employer.

" . . . so you can sssee, I am sure," Lady Time was saying, "why it issss important to me that you accomplish this tasssk?"

"Yes," he said.

"Good." Lady Time held out an article of clothing. A torn brown shirt. "Thisss was hersss. Taken from her cell. Iss enough?"

Luther took the garment. The air was filled with Lady Time's heavy perfume. Likely meant to suggest flowers, its odor conveyed nothing more than decaying flesh to Luther's sensitive nose, which held, thanks to genetic tinkering, as many olfactory sensory neurons as those of a wolf. However, despite the rank perfume—which had made him nearly gag when first entering the room—he immediately picked up another scent from the shirt in his hands. It was a pleasing one, suggestive not just of healthy sweat, but of wood smoke and desert soil. He held the shirt closer to his face, breathed in more deeply. Few of those he was set in pursuit of ever smelled as good as this.

"Enough?" Lady Time asked again.

Luther nodded. More than enough. All he had to do was get within a few miles of his prey or a place where she'd left a scent trail. From then on it would be easy. He could borrow the sight and will of a bird—crows or hawks were his preference—and send it circling into the sky in widening gyres until it located his prey.

"You know what I want?"

Luther nodded a second time. It was what they all wanted, what he had been designed to provide.

She held out a heavy plastic bag, one gaudily covered with a design of clocks that Luther immediately planned to bury at the bottom of his backpack.

"Her head in here."

A third nod. But then he felt the need of at least one question, just to make sure.

"The others?"

"Jussst kill them. Traitorsssss. Kill them all. Kill everyone with her. Kill them, kill them, kill them!" Lady Time's hands trembled as her voice rose to nearly a shriek.

Luther didn't even need to nod to that.

Of course. That was what he was planning to do anyway.

"Now, now . . ." Lady Time whispered. " Now, now . . ."

Her voice had become calmer, more rational—though never lacking that edge of madness. It was not easy for Luther to tell if she was speaking to herself or to him, so he said nothing. As always, he was ready for anything, including the unfortunate necessity of killing this mad woman—and her several attendants—should she slip into an irrationality too deep.

Such things had happened before. They didn't worry him.

She clapped her hands twice. The hunched little man rushed back into the room—like a lizard frightened out from under a rock.

"Yesmylady," he said, his words, slurred by his lack of teeth, as tightly compressed as his high, terrified voice, his hands trembling.

"Walter . . ." she said, then allowed a dramatic pause, which resulted in the little man's hands shaking even harder.

"Yesmylady, yesmylady!"

"Show him what you made, what we have for him."

The little man scuttled sideways, never taking his eyes off Lady Time as he did so, until he came to the object that Luther had noticed as soon as he entered the room. It was the size of a couch with a tall back, perhaps a throne, though the circular protrusions around it, discernable even under the cloth that covered it, suggested something else. A wagon, perhaps?

"SHOW HIM!"

The little man named Walter grasped the cloth and pulled so hard that the cloth came whipping back over him, tangling around his body and tripping him so that he fell on his side . . . painfully, from the sound of head and elbow hitting the floor.

But neither Lady Time nor Luther Little Wound paid any attention to her clumsy, terrified clockworker as he struggled to right himself. They ignored him as they approached the gleaming, three-wheeled object before them.

"You like it?" Lady Time hissed.

Luther ran his hands over it. The cool feel of the metal, its hard certainty, appealed to him. It seemed a mirror of his own controlled emotions. He wasn't sure he liked the insignia embossed on its side, a somewhat garishly rendered LT, but everything else? Ah. Perfect.

The metal on the side of the bike had been polished until it shone. Its surface was just like a mirror. He could see himself in it and was pleased at what he saw. It reflected back to him his broad face with its high cheekbones and firm jaw, his close-set eyes shaded by heavy black brows that joined in the center, the thick inky hair that framed that expressionless face, a single stray curl falling down in the center of his forehead. He reached his right hand up and ran it back through his hair, a gesture he did more often than he thought.

He slid into the saddle, the springs giving way under his considerable weight and pressing back up as if welcoming him. It had clearly been made for a big man, and that pleased him. He wrapped his fingers around the handlebars. It had been a long time—before the coming of the Cloud—since he had done something like this, felt something like this beneath him.

There'd be no roar of an engine, not from a vehicle driven by clockwork rather than internal combustion, but when he released the catch, gears would turn and it would move, pick up speed, and he would feel the wind in his face, race with the wind.

"How fast?"

"Walter!"

The little man, blood running down his face from his temple hitting the floor, limped over to them.

"Fiftysirmaybesixty," he slurred, wiping the blood from his

eyes and trying to stand up straight. Then, seeing he was being ignored again, he quickly moved back. It was only when out of the sight of his mistress, but still visible in Luther's enhanced peripheral vision, that his servile look turned into a stare of absolute loathing.

Useful though he might be, Luther thought, *I would definitely kill that one if he was mine.*

He turned his attention back to the new vehicle that would make his profession so much easier, leaned back to affectionately pat the side of the clockwork motorcycle as if it was a horse.

"It is yoursss for now," Lady Time said.

Of course it is, Luther thought, the wide grin on his face fully displaying his sharpened predator's teeth. *And not just for now.*

Lady Time nodded. With an imperious gesture, she tossed him a white armband, which he caught and fastened about his right bicep in a graceful movement that was almost, but not quite arrogant. Rather like the dutiful bow he gave to her, one hand on his heart, the other hand swung off to the side.

Lady Time stared at him through her mask. Finally, she gestured toward the door. Her audience with him was done, as far as she was concerned.

But Luther had one more question to ask. And while others might hesitate to be so bold as to continue a conversation after an overlord was ready to terminate it, he was not one of those. He knew two things about himself: his uniqueness made him valuable—invaluable—and his abilities, the twin facts that he was so hard to kill and found killing such an easy thing to do, made him someone that even an Overlord might fear.

And with good reason. He had already halfway made his mind up to add another head, one with a masked face, to that convenient bag Lady Time had just given him.

"Ah," he said, raising one of his hands, a hand as big as the front paw of a grizzly bear.

"Yesss," Lady Time hissed, unable to either hide the annoyance in her voice or to ignore that large hand with its lethal capabilities held up in front of her face. "What?"

"What about the other Overlord? Has he no part in this? I thought the two of you were the . . . Ones in charge."

Lady Time nodded. "A good question, yess. I may wish to ssspeak with you about that One when you return. But he has made planssss of hisss own."

Then she explained what those plans were.

An interesting strategy, Luther had to admit. A bit crude, but it might be effective. However, it was also a plan that would not interfere with his own task if he was swift enough about it.

CHAPTER TEN

A Dream

I wake up the way I always do. I don't move my body, even though the dream that I just experienced was a deeply disturbing one. I listen first. All I hear are the sounds of breathing from the sleepers around me, each inhalation and exhalation of breath so distinctive that I can tell one person from another. My mother, Victor, Ana, Hussein, Luz, Lorelei, the Dreamer—who is actually snoring.

Then I open my eyes just a little, just enough to look around. It's easy enough to do because I didn't lie down to sleep. I just leaned back against one of the wooden roof braces to the right of our fire and wrapped my blanket around me.

Again there is nothing for me to worry about. All I see are the figures sleeping around the fire. The only one not there is Guy, who is standing sentinel. He's not visible, hidden as he is in the shadows at the mouth of the shallow mineshaft dug in the side of the arroyo where we've set up our temporary camp. But I can feel him there.

My heart is racing, as if I had actually just been running and not just dreaming that I was sprinting as fast as possible. No matter how hard I ran I could not reach the place where a dark figure—a large man—leaned like a giant cat over my bound and gagged little brother, knife gleaming in his hands as he began to skin Victor alive.

I rub my hands together, hold them up. No flow of warmth comes to them. Nor do I pick up thoughts from anyone—or any thing. No enemy is close enough to be an immediate threat. But that dream was too real to be anything less than a warning. I trust my dreams. Somewhere, sometime—all too soon, in fact—I will meet that dark figure in the waking world. And if the intensity of my dream is any measure, he may be the worst human enemy I have yet to face. But not at this moment, and not in my dreams again this night. I've slept enough for now.

It's not the middle of the night. Dawn will soon be coloring the horizon, shadows running across the land. I can hear from outside the first stirring of the birds that will soon fly up into the sky to greet the new day with their songs. Even though the sky is different, their ancient avian melodies have not changed. There's still much to love about this life we're living. Perilous as our existence may be, my family and I are freer than we ever were under the rule of the Ones.

What was it Uncle Chatto used to say? All we can count on is one day at a time, one breath at a time.

My heart has slowed, that dream has faded. Not gone nor forgotten, but put aside for now. One day at a time. This day.

I slip off the blanket, feel the comforting presence of the Bowie knife on my left hip, the holstered .357 on my right. I take a moment to fold the blanket twice, roll it up, and place it to the side. A rolled blanket is faster to pack, and tangled blankets can trip your feet when you try to move fast. I stand and make my way silently to the place where Guy is standing to the left of the mouth of the shaft and the donkey cart filled with weaponry, which we placed strategically to block the entrance.

Quiet as I am, he has heard me coming. Without turning in my direction, he holds his fist out toward me and we bump knuckles.

"Nothing?" I whisper.

Guy chuckles. "Naught but a wee coyote pup come up to sniff me boot. Luz was taking a turn watching with me then. And it bounced over like it wanted to play with her. Made her laugh."

I smile at the thought of that. Normal animals—not the genetically modified freaks that are the awful legacy of our former planetary rulers—seem to trust Guy almost as much as they do me. It's not at all unusual for a crow to come down and land on his shoulder to tug at his sandy hair with its beak, or for a deer mouse to crawl up on his leg and beg for crumbs when he's eating.

"And then?" I ask.

"Ah, we jes gave the little beggar a bit of meat and told him to go back to his ma before he got into trouble."

That makes me smile even more. Almost the only time when Guy says more than a few terse words is when he's talking about animals.

Then he turns toward me.

"What?" he asks.

I understand his question as clearly as he understands that I am feeling troubled about something . . . more troubled than my usual concern, which right now is getting us safely to our Valley Where First Light Paints the Cliffs. By my reckoning, we should be able to get there within the next few days—barring any delays. Ahead, I hope, of the menace my dream warned me about.

Guy is still patiently waiting for me to answer his question. He's comfortable with waiting and will not ask again, knowing that I sometimes need to take my time. Sometimes a lot of time. Once, back at Haven, when Guy asked me "What?" in that knowing voice of his I didn't reply until three days later. Which was fine by him.

But this time I don't make him wait that long. I only breathe in and out a hundred times before I speak.

"A dream," I say.

"Ah," Guy says in a way that indicates another question is coming. This time I breathe in and out, counting one and one pony, two and one pony. I get to fifty before he speaks.

"Not just a dream?"

"No," I say, in a tone that indicates I'm done with this conversation.

So we both leave it at that. That's partially because I don't want to share those all-too-real details and partially because the light of the dawn is starting to touch the old mineshaft whose vantage point halfway up a hill is faced to the east. It was a good enough place to shelter us—at least briefly. I'm grateful that it provided these few hours of safety and that everyone with me has survived another night. Having a bit of peace in this world of constant turmoil is a sort of blessing, though it ended with that foreboding nightmare. I wish I could put that bad dream out of my mind for now—or at least a bit off to the side. Now is the time I should just sit with my old friend and enjoy the arrival of another day.

We're silent as we watch the distant hills being painted orange and gold beneath the streaked blanket of sky. We can see for at least twenty miles, the land before us stretching out with the promise of new life. A promise for us too, perhaps, despite this blackness I still feel inside me. Despite how raspy my throat feels right now. I am not going to drink yet from the little water we have left. We need to make it last. The last spring we came to yesterday had run dry. Nothing but dry sand

and stone smoothed by that vanished flow.

There's another bigger spring half a day's journey ahead. It's still flowing. I can feel it with my sixth sense. And our final destination is just beyond that farthest mountain. But I'll need to find some other water before that. The secret to survival is knowing priorities. Shelter, fire, food, and water. And of those four it is often water that comes first. We need it to keep hydrated, to cool our bodies. We need it to make tea and coffee and to cook the dried food that we have in our packs. Luckily, we found some old cans of beans and tomatoes on a back shelf in this old mine. Packed in their own juices, they need no water to prepare them for our morning meal.

Nearby shadows are now taking shape as small trees and bushes. Ocotillo, saguaro and sage, rabbit bush and creosote. A coyote barks once from somewhere close—maybe the mother of the cub that visited Guy. A striped lizard scuttles over the hollow skeleton-like dead branch of a saguaro and then scoots under a mica-flecked boulder.

"Good, eh lass?"

"Good," I agree, knowing that he means it is simply good to be alive, wishing I felt as good as he seems to be feeling.

Guy gets up and heads back into the mineshaft. It's his turn to make breakfast. I'll soon smell the wood smoke and then the bean and tomato stew cooking. No meat this morning, but the tracks I saw just before dark suggested that we might be able to remedy that lack today after locating water.

I close my eyes for a moment, take a few breaths. I'm trying to enjoy the way the morning air is filling my lungs when a hand suddenly grabs my shoulder and an arm slides across my neck in a choke hold.

"Did I surprise you, Lozen?" a small voice whispers in my ear.

"Yes," I say. "You really got me!"

Of course the real answer is no. I heard my little sister Ana sneaking up on me long before she reached me. It's fortunate for her that I did. If she really had surprised me, my reflexes would have resulted—at best—in her flying through the air and landing hard on her back with me on top of her and my knife at her throat.

But I am really pleased at how quietly she did that and I want to encourage her. She made no more noise than a snake crawling across the sand. She's been taking the stalking lessons that Hussein has been giving her very seriously. I'm doubly glad about that. Glad he's teaching her—because it's not something I have that much time to do right now. And glad that she is so focused on learning these skills because they can mean the difference between living and dying.

Ana is no longer thin as a rail. Her body has begun filling out. She never shirks her duty and has surprising strength. She and our younger brother Victor still laugh more than I do, but that laughter is most often these days because they're pleased about succeeding at something having to do with survival. It's amazing how much they've both grown since leaving Haven—

and how interested they are in anything that has to do with combat. Hitting a target with a spear, dodging a kick or a punch, and knocking an opponent down—those are the sorts of things that bring big smiles to their faces. Last night I caught Victor grinning as he studied the bruises on his arms—bruises that were a result of a repeated exercise Hussein was teaching him on how to use two hands to break an attacker's grip.

I've also noticed that their reflexes are a lot like mine, way faster than most kids their age. And both of them are more than just good with a gun. They have this ability that can't be learned, an ability to nearly always hit whatever they aim at. Hussein carries a bag of big foreign coins on his belt. For luck and memory, he says, since money is no longer worth anything. I watched as he tried throwing two of his coins high up into the air. First for Victor and then for Ana.

"Yours if you strike them." He laughed.

And, to his surprise, they each did hit those spinning little targets before they struck the ground. Victor carries that rial with a bent edge—it's now one of his most prized possessions—in his backpack. Ana looped a string through the hole in the center of her coin and wears it as a necklace.

Ana lets go of me and hops up. "I'm going to go tell Hussein how I got you,'" she says.

"You do that," I say, knowing how much it will please her to hear Hussein's approval. Although she is still a little girl, Ana has a mountain-sized crush on him.

I stay where I am, still soaking in the quiet—though it's not actually silent around me. I can hear so many things moving. Night creatures seeking their shelters from the sun's coming heat, and creatures of the day, such as the birds now flying up to offer their songs greeting the return of the light. The land itself is speaking as the coolness recedes and the warmth draws forth sounds from the rocks and even the earth. Even someone whose hearing isn't as keen as mine can hear that breathing of the stones and the soil if they just sit and listen.

Other feet are now approaching from behind me. Quieter than Ana's, though I know the owner of those feet is not trying to be silent. It's just the way he always walks, his steps never thudding on the earth. It's the way he told me his Uncle Ibrahim taught him that a true Bedu man is supposed to walk, always respecting the land as their holy book taught. What was it he called it? The Noble Krann? I think that was it.

Hussein drops gracefully down into a sitting position next to me. His knee is so close to mine—though not touching it—that I can feel warmth build in my own leg. My heartbeat is speeding up. I slide a foot farther away and turn toward him.

"Thank you," he says in that musical voice of his. "Ana told me what she did. It was kind of you not to kill her."

He's joking, of course. Aside from Hally, he's the only one who adopts that sort of teasing tone when talking to me. I like it, but I don't want him to know just how much I like it. So I do not smile and I make my reply short and straight.

61

"It's okay. I heard her coming."

"I am sure you did," Hussein says. "Just as you could hear my own clumsy steps approaching—like those of a wounded camel, no doubt."

This time I almost laugh, even though I have never seen a camel. Nor has Hussein, for that matter—aside from imagining what one looked like when he heard the stories his uncle told him. But I've learned that Hussein is good at seeing things in his mind that he's never been able to touch in reality—such as that sacred book he quotes from, a book that, like all the other books dealing with religion, was confiscated and destroyed "for the common good" after the Freedom from Religion Laws.

Hussein has raised one eyebrow and is looking at me with those dark eyes of his. There is so much kindness in him and at the same time he is so tough. I've never heard him complain, even when I know that his hand—where his little finger was cut off as punishment by the Ones—has to be hurting him.

I want to reach out and take that wounded hand in mine. But I don't. I can't.

I clear my throat and shake my head. Then I stand up and look back into the mine.

"I can smell breakfast," I say. "We need to get an early start."

CHAPTER ELEVEN

The Dreamer's Story

One dreamed," he says. "And that dream suggested something to me. It is this—that I should share with all of you the story of how it came to be that we are here in our present state, or rather the story of how our world—the world of those of us you have called Ones, came into being before *that*," he lifts one long elegant arm to gesture languidly at the sky outside the mouth of the mine, "put a stop to it all quite abruptly and inconveniently."

He pauses, cocks his head toward each of us, one after another, who've formed this small circle around the cooking fire.

"Shall I tell that tale?" he asks, his one-eyed gaze resting on me.

For some reason, the Dreamer is assuming that this morning, while we are almost done sharing food, is the right time for him to tell his story. I find it a little annoying, but I also have to admit that I am interested. There's so much that I don't know, so much that we mere mortals were never allowed to know.

The more you know, the less you will fear. That was what my father told me once.

The Dreamer is looking at me as if I am the one who has to give him permission to continue. Well, maybe I am.

"Go on," I say.

"Ah yes," he says, "I shall endeavor to do just that."

And then he does something quite unexpected. He removes his mask. It's always a bit of a shock to see the face of one of the Ones, a face that was once so perfect, so beautifully proportioned, and that now is maimed beyond repair. His face is not as badly scarred as Diablita Loca's was—there are no bones showing where once there was flesh, and his teeth are not exposed along one side of his face as were hers. His lips are fully intact, which explains why his voice is not as distorted as the voices of the other Ones I've encountered.

But the empty eye socket, the hard and blackened flesh all along the left side of his head, the melted skin that was once an ear, and the lack of hair on that blasted half of his countenance are such a contrast to the undamaged side that it makes me take a quick breath and bite my lip. I hear both Victor and Ana gasp at the sight. The pain he felt! When that happened, when all those implanted components melted down as the

Silver Cloud settled in and brought an end to the Electronic Age, it must have been close to unendurable. It had killed many of our former planetary overlords and driven others mad.

The Dreamer holds one hand up alongside that maimed side of his head. "This," he says, "was our power."

I nod. No need to go into that in any detail. Those who were higher in the hierarchy were so modified that they could kill with a glance, access information about anything and everything on our planet, quite literally see anywhere, were so immune to aging that they were close to immortal.

He slips the mask back on. Not a bad idea, seeing as how we've all just eaten breakfast.

"I could go into great detail about how we amassed such power and, if not confuse, then bore you all to tears," he continues. "So let me put it as simply as possible. By amassing wealth and making sure that wealth was not foolishly redistributed, by making alliances around the globe with those of similar status, we eliminated the need for such distractions as wars. We wiped out disease, found ways to improve ourselves both biologically and electronically. Rather than creating machines that were ever more intelligent—which might one day decide that humans were a distraction and eliminate us—we took the approach of incorporating the most useful elements of those machines that once were called computers into us, perfecting ourselves. In the end we created a planet-wide corporate entity that existed for the good of all."

He pauses again, which does not surprise me considering the sardonic tone his voice took on with that last long sentence.

"Shall I explain what I mean by *all*?"

Of course I nod.

"Not any of you," he says. "Just we few—we happy few. A few hundred thousand or so. Not all equal. There was a ladder to climb, more enhancement granted as we passed various tests and were permitted to ascend higher. I was on a rather low rung myself."

He rubs his hands together and then steeples his fingers. "At some point, some decades ago, it became clear to us that there were far too many of you. Simple logic told us that—and we had become ever more logical. Too many deer in a forest destroy all the vegetation. Too many fish in a tank foul the water. 'Carrying capacity' is the term that defines it. So, lacking wars and famines, diseases and such to serve as natural biological checks on population, there was but one logical alternative. Culling the herd from an unmanageable ten billion down to a more reasonable number."

I am squeezing my hands into fists so hard that I can feel my fingernails cutting into my palms. Culling. What he is talking about in that calm ironic voice is nothing other than mass killings on a scale that it is hard to imagine. It's hard to control myself from leaping on him and tearing out his windpipe. A low growl is building in my throat.

Whether he can hear that growl or his mind catches what is going on in mine, I'm not sure. For whatever reason, he unsteeples his hands and holds them out toward me.

"Please?" he says in a voice that is so lacking insincerity and superiority that it disarms me.

I relax. But I have to say something. "Why not kill us all?"

"Yes," he says, "That is the question. When the love for one's fellow man has been bred and enhanced out of those who see themselves as much more than human, a new species of being, why keep the relics of our anthropoid past?"

He holds his hands out to his side, then raises them, palms up. "The answer is simple—for our amusement. When one has before one the prospect of living forever, one must find ways to combat boredom. That is why one of our great pastimes was the creation of those you call gemods. The more monstrous the better. After all, we had them safely confined so that none of us were in danger—back then. And, in equal measure, maintaining communities of ordinary humans that we could watch and manipulate was nearly as amusing. We kept them occupied with the creature comforts we gave them—adequate food and housing; old, safe viddys to watch on their stick-ons; removing such unprofitable distractions as religion or politics. We held out to them the highly unlikely—but greatly desired—possibility of rising to our ranks. And we gave them jobs. Many of those tasks, mining for example, could have been done more quickly and efficiently with machines, but machines were nowhere near as . . . amusing."

The Dreamer leans forward and points a long finger at me. "There were also, every now and then, those such as you who showed some interesting abilities. That mind-reading of yours. Had that evinced itself before the Cloud came, we would certainly have taken note and either seen what we might be able to do with you . . . or done without you. Sorry. However, as you should see, having a nice pool of a few hundred million ordinaries made good sense. One never knew when something random might arise that would be of interest to us."

How nice to be wanted. Even if we were nothing more than pets or possibly useful pawns to them. Amusing, but generally powerless. No more important than the genetically modified monstrous beasts they made and then confined in their game parks.

I stare at the Dreamer. His one eye blinks, and he lowers his head with a sigh.

"I know," he says, his usually confident voice now no more than a whisper. "We made monsters, but we Ones were the worst monsters of all."

CHAPTER TWELVE

Presences

Story time is interrupted when I stand up, feeling the warmth in my hands. What have I just sensed? I need to get outside, find a vantage point. Guy and Hussein start to rise to their feet to join me. I motion for them to stay seated. Stay quiet.

They both nod, Hussein more reluctantly than my old weapons master, and settle back down.

I hold up both hands, fingers splayed wide.

Guy nods, taps the wind-up watch on his wrist. He understands that I've asked him to wait ten minutes before following me.

I walk out the hundred feet to the mouth of the mine, holding the compound bow I've just picked up from Guy's weapon cart. I am feeling that sense of a presence stronger, but not strong enough to be certain of what it is that I'm feeling. There's no digi-read for my power, no simple code that is easy to decipher. Its language is not in words.

Friend or foe? Or both? And who is that only a few yards behind me?

I look back. My sister Ana is standing in the cave mouth, holding a rifle. Somehow she slipped past both Guy and Hussein without them seeing or stopping her. And also quietly armed herself. Plus, this time, she really did come up on me without my noticing till she was close. Quieter than before. How did she do that?

I am going to have to talk with her. Seriously. I do not want her risking her life. I put a frown on my face and gesture for her to get down. She shakes her head. That almost makes me smile. I recognize that sort of stubborn determination. And I know how I used to react when I was her age and anyone tried to tell me not to do something dangerous. I need to take another approach.

Guard the entrance, I mouth at her. *It's important.*

The look on her face changes. I've given her a real job to do, not made her feel like a useless little girl. She nods and squats down, holding the rifle with a competence that is impressive.

I breathe a mental sigh of relief and keep walking uphill until I'm a hundred paces above the mineshaft. I round the corner, pass between the stumps of two big trees cut down so long ago that the wood has turned almost black, and leave the mine entrance out of sight. There's a boulder on an expanse of fairly level ground perhaps half a mile ahead before the hill rises up further. It's a perfect spot. I reach it, and then I climb up onto that boulder—a real boulder, I assure you.

I lift my hands and . . .

Crap!

I'm more sure of what I feel now. An enemy presence. But more than that. Two presences, one of which is truly strange, the other of which is hungry and following the scent trail we left last night before we found our current shelter.

I shade my eyes to look just slightly north of the sun that is now two hands high. It's the direction we came from, the direction of the prison we left behind. Then I lift my eyes higher. That first strange presence is up there, in the sky. I can see it clearly now. The sun behind is illuminating the spread fan of its tail. It's a red-tailed hawk high above, twisting its head to look down at me. But the presence I feel is not the hawk. It's as if another invisible being is with it, riding it and within it.

Then something even stranger happens. The presence accompanying the hawk vanishes as suddenly as a candle that's been blown out, and the hawk stiffens, begins to dive. But not at me. Its wings locked, it plummets downward to strike the ground a stone's throw ahead of me. It's a fall that would have killed it had it not been, as I know with an inexplicable certainty, dead already.

A shiver goes down my back. Weird. So weird that I've almost forgotten hungry presence Numero Dos.

But, unluckily for it, not completely forgotten. I've smelled it, even though it was at first concealed by a dip in the hillside. What little showed of it blended into the red soil and black sand. And I've been watching it out of the corner of my eye ever so slowly stalking me, now tensing its muscles to lunge forward.

Now!

I leap off the boulder, and a huge red-and-black beaded wide-mouthed head strikes where I was just standing. I land on my feet and start running, uphill, of course. I can hear wide feet scattering the stones as it writhes its way up after me, a heavy belly making a hollow, scraping sound on the earth.

It's fast, but not for a long distance. And even at its swiftest it's slower than me. Like the much smaller beaded lizards that were certainly a large part of the DNA mix that made it, this thick-bodied thirty-foot-long Gila monster, its jaws dripping venom, probably relies on a quick strike more than an extended chase to obtain its weekly caloric intake.

It is, however, determined. And just for a moment, as it happens now and then in stressful moments like this, I can hear something of its thoughts. Simple thoughts, admittedly.

Grab! Grab! Grab!
Bite hard, shake!
Chew up! Eat!

After all that stalking it is not going to quit. Its sole objective is chomping down on me with its curved teeth while shaking its head back and forth, until I'm torn to pieces. This is one big beaded lizard that's not about to give up.

Too bad for it.

Judging myself to be far enough ahead, when I reach the top of the slope, I turn, aim, and release the arrow I've nocked onto the compound bow I grabbed from the weapon's cart. That first feathered missile is followed by a second one quicker than a heartbeat.

TUNK! TUNK!

Arrow Numero Uno strikes the right eye, directly in the middle of the black pupil, while the other, a bit less well aimed, enters the left eye slightly off center. Despite my aboriginal ancestry I fear that bows and arrows, alas, are neither my best weapons nor my first choice in a fight. But they do have the advantage of silence. An arrow's flight cannot be heard from miles away like a gunshot. That's why I chose the bow rather than a more explosive armament.

Both the bow's effectiveness and my aim were more than adequate. One or both of my arrows pierced the overgrown reptile's small brain. Its whole body stiffens as if struck by a bolt of lightning and then its limbs go slack.

Bye-bye, Beady.

Guy and Hussein arrive while I'm still standing there at a safe distance, watching the beast for any sign of life.

As Guy makes eye contact with me, he holds up his wrist and taps his watch.

Right. They waited the ten minutes I requested before following me.

Hussein raises an eyebrow at the sight of the still body of my foe. He raises his left hand up shoulder high, his fist clenched. I know what he's about to do, what gesture he's about to make. I don't know if it is something from his Bedu traditions or just something he made up all on his own. Turning toward me and showing his perfect white teeth in a brilliant smile, he points his little finger up toward the sky before slashing down with it.

One more point for me.

Then he walks up to the creature, braces one foot on its nose—careful not to get any of its still-oozing venom on his boot—and leans down to pull the arrows from the critter's eyes.

Whick! Whick!

Two swift, easy gestures. I'm once again impressed by his strength and his competence. Less than six inches of each shaft was protruding and he still removed each with one quick, efficient motion. He cleans the arrows by twirling them in the sand, and then brings them to me.

"We Bedu," he says, "always retrieve our arrows." He goes down on one knee as he hands them to me over his left arm, the way another man might give a girl a bouquet of roses. Then he opens his hands and flashes that incredible smile at me. "Who but Allah knows what tomorrow may bring?"

That's not really a question, so I don't try to answer it. I just take the arrows and slide them back into the quiver slung over my shoulder.

Hussein spins up to his feet and turns back to the dead creature. As usual, he seems not at all insulted by my rudeness in failing to thank him. He begins to walk around the monster. Knowing Hussein, who seems to find something wonderful in everything, he is probably admiring it. And I have to admit that the beast is beautiful in its own way, the red and black of its skin, its fearful symmetry, its bulky tail that is almost as big as its body.

I wonder if it—like the super snake, the immense boa that attempted to ingest me—was once part of the collection at Big Ranch. That deserted home of reptilian horrors was a hundred miles east of here, though. Rather a long way for a critter like this to have traveled. Maybe some other bored and nearly omnipotent collector traded some of his own little creations with the late owner of Big Ranch back in the pre-Cloud days before such gemod-loving hobbyists ended up as entrees for their former pets.

Guy is also looking at the immense lizard's dead body and shaking his head.

"Meat aplenty here," he says, "but I would nae want to eat

it. Venomous beasties are nae my cup of tea, lass. Now why could you nae kill a giant deer or its like?"

"I'll keep that in mind," I say, looking briefly back over my shoulder, but not stopping as I make my way back downslope.

I'm trying to find the exact spot. Down there on that little plateau? Yes. There's the boulder that was my vantage point—and there, a stone's throw beyond the big rock, there it is.

I crouch down to look closely at the dead red-tailed hawk. It rests on its back, its claws curled up, tail fanned out, and wide wings stiffly spread as if they were frozen while still in flight. Its neck is twisted back, probably from hitting the ground, but there's no sign of any wound on its body. What killed it mid-flight?

"The big lizard," Hussein calls down to me, "it was a female."

I stand up and look up at him.

I'm about to call back to him the obvious question: How does he know that?

But he answers it before I can speak by holding up something as large as his head. It's large and oval and speckled. It's nothing less than an egg. Then he bends down and holds up another egg. The critter whose vision I permanently impaired was a mama. Was it just trying to protect its nest from us? Did I really have to seek it out and kill it?

But that thought quickly vanishes to be replaced by something else. That fact that it was a gravid female, one that needed to eat, and the tingling I'm feeling in my hands tell me I have been stupid. Why have I forgotten that where there is one monster like the one I just dispatched there might be a second one—its mate—not far away?

And the sensation of something dangerous is coming from downslope and around the hill. It's the direction where, a quarter of a mile away, my family and the others are waiting inside the abandoned mine.

Waiting without the protection of Guy or Hussein or me.

I start to run, knowing I am going to be too late and hoping that, for once, my knowing will be wrong. I've taken only a few strides before I hear the cracking sound of a rifle being fired.

Ka-pow!

A second of silence and then more shots.

Ka-pow! Ka-pow!

And I run even faster.

CHAPTER THIRTEEN

Four Deaths

Luther crouched close, studied the snake. He could have taken over its mind, made it do whatever he guided it to do.

But where was the fun in that?

It studied him right back, its tail whirring from the center of its heavy coils. If this human just left it alone and backed off, it would stop its warning rattle, turn, and crawl away. It would only strike if the human made it strike.

Alas.

Luther poked at it with one finger. Then, even though it was a blur of motion too fast for most human eyes to see, too swift for most human reflexes to defeat, Luther Little Wound dodged that strike. He caught it just behind its lethal head and, with one quick snap, broke its neck.

He held it up above his head. Its twitching tail still dragged on the ground. Nine feet long perhaps, and thick-bodied. A normal rattlesnake, nothing modified about it, but one of the largest and heaviest he'd ever seen.

Good.

He liked snake meat.

He opened his mouth and bit down twice to sever its neck. Dropping the still-squirming body, he grasped the rattler's head and pressed on either side so that its jaws gaped open and the lethal fangs protruded. He held it up between his thumb and forefinger leaned back his head, opened his mouth, squeezed the head again so that the poison from the sacs behind its cheeks oozed out. As it fell on his tongue it burned slightly. It was a taste that he enjoyed.

Tossing the head aside, he picked up the snake's body and bit again, tearing its chest open to expose the heart, a heart was still beating as he scooped it into his mouth and bit, the sweet warmth of its blood filling his throat.

It almost made him feel happy.

But not quite.

He was still feeling disappointed about that hawk. It had been just what he was looking for, asleep in its nest at the top of a pine. He'd felt its presence in the dark hours just before dawn. He'd caught it with one quick, brutal thrust of his mind, sent it flapping frantically up and up into the sky that was just beginning to be tinged by the rising sun. He'd made it circle up, higher, higher, then sent it sailing off, over the hills and canyons, unimpeded by the need to keep to roads as he was now that he was using a wheeled vehicle. Southwest, that was the way he sent it, using its eyes to see, burning out its own vision to replace it with his own.

No bird could sustain his presence for long, even one as strong as this hawk seemed to be. But it was doing well, circling high and then arrowing forward mile after mile, its telescopic sight scanning even more of the land ahead of it.

Luther had sat cross-legged, leaning forward as his vision was carried by the hawk. He could feel it weakening.

He'd pushed it harder. Soon it might locate the ones he was tracking.

Then there was something, something off at the edge of the bird's line of sight. Yes! He made its head jerk toward that side. But in his eagerness, he did so a bit too abruptly, too violently. Something in the hawk's neck snapped, and it fell like a string-cut puppet, darkness filling its eyes, death breaking the connection.

Alas.

Yet despite losing that connection a bit sooner than he'd wished, the usual feeling of satisfaction had come to him. The feel of death. He'd always been able to feel such mortality—to deeply sense the moment when life left a body he'd briefly inhabited. He could also feel it, though in a different way, when he physically killed something or someone with his body or a weapon of some sort. That was one of the things that had always set Luther apart and made him of such interest to those who employed him—his unusual competence as a dealer of death.

They had noticed it when he was a small boy in the Lakota community that had once been a reservation before it became just a place from which the Overlords could draw workers for the nearby mine. The Lakota elders who had found him in an abandoned shed, crouched over the body of a dead dog, had tried to help him, but to no avail. There was something worrying about him. They noticed him smiling as he crushed grasshoppers with his fingers. They began to fear that something twisted had taken residence within him after the strange death of his parents.

Luther remembered their deaths. He'd been crouching in the darkness, the image of their deaths as bright as a fire burning in his eyes. The man who killed them had laughed as he did it, laughed as he took his time before he cut their throats and drank their blood. Then he had looked at the boy Luther was then, the boy who had sat there in the corner, eyes wide open, watching.

The man looked at him. No, not looked at him. Looked into him.

"They deserved that," the man said through the mask that covered his face, his voice more like a snake's hiss than human speech. "Dared speak up against our masters. Sent me as their messenger. Understand that, boy? I think you do. I see something in you. You're me, aren't you?"

The man had taken his finger, a finger red with blood, and made a mark on Luther's forehead.

"This won't wash off," he said. "You'll come to me before long."

Then, like a shadow disappearing back into the night, the man was gone, leaving Luther sitting there.

And when the boy walked out into the night, leaving behind the death of his parents, he heard another voice. One not spoken.

My child, the darkness said.

My child, my child.

It opened its arms, black wings.

And he walked into it, embraced it, felt the light leave him like a candle blown out by the breath of a giant.

Some of the elders saw that darkness in him.

There is still medicine, they said.

And there was medicine that some of them still secretly knew, a medicine to combat that dark presence.

But it was too late. Before they could do their ceremonies, someone came looking for the boy, that boy who drew a black circle on his forehead with dirt each time it was washed off.

He was taken away. Screened, approved, to be trained for a role toward which he already had a useful inclination.

Because he was still a prole, and an Indian at that, there were no modifications made to his body as there would have been for one of the elite. No electronics wasted on him. But the various drugs, the gene therapy, the stem-cell implants, and his own biological heritage, a child of a family whose members were known for their strength and height and endurance, had made him much more than a normal human. Then there had been the training. It had taken decades, but those who were turning him into a weapon were patient. After all, their own near-immortal lives had no foreseeable end.

Those who trained him were men also good at killing. They held nothing back, punishing his body. If he was killed during training, it would simply prove he was not up to the task. He suffered wounds, broken bones, heat and cold, burns and bruises beyond most normal endurance. And he shook them off, healed, grew stronger.

The day he killed his first teacher, a man whose hissing voice seemed familiar to him, was one of the proudest days of his life. Their combat had been with swords that day. It had begun as what was meant to be a lesson but became more than that, a contest that could only end in one way, a fight in which nothing could be held back. Sensei

Kobiyashi's blade had pierced Luther's shoulder—in a move Luther had never seen before, one that he admired greatly and promised himself he would not forget. Undeterred, spurred on by the pain, he had pressed forward, driven the point of his own katana into the surprised man's throat, then twisted it.

Good but not good enough.

He was not the first man Luther killed. There had been others, fellow students not as gifted or as determined. Pathetic failures whose deaths Kobiyashi always responded to by saying those words.

"Good but not good enough."

Perhaps that was why, for Luther, the swordsman's death was the first death that truly counted, the first killing that he felt like a surge of fire in his belly.

Good and quite good enough.

Luther drew the long, sharp fingernail on the index finger of his right hand down the snake's belly. The skin slit as easily as if he'd been using the machete that remained sheathed at his side. Then he peeled the skin away down the snake's length, exposing its pale, muscular length. He coiled it up into a ball, using the skin to tie it in place. Then he tossed the heavy bundle of meat into the center of the glowing embers from the fire he'd kept burning through the night as he'd sat without sleeping, his back against a large saguaro.

The fire had both kept him warm and helped him see anything that might be approaching out of the night. It had hardly been necessary. The two near-human creatures that had tried had been so easy to hear that he had more than enough time to draw his machete long before they were close enough to leap toward him. Then, before they could leap, he'd moved swifter than thought.

Whick! The comforting sound of a blade cutting through cartilage and vertebrae on the forward stroke followed by the same Whick! again as he brought the machete back to his left, and a second head went rolling off.

He'd kicked the two surprisingly light, dry bodies of the Bloodless he'd killed back away from his fire. It had been a while since they'd fed. Not even a drop of blood had come from their severed necks. He'd wondered, but only for a moment, how these things had come to be. Not the result of gen-mod tech. More like something out of an old legend. But it hadn't worried him. After all, in the Valley of Death, he was the one who best embodied the bringer of mortality.

The scent of the rattlesnake's meat cooking in the embers was pleasing to Luther. He enjoyed eating. It would take his mind off the disappointment of that hawk dying just a little too soon before he fully caught sight of what was down there. He'd wanted to know if it as her, the Little Killer he had been employed to terminate. He was looking forward to meeting her, hoping that she might be something of a challenge.

But he doubted it.

CHAPTER FOURTEEN

Gunshots

I'm dreading what I might see as I race down the hill. Images of torn and crushed bodies are filling my mind, hard as I try not to see them. My heart is pounding in my chest, and I'm going so fast that I'm nearly flying, heedless of the loose stones that clatter under my feet. I almost fall time and again, but I won't slow down. I can't slow down.

The only thing that is giving me hope is the gunshots. One shot, then two. Not just a single shot. And there was the space of a long second between that first and the next two. It means that the one who fired that gun—and it had to be Ana—was still able to aim and shoot again. That her gun was not just discharged by accident as something attacked her. That she was not immediately overcome.

There are the two blackened tree stumps. I leap over them rather than between them and what I see makes me finally slow down and come to a halt. My heart no longer feels as if it is in my throat. There was indeed a second Gila monster that tried to attack my family.

Operative words in that sentence being "was" and "tried."

Its dead body, which rolled partway down the steep slope from the mouth of the mine, is the evidence of its failure. It's maybe two-thirds the size of its equally decimated mate. The two large-caliber bullet wounds in its pale exposed throat were not what killed it. They were just the "let's make real sure" shots after the first one entered its right eye and blew out its brain.

And just in case I might have had any doubts about who fired those shots, there's my sister Ana standing in front of the mine entrance. My mother and Victor are close behind her and so, standing slightly off to the side, are Lorelei and the Dreamer, who has his head cocked as he looks down at Ana in an appraising sort of way. On Ana's other side is Luz, who has placed her hand on my sister's shoulder. It makes me notice even more just how much she has grown in the last few months.

Ana is holding up the 30.06 she just fired—with such obvious effect—in her right hand. Her left hand is clenched in a fist at shoulder height. She extends her little finger and slashes it down, a wide grin on her face.

Now just who did she learn that little gesture from?

And who, rather than me, is she looking to for approval right now?

The clatter of stones behind me is the answer to both those

questions. I look back at Hussein, who barely catches himself from falling again on the stones I loosened in my headlong dash. I've just said "again" because of his torn trouser leg and exposed bloody knee. But even though he limps a little as he comes up next to me, there's an equally wide grin on his face to match the smile my not-so-little sister is beaming at him.

Then—what else did you expect?—Hussein raises his own left hand in a fist, sticks up his little finger and brings it down before limping the rest of the way over to Ana and hugging her.

I'm not sure if I want to hug them both or slug them both. Instead I just shake my head.

Keep it together, Lozen.

Victor runs up to me and hugs me.

"Do you see what Ana did?" he says. "That thing was coming right at us, but she just stood there and then she shot it. Just like you, Lozen."

"Yes, sweetheart," I say in a soft voice. "She done good."

Guy has also reached us now. He's holding the compound bow and quiver of arrows that I tossed to the side when I heard the gunshots and took off down the hill.

Everyone is looking at me again. As if I know what to do, after our little party of refugees was attacked yet again by not one, but two monsters. Plus there was that unsettling presence riding that hawk, a presence that my gut tells me may be one of the worst dangers we have yet to face.

Hally, I think. *Are you there?*

I think I sense something, something as thin as a wisp of spider web blown on the wind. Or maybe it's just wishful thinking because nothing comes back to me, not even one of those maddeningly oblique wisecracks he used to make.

Please?

No reply. Nada. Nobody home . . . "and left no forwarding address" as I heard someone in one of those old dumb detective viddys say, though I have no idea what it means.

Everyone is still looking at me, waiting while I am standing here looking stupid and feeling totally clueless.

I guess the only thing is to pretend that I know what to do.

"Clean up your knee and bandage it," I say to Hussein. "And everybody else get ready. We need to get moving."

I squeeze Victor's shoulder. "You too, big guy. Go help Mom pack up."

To my surprise, he does exactly what I've asked. And so does everyone else.

My problem now is that I am not sure either what to ask of myself or how to do it. I sit down and rest my head in my hands. While I'm sitting there I feel someone approach.

Lozen? Are you all right?

It's an unspoken question that I hear through those ears, or whatever they are, inside my head. And I recognize right away that it's my mother asking me.

I open my eyes and look up into her concerned face.

"You heard me, didn't you, dear?" she says, her voice as soft as I remember it being when I was a little child and woke up from a bad dream to find her comforting presence right there with me. Right there when I needed her.

I think back a *yes* to her. But I can see my thought didn't reach her. So I nod.

She sits down next to me.

"Is it still just happening now and then?"

I nod again. "Except with Hally. With him I can have real conversations."

Mom nods. **Go on**, she thinks. And I hear that.

Mom?

She just looks at me. She clearly didn't hear my attempt at a mental reply. It's maddening. It's like having a phone inside my head that turns itself on and off at will. So I go on, but out loud.

"Why is it that sometimes it works and sometimes it doesn't? And the weirdest part is that sometimes I can hear not just people but also those things, those monsters. How come I hear what they are thinking and I hear it in English?"

Mom nods. She has a thoughtful look on her beautiful face. I know that look. It always comes before she says something that I never would have thought of, often something from our old traditions. I would really like to read her mind again and know what she is thinking right now. But that doesn't seem to be about to happen, so I just listen, listen real hard.

"Our old people said," she begins, putting one arm around my broad shoulders as she does so. She's speaking in what I've always thought of as her storytelling voice, and I am listening as if I was once again a four-year-old and believing that my mother knew the answers to every question.

"Uh-huh," I say, showing her that I am listening. "Our old people said . . . "

"They said that everything in the earth is alive. You know that."

"Uh-huh," I say again.

"Everything. Not just the animals, those that walk and swim and fly and crawl and dig in the earth. Not just the plants, the trees and bushes, the grasses, the corn and beans and squash, all the plants that grow on the land or in the water. But everything. The winds are alive, and the waters, the rain, the streams that flow. And the rocks are alive. They are the bones of the earth. Like the bones of our body, they help the earth take shape and keep its shape. Otherwise it would all just be mud.

So we have to respect everything around us, animals, plants, wind, water, stones."

She pauses, letting me think about what she's said. And I do. I think about it, picturing all those living things before yet again saying, "Uh-huh."

"You know who the Hactcin are, the Holy People who were here from the beginning. They were here before there was earth, when there was nothing but Darkness and Water and Wind. They were the ones who had the material from which everything was made. Black Hactcin and White Hactcin. In those beginning times, it's said, every living thing spoke the same language. Rocks and trees, the wind and rain, the animals and plants. But the Hactcin decided that was not good. It was too monotonous. So different voices were given to all the living things, even though all things remained aware and able to speak. Birds sang in their own way, the wind's voice was only its own, and people began to speak different languages. Some were loud, some so soft you could barely hear them. But every being still kept its own inner voice, even if it now seemed as silent as a stone."

My mother looks up and makes a circling motion with her upraised hands, taking in everything around us, not just here inside this place of temporary refuge, but everywhere on earth.

"So it is, we've always said, that everything around us is listening. Sometimes those things find ways to speak to us. Rocks, plants, animals. And they always used to speak to us in our language, in Chiricahua. Saying things like, 'I can help you; make use of me.'"

She drops her hands back onto my shoulders. Now her voice changes. It no longer has the tone of storytelling but is more matter-of-fact, the way her voice always sounds when she is talking about practical things—like when she's telling me how many spoonfuls of coffee to put into the pot to make it just right.

"What I think, Lozen," she says, "is that you have found—or you're being given—a gift. You've begun to find ways to listen, to hear the inner voices of others. And when they are not people, it's your mind that translates their voices into words you can understand. If you spoke Chiricahua, then you'd hear those voices that way. But since you only know a little of our language, your mind is translating it into English."

"Uh-huh," I say.

"There's more," she says. "Now that you are hearing those voices, you may be hearing others. Others of the ones we call the Holy People."

Like the gans, the Mountain Spirit who showed himself to me in the shape of a cowboy, I think.

"You may even be hearing Coyote." The look on my mother's face is even more serious. "Especially Coyote. These times are perfect for him, with the world in chaos. In many ways this is Coyote's world now. That's why I think that Coyote may come

93

to you, Lozen. And if that happens, remember who he is. Sometimes he's a helper, especially if he likes you or the things that those close to you have done. But sometimes he does things for almost no reasons at all."

I nod. I've been hearing Coyote stories from my mother ever since I was old enough to understand English. She's always loved those stories and the lessons that they teach. I've always thought my mother was wise, but I now think she's even wiser than I'd realized.

"So," she says, spreading her hands out in front of her like a fan, "if you do meet Coyote, be careful. Remember, he's always a trickster. So don't expect too much of him . . . or too little."

We sit together in silence for a while as I think about what she's just said, about the Coyote tales she's told me in the past. Finally I stand up.

"Thank you, my mother. Your words have helped me."

And they really have. At least a little.

CHAPTER FIFTEEN

Hunting

The nice thing about doing something, even something as automatic and mindless as stuffing your few possessions into a pack is that you can feel as if you are actually doing something. You get a sense of accomplishment ticking the list off—three pairs of socks, a spare pair of jeans, two shirts, a few pieces of underwear, the blue hair brush that was my grandmother's, the white bone comb my dad gave me, and the plastic bag with the soap and my other toiletries in it.

It's a small pleasure, admittedly, but it's better than sitting with your thumb in your mouth and your other arm wrapped around yourself, rocking back and forth, which is about where I am right now in my head. My mother's story about the inner voices of all things has helped some. Even if that mention of Coyote was sort of disquieting. As if I needed more chaos in my life?

But her story, her sense that things are trying to talk to me, helpful things? It's something to hold onto, like a thin line when you're trying to climb up a cliff. Or maybe a short piece of thread to hold together a seam that is about to burst open.

Like me. I feel right now as if am so close to completely falling apart that you could not slide a piece of paper between me and a total hysterical mental breakdown.

But what can I do about it? This is not all about me. I'm not usually the kind of person my dad used to joke about, the one always talking about himself who finally says, "But enough of my talking about me. Now tell me what *you* think of me."

I'm way too aware of the role I've had to play and need to keep playing, the responsibility of protecting and taking care of the people who trust me to know what to do. Right now those weights seem too heavy for me to bear. How did I end up here?

Actually that's a question I can answer all too easily. I ended up here because of the choices I made, choices I had to make.

It's the next questions that have me stumped.

Numero Uno: what to do now?

Numero Dos: how to do it?

Help? Hally?

No answer again.

"Lozen?"

I stand up, shrugging my pack onto my shoulder before I turn to Guy.

"What?" My voice comes out in such an impatient tone that I regret saying anything. But Guy ignores it. I want to hug him for that, but I don't. I just keep my face blank.

He raises his finger up to tap it on his chin.

"Those tracks we saw last night. After we find some water, we might get ourselves a wee bit of meat before we take to the trail. Nae need to rush. Your valley will still be there, will it not?"

The slow, soft way Guy spoke reminds me once again how well he knows me. He's calming me down. It's made me remember once when my dad and I were watching an old viddy that had this cowboy in it talking to a skittish horse—back when there were horses.

"That's the way we did it with our horses," my father said. "We'd whisper to them, let them know they could let go of their fear, cool their insides."

Man, what must it have been like when everyone had horses? The only one I remember was Black, the horse my family had when I was very little. I was small then but I will never forget him, brief as my time with him was. Because of that memory, and the stories Dad told, a part of me, I've always felt as if having a horse would unite me with a missing part of myself. But enough of such futile thoughts.

I shrug off my pack.

"You're right," I say. "Water, then meat, then hit the trail."

Ana comes up to us, carrying the rifle that has scarcely left her hands since she shot the giant lizard. "Can I go along?"

I shake my head. From now on I am going to make sure that there are at least two well-armed people left behind whenever I head out for whatever reason.

"No, just Guy and me. You stay here, help Hussein guard our camp. Okay?"

Ana nods.

I have armed myself once more with that nifty silent bow—a weapon I have become more fond of since it proved so effective against that giant Gila monster. Its silence will make it more useful for hunting than a rifle, which may have a greater range but will send the game animals we're after scattering in all directions after the first shot.

I am also still packing my trusty .357 magnum. And my Arkansas toothpick. A girl these days just can't have too many accessories when it comes to armaments.

The water turns out to be easier to find than I'd expected. As soon as we reach the base of the hill, I feel its call. I turn off the trail, climb over a little hill, pass through a stand of bushes and trees, and there it is. A spring as clear and clean as any person might wish. Or any animal. The patterns of their tracks in the sandy soil around the spring are evidence of that. We drink deep, fill the canteens, and carry them back to the mine, where everyone is as pleased to see that water as I was.

"Drink as much as you want," I say. "The spring is that close. We can refill the canteens again before we all head out."

Time now to turn our minds to hunting.

Guy and I head farther downhill, to the flat area where we crossed those tracks leading into a sandy arroyo yesterday afternoon when finding shelter was our first priority and the mine shaft above us caught Guy's eye.

I look back when we get to the base of the hill. Ana waves to us from her post by the mouth of the old mine. She is holding her gun across her chest and her back is straight as an arrow. There's no question about how seriously she is taking her job of being a sentry. Everyone else is back inside the mine. Except for one person.

Hussein, also armed with a rifle, has stationed himself behind and a little above her. He's sitting on an old beam that was left outside when the shaft was deserted. I raise my free hand to both of them, and Hussein flashes that smile at me, so bright I can feel its warmth even from half a mile away.

I turn quickly toward Guy and start walking. I keep going until when I look back again the mineshaft is no longer in sight.

Turkey buzzards are already kettling in the sky high above. They've caught sight or scent of the punctured predators that will provide their next feast.

I nod at the sight of those scavenger birds. I know some people don't like them, and in the viddys they were always a sign of doom and disaster, hovering over the heads of lost travelers stumbling through the sands. But seeing them is a reminder that despite all the insanity loosed upon the world, despite the deep imbalance among us humans that existed even before the coming of the Cloud, there's still a balance. Things die and become part of other lives. Those buzzards, birds that clean the world as our old people called them, are part of a continuing cycle. There is beauty in that.

We're at the arroyo now.

"Ah," Guy says, pointing with the compound bow he's carrying that is nearly an exact mate to mine, aside from its being black where mine is camo green.

I agree. It's just as we hoped. Not only are the cloven hoof prints left by the herd of peccaries still there, the sand is churned by fresh prints over the top of the old ones. We could probably sit here and wait, and as long as we were downwind, those little wild pigs would come back again right past us.

But we want this hunt to be over as soon as possible so that we can get back to the others. We follow the prints and come to a place where the arroyo diverges around a strew of tall stones and a stand of yellow aspen. Some of the herd went to the right, others to the left.

Guy looks at me, points right, then left with his bow.

I nod my agreement. We'll have a better chance of each bringing down an animal if we split up here.

"I'll take the road less traveled by," Guy says with a grin as if he's making a joke.

I'm not sure I understand it, but I nod again and follow the tracks to the left as he heads to the right and soon is lost to my sight.

The clean white sand is soft under my feet and makes a swooshing sound as I walk. I picture for a moment what this dry wash must be like when thunderstorms in the mountains send rivulets of water down the slopes to gather in this dry riverbed and turn it into a torrent. No worries about that today. There's not a sign of a single dark cloud gathering in the silvered firmament, no distant rumbles of warning thunder from the peaks to the east.

What little breeze is stirring today is in my face. It's dry and redolent of earth and stones and desert plants, as well as the musky, sharp scent of the herd of perhaps a dozen or so animals not far ahead. They are coming my way from around a curve in the riverbed. I can't see them, but I can hear them, the sounds of their feet in the sand, the small noises, soft grunts and little squeals, they are making to each other.

It's a sort of conversation between them.

Hey, look at this. Hey check this out. Over here. Hey! Over here. What's this? Hey!

I take a slow step back and then another, moving to the side toward the trunk of an old tree that was left wedged into the bank of the arroyo by the last flood. I crouch down behind the tree, the arrow nocked into the bow, just before they come into sight.

There's more than a dozen of the javelina. Not just grown ones, but also half a dozen little striped piglets scampering back and forth and butting into the side of their mothers.

It's sort of a shame to have to do what I'm about to do. But it's also as natural as what those turkey buzzards are doing on the hilltop behind me. And I'm going to do it in the way I was taught.

I've picked out the one I'm going to take. Not one of the mothers or the older boars and certainly not one of the little ones, tender though they might be to eat. I've chosen one of the chunky well-fed males that looks to be about a year old and probably weighs forty pounds.

"Thank you," I whisper under my breath, "for allowing me to use your body to feed my people."

The javelina I've chosen stops, turns sideways as if it has heard me, as if giving me a sign that it is willing to give its life knowing its spirit will keep running on.

I release the arrow and it speeds straight, pierces the wild pig's side. Its front legs collapse and it falls over to its side. There's a moment of confusion in the little herd. I could easily have fired another arrow, taken a second, even a third. But one is all I asked for, and that is enough. I stand up and the peccaries catch sight of me.

"Go," I say to them. "Good travels to you."

Some people have told stories about how dangerous a herd of javelina can be, how they will chase you, trying to tear you apart with their tusks, if you disturb them. But those are not the stories told by my Chiricahua people.

The herd of wild pigs looks at me. One of them, an older sow, bends her snout down to snuffle at the body of the one I shot. Then she looks up as if seeing something, as if seeing the spirit of the one whose body died here. She turns and trots back the way they came, followed by all the others. Not a panicked flight, but a departure without fear. They vanish around that curve in the streambed, leaving me alone with the meat left by that one I chose, the one that chose to leave me its flesh.

I walk over, kneel, and take out my knife.

I've just made my first cut, the one to open its paunch and take out its entrails, when the hair stands up on the back of my neck. It's not my power speaking to me in its usual fashion, but it's something or someone watching that I've sensed in a very ancient way.

Is it friendly?

Or dangerous?

Or both?

Does that means it's . . . ?

"Hey, Little Girl," a high nasal voice whines more than says. In Chiricahua.

I turn around slowly. And I'm surprised when I finish

turning to see how close he is to me. The grin on his face shows me he's pleased at the way he's surprised me. But I suppose I shouldn't be surprised. That's the way Uncle Chatto said he always was. Sneaky and cheeky.

He's sitting on his haunches, an arm's length away, his tongue hanging out.

Coyote.

"Gonna give me some a that?" he says. This time his words are in English, in a tone that's a combination of a whimper and a demand.

I almost laugh. Which is not a good idea. When you laugh at the trickster you are about to get tricked yourself.

How crazy is it that I am about to enter into conversation with a character out of our oldest tales? No crazier than anything else these days. After all, my mother's story prepared me for this. I just didn't think it would happen this soon.

Once again I am wondering what the coming of the Cloud let loose in addition to those genetically distorted beings that want nothing more than to destroy all human life. Did electricity have a dampening effect on the things western civilization called supernatural? And, with the loss of that technologically generated power, are all the older powers becoming stronger again?

Yeah, Lozen. Do you really have to ask that of yourself, considering just what's been happening to you?

I shake my head as if to clear it of cobwebs. All that internal dialogue is taking my mind off the one sitting right there in front of me. The being whose very presence is a general source of confusion. Who wants to confuse me.

"Stop it," I say.

"Stop what, Little Girl?" Coyote says. Way innocent, as if butter wouldn't melt in his mouth.

"Just stop it," I say. I don't take my eyes off him.

Coyote smiles even broader. "Gonna give me some?" he asks again.

That is a question you do not want to answer with a simple yes.

"That javelina gave itself to me," I say.

"You sure about that?"

I reach back behind me and put my hand on the still-warm body of the javelina, just to make sure it is still there. I do not turn around to look. If I did I would probably see the black, carbon fiber shaft of my arrow had been replaced by another arrow, one roughly crafted from a twisted branch with bird feathers haphazardly glued onto it. Then, just as he did long ago, Coyote would claim that his arrow was the one that hit it and so the kill was his to take.

"Trade," I say.

If Coyote's grin got any bigger it would split his head in half. "Trade? Nice. Me, I like to trade."

"First back off a little."

"Like this?"

In an instant he's a good twenty feet away.

"Better," I say.

"Is this better, too?" he asks. The air seems to shimmer and dance around him and, then, like dust caught in a beam of sunlight, his shape disperses and reforms itself. Now, instead of a mangy dog-like creature, I'm looking at a scrawny old brown-skinned man wearing an eared fur cap, a torn buckskin loincloth—and a very snazzy pair of new leather boots. Leather that looks to be red-and-blue-beaded lizard skin.

I furrow my brow as I study those boots.

"Hey-hey-hey," Coyote whines, "wasn't like you was gonna use any of that skin, Little Girl. Why should I leave it all for them buzzards?"

I shake my head and let it go. No point arguing with Coyote. Once he possesses something, it's his—at least until he does something foolish and loses it.

"Trade," I say again.

Old Man Coyote nods. "Trade," he agrees. "What do I get?"

"Entrails," I say. "Nice and warm and juicy."

His mouth waters at the thought, but he doesn't nod.

"More," he says.

"What have you got?" I ask in return.

"What you need to know," he says. "One thing."

I have no doubt that he does know one thing that I'd like to hear about. Tricky and foolish as Coyote may be, he is always looking and listening. But I can't give in too quickly.

"More," I reply. "Two things. Then you get the liver, too."

His eyes get brighter at that, and the same dance of molecules around him begins once more, ending with him back in the shape of the animal he was when I first saw him. He leans forward, a string of saliva hanging out of his gaping mouth. But then he catches himself.

"Two things," he whines in that nasal voice. "Two?"

I nod.

"Entrails, liver, and lung. Last offer," he says.

"Deal," I say.

He starts forward. I hold my hand up.

"What?" he whimpers.

"You promise, promise on your mother's life."

A little growl escapes from his lips, and he shows his teeth. He no longer looks as foolish or mangy as before, that appearance he chose to make it seem as if he is not the dangerous old creature he truly is. He's looking bigger, more menacing. But I don't let him frighten me.

I just repeat what I said. "Promise. Promise on your mother's life."

He leans back onto his haunches again. "You bargain hard,

Little Girl." Then the grin returns to his face. "Okey dokey. I promise. May my mother drop dead if I lie to you now."

The image goes through my mind of an elderly Coyote lady walking along and then suddenly clutching her heart and falling over. But what else can I do but trust him—at least a little?

"Okay," I agree, "I swear to honor our bargain. And to show you I mean it, you can take your part of the trade now."

I take my hand off the javelina's body and move aside.

Coyote raises one eyebrow, as if to say he cannot believe just how trusting this foolish human is being. All of a sudden, faster than a speeding bullet, he's past me and is there at the carcass, digging his snout and his hand-like paws into it. Then, whoosh! he is sitting across from me in the shape of that old man, his hands full of pig guts, his face bloody as he gulps them down. No exactly a pleasant sight, but what did I expect? After all, he is Coyote.

I wait till he has finished eating and he is looking at me, wiping his mouth with his arm.

"Well?" I say.

"You trust me, Little Girl?" he asks.

"No," I say.

He grins at that. "Good. You will live longer that way."

"Two things?"

"Two things." He wipes his hands together and then picks up a handful of the white sand, watches it as it trickles through his clawed fingers.

"First thing," he says, "You are sick."

I open my mouth, but before I can say anything, he holds up his hand. "I know that you know that. What you do not know is how to get better." He turns his head. "Someone is coming from the winter land way. She knows the medicine to make you better." He grins. "Just as long as she doesn't kill you first."

He picks up a stick, breaks it in half and begins to trace patterns in the sand he has smoothed in front of him. Shapes begin to take form there. They're clouded, constantly shifting, but they're images that hold meaning.

Old Man Coyote drops the stick and places both of his paw-like hands on top of the patterns he's made.

"Second thing. Second thing is . . . " He suddenly raises one paw and points. "LOOK OUT BEHIND YOU!"

I don't. I also don't take my left hand off the body of the javelina. But I do use my right hand to draw my Bowie knife in a motion that is even swifter than usual. Good thing, because it stops Coyote halfway through lunging forward, back again in his mangy animal shape.

"That works sometimes," he says, not at all apologetic.

"Second thing," I say.

"Second thing," Coyote says, bobbing his head up and down. "You need to keep moving. Someone is after you, dangerous and hard to kill."

Somehow I know, in a way, who he is talking about. It's not someone I've seen, but someone I've felt—the hostile presence held in the hawk that fell dead from the sky. A shiver goes down my back.

Coyote grins. "I like you, Little Girl. I like your old one-eyed friend, too, that big man who gave food to my nephew. So me, I will tell you one extra thing now."

I lean forward, listening closely. There's always meaning in the trickster's words. Deceitful though he might be at times, Coyote always tells the truth. Even when he has to lie to do so.

"Go on," I say.

"Okey dokey. Your big friend, the one you are looking for? *Hally.* I nod.

"He is busy now. But he will find you again pretty soon."

I nod again. Nothing new in that, but it is reassuring to know that my big hairy giant ally will be reappearing.

Coyote grins, showing all his teeth. "Just be careful. You big friend is more than what he says. After all, he's not from around here."

Suddenly Coyote lifts up his hand-like paws and hurls sand at my face. I close my eyes, duck and wrap my left arm tightly around the javelina's carcass. A lanky body is wrestling briefly with me, hairy hands trying to pull the carcass away from me. But it retreats even faster when I poke the Bowie knife in its direction. I sit up, holding the body of the javelina to my chest.

"Had to try," a nasal voice whines from somewhere in the brush behind me. "After all, I am Coyote. Bye-bye, Little Girl."

When I turn around to look, no one is there. Just as I expected, Coyote is gone.

CHAPTER SIXTEEN
High Road or Low Road

I sit there for a while, cradling the body of the javelina. I have been given a lot to think about. A whole lot.

Yup.

But I'm still sitting when I hear the sound of approaching feet, feet falling a bit heavier than usual. I know who it is before he appears around the bend. It's Guy, and he's carrying the weighty body of a second javelina over his shoulder.

"Lozen," he says, looking at the pig I'm holding. "Good one."

"Thank you," I say.

"For what, Lass?"

"For being kind to coyotes."

He looks slightly puzzled at that, but then being puzzled by things I say or do is nothing new for Guy. Though he does have one question.

"I see you dressed it out nice and clean," he says. "But where's the liver? Good meat, that."

"Good enough," I say, standing and slinging the carcass over my shoulder. "Let's go."

As we walk back toward our camp in the hillside mine, the things Coyote said keep running through my mind. He'd said there were two things I had to know, but there were more than two things in what he told me. Way more. Just his showing up the way he did was a message, a reminder that just about anything seems possible these days and that I can never let my guard down. Expect the unexpected.

I think about the stories that my father used to tell me about Coyote. Those stories were always fun to hear, but they always, always taught you things. Because they were so powerful, those stories had to be told indoors and only at certain times of the year. And you had to be really careful about mentioning Coyote's name out loud because whenever you did there was a chance he would hear it and come to you. And as soon as Coyote comes to you, my father said, he brings trouble with him.

Hmmph.

I smile grimly at that thought. Trouble? I already have more than enough trouble, so much that whatever Coyote might bring is just a drop of water in this ocean of problems that tries to drown me every day. Somehow, though, I've managed to keep surviving. And that is like Coyote.

In one of the stories my father told, Coyote lost his wife. That was always happening to Coyote. No woman could ever live for a long time with Coyote without getting disgusted with him.

As soon as his wife walked out on him, Coyote wanted to find a new wife. He went to another camp and asked a young man if he could marry that young man's sister.

I'll help you if you agree to help me, Coyote said.

Every day he went hunting with the man and chased the deer to him. Coyote was so helpful that the young man agreed. He went to his sister.

Coyote wants to be my brother-in-law, he said.

I do not want to marry Coyote, his sister replied.

Coyote did not give up, though. He hung around the camp and did everything he could to be helpful. That young man kept talking to his sister about Coyote.

Look how he helps us, he said. He would be a good husband.

Finally the sister gave in.

I will marry him, but he has to let me kill him four times. If he comes back to life four times I will marry him.

The young man went to Coyote.

My sister will marry you if you let her kill you four times.

Good, Coyote said. Good.

Coyote used his power then. He went off where no one

could see him and took out his heart. Using a flint knife, he cut it in half and stuck half of his heart on the tip of his nose and the other half on the tip of his tail. He came back to the camp and went to the sister.

Okey dokey, Coyote said to her. Come on and kill me, my wife-to-be.

The sister picked up a big wooden club. She hit Coyote with it and killed him with one blow. She kept on hitting him with that wooden club and broke all his bones.

He's dead, she said.

The next day, though, Coyote came walking into the camp as if nothing had been done to him.

Here I am, he said. Want to kill me again?

This time the woman used a stone club. She hit him in the head with it and killed him. She pounded him with that heavy stone club until he was all mashed up and completely flat.

He is really dead now, she said. She felt certain of that.

The next day, though, just as before, Coyote walked back into the camp.

Hey hey hey, he said. Here I am.

So the woman tried again. She used an ax. She killed Coyote with one blow of the ax and then chopped off his head and his legs.

He is good and dead this time, she said.

Once again, though, Coyote walked into the camp the next day as good as new.

I really slept well last night, he said. Come on now. Kill me again.

The woman was determined that this fourth time she would kill him for sure. She took a sharp knife and cut him into little pieces. She scattered those pieces of Coyote all through the desert.

However, when the sun rose the next day, just as before Coyote came walking back into the camp.

"Must be our wedding day," he said to the woman.

And it was.

We've walked most of the way back now. I'm not that tired and could keep going, but it's now mid-morning and the heat of the day is making both of us sweat like crazy. Plus I want to ask Guy something before we get back to where everyone is waiting for us to return. There's a place just up ahead that is shaded by a flowering bush. The ground beneath it looks firm and is raised almost like a bench.

"Let's rest here," I say.

"Good enough," Guy agrees.

We drop our loads and sit together there, neither of us saying anything for a while. It's the sort of companionable silence I've always enjoyed sharing with Guy and I am usually not the one to break it. Not this time, though.

"Guy," I say, "I have a question."

"Aye," he says. "And do I have the answer?"

"I think so." I've picked up a stick and I'm tracing lines and circles in the dirt, sort of the way Coyote did back in the arroyo, though the earth does not start swirling and shaping itself into patterns the way it did for him.

"Ask," Guy says.

"Luz," I say.

"Aye."

"Luz?"

A long silence follows.

Finally Guy sighs.

"And if I cannot trust you, who can I trust, eh, lass?"

That's not really a question, so I don't say anything.

A longer silence this time.

"She looks like her mother," Guy says in a soft voice. Then he smiles. "At least when her face is clean."

"Maybe more like you," I say.

"And that would be a curse, would it na?" he chuckles. "When we first came to Haven, back before you were brought there and back when I had two eyes, her mother was already gone."

Guy lowers his head and starts humming a tune I've never heard before, a sweet song that he begins to add words to.

Ye take the high road
and I'll take the low road,
and I'll be in Scotland afore ye
But me and my true love
will never meet again
on the bonny, bonny banks
of Loch Lomond.

He looks up at me. "Ever hear that 'un before, lass?"

I nod at him. Just two nights ago Hussein had been playing that melody on his guitar as he and Guy sat together waiting for their turns to keep watch. Since I was on sentry duty, I wasn't paying all that much attention then to the words Guy was crooning—almost under his breath—as Hussein played.

"The high road and the low road," Guy continues, "the living and the dead. Her mother dead and she our only child, the two of us yet walking the road of those who breathe? But once we got to Haven, the best role I could play with me daughter was to pretend she was just some lost child that me and the others seeking shelter—none of whom we knew that well—picked up along the way. A child good with her hands, fit to be an apprentice in the work with weapons the Ones gave me. But not a child I cared about. That way they could na threaten her to make me do anything. Ye know well enough how they can use a family against ye, lass."

I scratch a line through the pattern of four intersecting circles I've just drawn.

"I do."

"Na reason for me to keep that up anymore, is there?" Guy asks. "Na." He smiles. "She might look a bit older, but she's the same age as yer sister. Yesterday was her birthday."

He stands, slings the carcass of the javelina he killed over his broad shoulder, and points with his chin in the direction of our camp.

"On we go then," he says. "High road or low road."

CHAPTER SEVENTEEN

The Burned Man

The road in front of Luther, old Route 10, was so straight that it almost seemed to disappear into itself in the distance. It made Luther wonder if he went fast and far enough he might not vanish himself.

The ruins of what had once been a city called Tucson were behind him now. The city had been quite large and, it was said, picturesque. But after the global corps were firmly established, the Southwest Regional Admin of New America had deemed Tucson and most of its inhabitants of minimal value. The sprawling city back then, like most now-decimated metropolises, had been home to many inhabitants who stubbornly attempted to persist in such counterproductive practices as religion and democracy. They had done so, amusingly, through non-violent protests.

Sweet, innocent—and dead—little non-violent protestors.

The SRA had applied the usual reductionist measures accordingly, leveling buildings, removing interesting objects for their own private collections and, of course, culling.

Luther himself had only stopped there briefly to see if there might be something worth scavenging from its remaining buildings devoid of human life. He'd run into a few non-human things in his search, but none had caused him much difficulty. That included a sizable and aggressive nest of Bloodless. He'd gone through them like a scythe through a wheat field.

Only one of them, a slightly larger male with a thick head of greenish hair, had gotten close enough to actually grab his wrist and attempt to bite him.

That had provoked a grim laugh on Luther's part. The hardened skin of his arm where the creature tried to inflict an injury was not even dented by its sharp fangs. One tooth even broke off in the process before Luther absentmindedly snapped its neck.

There was a legend that being bitten by one of them would turn you into a Bloodless yourself. Some sort of viral infection through the circulatory system. Luther was not sure he believed it. Does getting bitten by a mosquito turn you into a mosquito? Plus if the legend about infection was true, wouldn't the end result produce far too many predators for them to sustain themselves?

Luther didn't care either way. The one thing he did care

about was what he obtained in a former apparel provider after invading their nest. Seeing that coat displayed on a mannequin—like bait on a hook—was what attracted him there, to the eventual dismay of his thwarted attackers.

It had been crafted for someone with a physique as large as his—perhaps one of the larger ball players in the leagues that had thrived for the amusement of the Overlords. It fit him perfectly. A fine, sturdy jacket hand-crafted from supple black leather, lined with purple silk. The pockets on the side and the loops inside were perfectly designed to hold concealed weapons—another thing the best ball players had been allowed by the Masters.

He put it on and it fit him well, loose enough to allow him to move easily. The sleeves were not too tight, either. Plenty of room to conceal one thing or another. Unsuited for the heat of the southwest, some might think. But not Luther. It was cold that always had bothered him, never warmth. Cold brought him back to the unheated trailer where he had lived as a parentless child, scavenging for food. One of his worst dreams was of being trapped in one of those trailers as it slowly filled with ice—as bad as his other recurrent nightmare of drowning in rushing water.

Luther stroked his hands down the sides of the jacket. It reminded him of the one worn by the motorcycle-riding wild hero of one of his favorite old viddys. Now that was something he missed, viddys. But now, with a bike of his own—clockwork, true, and with three rather than two wheels—he could picture himself in that role as he roared along the highway (well, actually glided silently, aside from the soft ticking).

That image pleased him almost as much as killing, though not quite.

Something was moving on the road ahead. His biologically enhanced vision allowed him to identify it quite clearly from several miles away. A group of men bearing a variety of weapons, including one object that required three men to carry it. They were heading his way, led by one whose clothing was blackened, hair singed short. The charred armband he wore appeared to have once been as bright forest green as those worn by the ten others in his party.

It was clear whose minions these were. Luther had discarded his own white armband, not at all stylish, as soon as he'd left the confines of Haven. But even without it, he suspected the men he seemed about to meet would not welcome him in a comradely fashion. Even though—or perhaps because—they wore the Joker's color.

Alas.

None of the men's weapons had scopes on them. Any bullets fired his way at this range would certainly miss. Luther could have turned around. But that was not the sort of thing he ever did. If a confrontation lay ahead, so be it.

Let's hope.

The clockwork motor ticky-ticked beneath him, and the three wheels whirred on the sun-cracked pavement as he proceeded on at a pace far faster than any normal human could run. The hazy sun was hot, the wind warm in his face.

The men were now fanned out across the road, the burned man in front holding up a hand.

"STOP!" the man shouted in a harsh, dry voice.

Luther applied the brake and did just that. Rather sooner than they expected. He was still fifty feet from the armed men. Then he waited.

"Will ya lookit that!" one of them, a bulky sandy-bearded man carrying an AK-47 said in a low voice as he stepped up next to the burned man. "Motorbike! Never thought I'd get to see one of them again."

"Shut it, Sandy," the burned man said. "Do I need to kick your ass again?"

Sandy. How unimaginative.

"Sorry, Rourke, sorry," the man called Sandy said, retreating back a quick two steps.

Rourke, Luther thought. It did suit his voice.

The burned man named Rourke gestured with his raised hand.

"Closer," he rasped. "Come on closer."

Luther re-engaged the clutch and lifted his foot from the brake. Ticking softly, the clockwork cycle glided forward at a slow, non-threatening speed, straight into their midst and past

124

their burned leader—who had to step aside—before he applied the brake again. Now Luther could tell from the yellow color of their eyes and the way their fingers were shaking—not just from their rank breath—that all were on Chain, the highly addictive drug that not only increased strength, energy, and aggression, but also drastically shortened its users' lives while affecting their judgment.

As proof of that, none, aside from Rourke, were pointing weapons at him.

Alas.

A pale-skinned, lanky redhead with what looked to be a painfully sunburnt neck, pointed a crooked finger at the insignia on the front of the cycle.

"LT," the redhead said. "That must stand for Lady Time, don't you think? I heard they was working on something like this in her workshop."

"Zip it, Red!" the burned leader said.

Red. So predictable, Luther thought. In a way that cognomen displeased him.

"So who are you?" Rourke growled. "Where you going?"

No point in being uncivil. That could come later. "Luther Little Wound," he replied.

His voice was calm, matter-of-fact. But for some reason his mention of his name made the man called Red turn paler than before and stumble back against the three men behind him who were still bearing that large object.

"Four Deaths," someone whispered near the back of the group. Luther was not quite sure who it was. Perhaps the stocky blond man. It pleased him to be so recognized.

Out of the corner of one eye, Luther looked at the contraption borne on the shoulders of the three men (so foolish of them not to put it down). A metal tube blackened at one end, connected to what looked like a double set of bellows and a tank of some sort at the other. The odor of gasoline was quite strong—unpleasantly so, to his sensitive nose. He'd be happy to leave that scent behind.

Rourke swallowed audibly. Perhaps his throat was dry from the burning they'd been doing with that object, work that Rourke obviously had controlled while standing at its front and grasping it with the heavy asbestos gloves that hung at his waist.

Luther jerked his thumb toward the metal tube.

"Flame thrower?" he asked, not really meaning it as a question.

Rourke did not try to answer it. "Where you going?" he asked.

Rude.

But no harm in giving a civil reply. Repay unkindness with a gracious answer.

"An errand for Lady Time. Eliminate a nest of resisters in

a place rather picturesquely described as the Valley Where First Light Touches the Cliffs."

"Haw!" laughed the bulky man Rourke had called Sandy. "We brought some light there already! Didn't we, boys? Burned the whole place up real good."

Rourke turned his head to say something to Sandy.

Those words failed to reach his lips. Luther, who had finally become bored with the whole conversation, lifted both palms from the handlebars of the cycle and flexed his wrists. The two automatic weapons, propelled forward by a spring mechanism, began firing, almost as if on their own, as soon as they were firmly grasped by his hands.

Pow! Pow-Pow!

The first shot blew out Rourke's throat. The second and third accounted nearly simultaneously for Sandy and Red. Both rounds were neatly placed in the midst of their forehead, as if to open that third enlightened eye of which his old martial arts teachers spoke.

Seek more creative nicknames in your next incarnations.

Rather than shooting back, the remaining men bumped into each other, fell down, attempted to run—but brief results of their panic, as Luther emptied the chambers of his .45s with quick efficiency.

He saved the last shot for the stocky blond who might have

referred to him as Four Deaths—the gift of a few more breaths for speaking his name with the proper respect.

It was the work of but a few minutes to neatly stack the corpses, empty the reservoir of the flamethrower upon them, then toss Rourke's lighter onto the pile from an appropriate distance. The resultant conflagration was pleasantly warm on his face and dispelled the nasty gasoline odors.

CHAPTER EIGHTEEN
In My Head

As I reach the place where the road reaches the crest of a hill I scan to either side. Hills come down to my right. To the left the folded land is open, sandy, and empty of vegetation until it reaches a black mesa about three-quarters of a mile away that has a small patch of green at its base. In front of me, the road curves along like the body of a great black snake. In the far distance, perhaps four miles from here, I can see a fairly large building by the roadside. Nothing is moving anywhere that I can see, either to the right or left of me or in the broad expanse ahead. And although I feel the twinge of a headache starting—maybe from the heat of the day—I am not sensing anything dangerous.

That's a relief.

Since the Dreamer joined us with his cartload of weaponry, we're no longer taking the narrower trails I'd prefer. It's meant that we are potentially much more exposed to enemy eyes, but I'm trusting that my power will warn us in time of any threat before we get too close to it.

I turn and look back downhill the way I just came, toward the rest of our party. The nine of us make a strange-looking parade. I'm twenty yards ahead of everyone, Hussein the next in line behind me. Both of us have been holding our rifles at the ready as we stride along—although Hussein's stride has been falling into a limp whenever he thinks I'm not noticing him. The next down, another twenty yards or so behind, is the Dreamer. His stamina is amazing. Even when he is dragging that bulky cart uphill—a cart even heavier now since, at his suggestion, we've loaded it with our heavier packs and even Hussein's precious guitar—he hardly slows down. With his long fingers wrapped around the shafts, he walks with the ease of someone just out for a casual stroll.

Although he's said that his insolence was merely a pose to shield him from the suspicions of the three other Ones who ruled Haven, there's an air of assumed superiority that seems to always settle around the Dreamer. For some reason, though, that attitude of his no longer bothers me. It actually amuses me a little—though any feeling of amusement I might have never lasts long. Whenever a laugh or a smile bob up in me, the weight of my responsibilities and the dark sickness eating at my core submerge my mood back beneath the surface of an ocean of depression.

Lorelei is walking to the right of the Dreamer, holding onto one of those shafts and helping him pull. You can see the effort she's making from the way she is biting her lip, even though I'm not sure she's helping that much. My brother Victor has stationed himself right behind the cart and is leaning into it, pushing. Unlike Lorelei's efforts, I am sure that he's actually helping. He's been getting stronger since we left Haven, and I think he's grown an inch taller.

But what he is doing now is not good. Seeing it is making my headache worse. Victor was supposed to be hanging back another twenty yards behind the cart. I'd told everyone to stay spread out, not bunch up.

Saying that to my little brother's face was a mistake, of course. Victor is as stubborn as his sister—well, his sisters. Telling him not to do something is like a challenge. He wants to be as useful as he possibly can, prove that he is not a little boy anymore. Show off his competence and his strength.

And not just for Hussein or Ana or Mom, I suddenly realize. He is looking back, past the barrel of the rifle he has slung over his shoulder. He's looking at Luz—who turns her face away from his gaze, hiding it behind her thick black hair. But not before I think I catch a glimpse of a smile. Which Victor seems to have also seen because now he is pushing harder.

Next in line, as I've indicated, is Luz. And then Mom behind her. Each of them is keeping the twenty-yard gap I asked for. The last two in line are Ana and then Guy—though he's not in sight right now. Ana looks as if nothing is on her mind other than her duty of being watchful. She is constantly scanning from one side of the road to the other and walking a path that ranges back and forth, not a straight line. I feel a surge of pride at how competently she's assumed this new role.

Guy comes into sight now. He's walking backward from around the bend that is obscured by the shoulder of the mountain. He is staying, as he should, much farther back, bringing up the rear in the position my father and Uncle Chatto called drag.

Aside from Victor being slightly out of place, everything is going as I planned. That's good, I suppose. But I can't afford to be complacent. That is the wrong way to feel on this more exposed trail we've now taken. My ancestors in the old days knew that death was always waiting for the unwary. That's even more true now.

Something is starting to feel wrong. But what is it? And why is this headache getting worse?

The Dreamer's cart has just reached a place where the grade is level. I raise my rifle high over my head. It's a sign for everyone to halt. The only one who doesn't is Victor, whose view of me is cut off by the back wall of the cart. He actually pushes the donkey cart another six feet forward all on his own before he realizes the Dreamer has stopped pulling.

There's a sharp pain stabbing behind my eyes now. I put

my rifle down, press my palms to my temples. It's not as if someone or something is trying to contact me. It's as if chittering waves are washing across my mind, twisting through my brain, joining that dark despair in the core of me, blanketing my thoughts. My knees start to buckle.

"Lozen!"

Hussein's voice brings me back to myself. There's a pained look in his face, but he's not half-trapped in a suffocating blanket of darkness like me. His right hand is on my shoulder, steadying me, shaking me. My .308 is in his left hand.

Why did I put it down? What is wrong with me?

And then, as if the firm grasp of his hand—like that of a lifeguard in an old viddy saving a drowning swimmer—has pulled me up out of deep water, I come back to myself. My power surges in my hands, directing me toward the source of the attack I've felt in my mind. I grab my rifle from Hussein as he turns and swings his own .308 up to his shoulder.

"There!" he shouts.

There, a nightmare sight is rising up out of the sand where it was buried. A stone's throw away from us, venom-dripping tail raised above its back, big claws open, it's a sand-colored eight-foot-long scorpion. My power recognizes it as the source of that attack on my mind, meant to paralyze me until it was close enough to grasp and strike with its lethal sting.

And not just me! My peripheral vision has taken in the rest

of our party downhill from me, everything seeming to move in slow motion, as so often happens when my power rises through me.

The Dreamer and Lorelei have both dropped to their hands and knees. Luz is lying curled up on her side and Mom is bent over with her palms pressed to her cheeks. And there, where the road bends, Guy has his arm across his one eye.

But not Victor. And not Ana. They are raising their rifles and taking aim at the half dozen or so other big poisonous arthropods now showing themselves along the trail and beginning to scuttle toward what they intended to be helpless prey.

I pull my trigger at nearly the same time that Ana and Victor start shooting. Hussein's gun goes off a split second later.

BLAM! BLAM! BLAM-BLAM!

My first shot strikes the nearest scorpion in the center of its neckless head between its eyes. Yellow ichor spurts out and it thrashes off to the side, its long stinger striking down into its own body as it writhes in its death throes.

I shoot at a second scorpion as it starts to scuttle around the body of the first one, blasting a segment out of its tail so that it hangs limp before my next bullet kills it. As I take aim at a third one I realize how slowly they're moving to the attack. Clearly that ability to stun the mind is their main weapon, and not speed.

BLAM! BLAM! BLAM-BLAM-BLAM. BLAM! BLAM!

And then all the shooting stops. Three of the enormous

scorpions lie in front of me, the closest one now more than four feet away. I look downhill. Three more dead ones there. Ana and Victor both wave up at me with triumphant looks on their faces. But they only wave with one arm, each of them still keeping watch in case there are more scorpions yet to come.

But there are not. I can feel that through my power. The tingling in my hands subsides with the last twitch of a claw from the closest dead monster. Three feet from my boot.

If Hussein had not brought me to my senses, I might have been the one dead.

Hussein! Is he all right?

That thought hits me like a punch to the guy.

"Hussein?" I blurt out, turning to look behind me—and almost running into him as I do so.

"Lozen," he says. "I am here."

He holds out his hand toward me. I want to take it. In fact I want to hug him. But I don't. I'm feeling angry at myself for being so concerned about him. And angry at him for making me worry. Totally illogical, I know. But I still glare at him and step back.

He lowers his hand. A wry smile comes to his face, "Ah," he says. "Good. You are back to yourself again."

"How?" I say, my voice coming out as a growl.

Hussein's smile grows larger. "Totally yourself," he says, whatever that means. But he has understood my question because he pivots and makes a sweeping gesture that takes in not just the three super-scorpions I terminated, but an additional four—four!—that his own competent shots accounted for.

"I have seen such things before," he said. "Not here, but far away. The djinn who befriended me taught me how to resist the net they throw over the thoughts of their prey."

He walks back up to the crest of the hill and looks down toward the rest of our party. All of those affected by the monsters' mind attacks are back on their feet again. They are gathered around Ana and Victor, who are attempting to both keep watch and explain what happened at the same time.

"How?" I ask again.

Hussein, who seems to be able to understand my verbal shorthand as well as Guy always did, knows right away what I am asking.

"They are like you," he says, his voice soft and certain. "Your brave sister and your strong little brother. I see them growing more so each day. That is why they were able to fight off the touch and the poisonous ones. You would have done so yourself if not for what I see happening in you, my dear friend."

What do you see? That's what I start to open my mouth to ask.

"Lozen?" a voice says.

"Lass?" says another.

Both Guy and my mother have come up the hill to within arm's length of us and, once again, I have not been aware of anyone walking up behind me.

What is going on with me?

"We shall talk later," Hussein says as he turns and walks back down the road toward the others.

"Are you all right?" Mom says.

"What now?" Guy asks.

I have to look strong for them. I have to act self-assured. I paste a smile on my face.

"I'm fine," I say. "But now . . ." I look up as the hazy sky, where the sun is four hands above the western horizon. Then I look down the snake of road that leads north and west.

"Now," I say, my voice ten times as certain as I am actually feeling, "we need to find shelter for the night." I point with my chin toward that square building four miles ahead of us. "And that might do."

CHAPTER NINETEEN

Running

I'm running. But as fast as I run, it's faster.

I don't know what it is that's after me, but I know my only hope is to run. I reach down to my belt. My belt isn't there. My knife isn't there. All of my weapons are gone. I don't know where they went. Why am I running? Why don't I turn around and fight? I can't beat it, but at least I can die trying.

It could catch me if it wanted to. I know that, too. But it's playing with me the way a cat plays with a mouse, enjoying every moment of this chase. Someone told me that a cat does that because the meat tastes better after it's been flooded through with adrenalin.

Was it my father or Uncle Chatto who told me that? I could always remember before, but now I can't. I can't think clearly. All I can do is run.

There's something ahead of me. A big stone at the base of

a cliff. It's moving. No, it's being moved by a large hand reaching around it. It's a door and I know who is behind it, who's opening it just in time to save me. I dive through the doorway, and the stone swings back into place with a reassuring thud. I hear the muffle sound of my thwarted pursuer striking the stone on the other side. It's snarling, gnashing its huge canine teeth, roaring in frustration. But it can't get through. Not now. I'm safe.

I look up from the floor of the cave at Hally.

"What took you so long?" I ask him.

But he doesn't make a wisecrack in reply. He doesn't show his teeth in a smile. He just stares at me, his face blank of all expression.

"Hally," I say, changing my voice so that it sounds like the cartoon rabbit in an old viddy, "Uhhh, what's up, Doc?"

No response. Neither spoken nor mind to mind. I might as well be talking to the stone door he opened to give me refuge from the creature that was about to tear me limb from limb.

Then it comes to me. I remember what Coyote said about Hally. That Hally is more than I think he is. That he is not from around here.

"Yes," Hally says, opening his mouth at last. But he does so in a stiff, mechanical way. "Yes." His hollow voices echoes through the cave and I am pushing myself backward until I feel the cold cave wall against my shoulder blades.

"Time to show you," he says, his voice booming. "TIME."

I hold up my hands in a T shape. "Time out?"

No response to that, no sense of humor at all.

"We came here," he says, that emptiness of emotion in his voice, "to serve you."

He's holding a book in one of his hands now. With the other he peels the skin back from his arm, disclosing the gleam of metal. He's a cyborg, part organism and part machine.

"We get power from the Cloud," he says. "Another kind of power than the electricity you humans generated. That power has been building, and we have been getting stronger. Now we are strong enough. Now we can reveal ourselves. Now you must know."

He tosses the book into my lap. I can now read the title on its cover.

HOW TO SERVE MANKIND

I open it up.

It's a cookbook.

He's got on that corny chef's hat and the apron we saw him wearing in his cave. His big hand reaches out and grabs me by the shoulder. I try to pull free, swing my arms trying to hit him, kick with my feet.

"Nooo!" I'm shouting. "Nooooo!"

Lozen, Lozen! Wake up!"

The hands that are holding me are not Hally's. Nor are they the hands of one person. Guy has one of my arms and Hussein has the other. Ana and Victor have their arms wrapped around my legs. My Mom and Luz are standing as far away from me as they can. Mom is holding my gun belt in one hand and my sheathed Bowie knife in the other.

As soon as I see that I stop struggling. There's enough morning light coming in through the small windows high in the walls for my confused brain to see where I am.

We're not in the cave I saw in my dream. We're in that square building I spied from the road yesterday afternoon. It had turned out to be a big three-roomed stone house, built almost like a castle in some previous century when such heavy walls provided protection against enemies. Its two giant oak doors were intact, and after we'd wrenched open the big padlock that held them shut, we'd found the place entirely empty. It was big enough to fit us all and even bring in the Dreamer's beloved cart. We thought it would be a perfect refuge from danger for us. Which it was, until I turned out to be a threat all by myself.

A dream. It was just a dream, and one that ended with a corny punch line out of an ancient science fiction story. Crap! You'd think my bad dreams would at least be more original.

"I'm awake," I say. "You can let go. I'm all right."

"Unlike some of us," an ironic voice says. I look up at the Dreamer, who is pointing to the bruise on his left arm.

"Sorry," I say. "It was a really bad dream."

"For us as well," the Dreamer says.

Everyone lets go of me, and I stand up. I'm all right, as I said before, but I get the Dreamer's point as I look around the room. Things have been thrown in all directions. Guy has a bloody lip, and it looks as if Hussein took the worst of it. His face is marked in more than one place, and he is surely going to have a black eye. The look of concern in Hussein's eyes makes me feel ashamed of myself, but when I turn my gaze away from him I see something that makes me feel worse, lower than a snake's belly. Both Victor and Ana have scrapes on their faces where I must have kicked them.

"I'm really sorry," I say again. "Really."

The Dreamer turns back toward Lorelei, who is looking at me from around his broad back. He puts his hands gently on her shoulders.

"All is well, dearest," he says, his voice both sardonic and reassuring. "She'll kill us all some other day."

My mother has handed my gun belt and my knife to Victor.

"Lozen," she says, speaking my name in a way I've never heard it spoken before. "Come with me, daughter."

She takes me by the hand and leads me away from the others, to the farthest back room of the building where a bench is built into the walls.

"Listen," she says, sitting me down. Her voice is soft but intent. "Listen."

My mother is so serious, more serious than I've seen her before. It's as if she has determined to show me some part of herself that I've never seen before. I've always thought of my father and Uncle Chatto as the strong ones in my family. But there's something about my mother right now that reminds me how strong our Chiricahua women have always been, and that my connection to the powerful woman who was my namesake came to me from my mother's side of the family.

"There is a story I have to tell you," she says. "It's not winter time, I know. But you need to hear this now. And though it is not night, it is dark enough back here that the sun cannot see us. So, are you ready to listen?"

"Yes. I'm listening."

Long ago, so they say, a girl and her little sister and some other children were playing in an arroyo. They dug a hole in the bank of the arroyo to make a cave.

I will be a bear, that girl said. I will go into my cave and you call me to come out.

She crawled into the hole and the other children called to her from outside.

Here we are. Bear, try to catch us.

As soon as they called to her, she crawled out. She turned to the east and the started after the children. She chased after them but did not catch them. It was so much fun that they did it again.

This time, though, when they called her and she came out she had the paws of a bear. None of the children noticed that as they ran from her. Her mind was still that of a human being. She turned to the east and the south. Then, just as before, she chased them and no one was caught.

A third time she crawled back into her den.

Here we are, Bear. Try to catch us, the children called out a third time.

When she came out, her whole body was that of a bear. But her head was still that of a human being, and her thoughts were those of a little girl. She turned to the east, the south, and the west. No one noticed how she had changed, and all the children got away when she chased them.

The fourth time she crawled into her den was different. When the children called her out, every part of her had become a bear. She turned to the east, the south, the west, and the north. The children screamed in fright and ran from her. She caught them, one after another, and killed them all until she came to her little sister.

Please, her little sister said, do not kill me. I was your sister. I will help you.

So the bear spared her. She took her into her hole and made

it bigger. Then the bear ate the children she'd killed. She turned their skulls into water buckets. Every day the little sister had to get water in those buckets and bring it back to the bear.

Each day the father of the girl who had become a bear and the five fathers of the other missing children went by the mouth of the cave looking for their little ones.

Do I hear people passing by? the bear would say each day.

No, it is only the wind in the trees, the little sister would say. She did not want the bear to kill her father and the other men.

On the fourth day, when the men went by the cave, the little sister saw that the bear was asleep.

She crawled out to the men and told them what had happened.

Soon the bear will come out and kill you all, she said. You must run away.

Her father and the other men were all frightened. They had a council to decide what to do.

We must gather wood, the father said. Pile it in front of the cave and set fire to it. Then we can run away while the fire keeps the bear inside the cave.

That is what they did. They lit the fire and started to run as far as they could toward the east. When the fire burned out, the bear came from the cave and ran after them to kill them.

The six men and the little sister ran till they came to a big mountain, a holy mountain. They climbed to the top. When they got there, they prayed for the wind to help them. The wind blew a cloud to them, and they climbed into that cloud. It carried them up into the sky where they became the Seven Stars we see each night.

So it is that we see those stars. And we tell our children they must not pretend to be a bear. They must keep their thoughts the thoughts of a human being.

By the time my mother has finished her story I've put my arms around her and leaned my head on her shoulder the way I used to when I was just a little girl. She kisses my forehead.

"Lozen, my daughter."

"Yes, Mother."

"You know who you are. No matter how much you have to carry, no matter how much your power gives you, you will stay who you are."

"I'll remember that."

"I know you will."

She pulls me to my feet. "Now go help clean up the mess you made."

I'll try to do as she says. Despite the fact that I seem to have just made a decent attempt at slaughtering all of my companions in my sleep, her story has made me feel a little more like myself. I'm not a bear. I will not try to kill my friends and my family.

I'm not healed. I can feel that sickness in my heart. There's still a blackness in me that I have to struggle against. But my mother's story has reminded me of my human identity, the role I need to accept and continue to play.

I walk into the main room. There's no real cleaning up for me to do. Everyone else took care of it while Mom was talking to me. The Dreamer has already loaded his cart and pulled it outside. The sweet scent of wood smoke is wafted to me on the dawn wind. Someone has started a fire on one side of the building, and I can smell coffee being brewed.

I walk through the open doors, the morning sun touching my face. I look out at the land, at the mountains that are glistening as bright as turquoise in the light of the new day. This world is still worth living in.

Worth fighting for even if I have to fight myself to do it.

CHAPTER TWENTY
Tahhr

Tahhr. Tahhr. Tahhr.

He woke to the sound of his name. The little ones were speaking it as they crawled over his chest seeking play.

Tahhr sat up. He pushed them off him gently so that they fell onto the grass piled deep on the floor of the shelter. As soon as they landed, they rolled over and leaped back to attack his feet with small growls.

Tahhr picked them up, one in each hand. He held them close to his long-snouted head, opened his mouth to show his rows of long sharp teeth.

Tahhr will eat you.

No, no eat. Play with us.

Laughing at him as they said it, Tahhr joining in their laughter as he rolled onto his back, dropping them onto his belly.

Tahhr.

His mate, speaking his name.

Derhha?

Smoke. Smell it?

Tahhr sniffed the air. Smoke. Not close. Smoke carrying a meat smell and the sharp odor of something else.

He crawled to the entrance of the shelter. Good shelter, he thought as he grasped one of the bent branches. They had woven it together in this high place with a good view, finished it just before the day fire dropped behind the hills.

A good place for a shelter, Tahhr thought again. Many flowers all around, flowers that smell much better than smoke.

There, Tahhr said, pointing toward a plume of rising smoke beyond the farthest. hill. Far, but not far far.

Derhha pushed him. Gently, but firmly.

Go, she said. See what makes smoke. Then come back quick.

The little ones growled at Tahhr's feet.

No go, they said. Stay and play.

Smoke. It meant fire. It might also mean bad humans. And that was not good. Derrha was right. He had to go and see. There were humans in the hidden valley that was even farther beyond that smoke. But those humans were not the bad people who hunted those like Tahhr and his family.

Tahhr picked up the little ones and hugged them.

Tahhr will come back quick, he said. Then I will eat you.

He put them down, started to leave.

Wait. Derhha was holding up something. Flowers she'd picked. She wove some of those white flowers into Tahhr's hair, stepped back and looked at him.

Good, she said. Now go and come back quick.

Bending his head as he crawled from the shelter, Tahhr stood and then paused for a moment, feeling the warmth of his family behind him. He stretched his long red-furred ape-like arms—ape-like aside from the retractable claws on the ends of his fingers. The eyes in his massive head, like that of an immense tiger, were—if anyone had been looking into them at that moment—surprisingly human. Another evidence of the genetic splicing that had made him and his mate. Both of them, and their two cubs, were an equal blend of great cat, orangutan, and human DNA.

He smelled the air. Familiar odors, natural things. Pine nuts almost ready to gather. A rabbit under that bush over there. Blossoms just opening on the cactuses after the rain that fell two days ago.

Good smell. Good smells.

The only thing different was that troubling smoke. It might mean bad humans.

Nothing of a bad human scent anywhere near yet. That was good. To avoid such humans was important. They were the ones who had caged Tahhr and Derrha, disappointed when neither of them was fierce enough, and so had planned to terminate them. Tahhr knew this because he had learned enough of their speech. Even before the pulse fences vanished, allowing the two of them to get away, he had been planning their escape.

Tahhr was a good hunter. A good gatherer. So was Derrha. They lived well, sometimes eating fruit, berries, nuts, sometimes hunting deer, antelope, smaller animals.

Never be seen by humans, even the good ones.

Stay away. Stay away.

Sometimes they were attacked by strange creatures, ones that smelled wrong. But Tahhr and Derrha were good fighters. One thing they could do that those other nasty creatures could not was throw rocks, heavy ones. And when they made their nests for the night they always put them in high places like this, places nothing dangerous could easily reach them without being heard or smelled.

Their lives were good. Better since the cubs.

Tahhr dropped to all fours. He could run more easily that way than up on two legs. With great bounds he went down the slope, out onto the plain. That valley where the smoke rose was a place he had not yet been. If there were humans there, then they would have to move farther away. But best to see, best to know.

And then come back soon.

CHAPTER TWENTY-ONE

Enemyway

We've paused for a mid-day break. The road was so hot that the soles of our shoes were sticking to the pavement. Everyone was feeling drained of energy by the relentless heat.

Continuing on at this time of the day would have been too hard on everyone. This spot, though, is an amazing break from the dead-seeming land we've been trudging through hour after hour.

I felt the spring that gives life to this little oasis before I smelled or saw it, my power responding to the throb of its waters. It is just a short way off the road, a hundred yards back in a notch where two hills shoulder down, the water flowing from a break in the layers of stone.

There are a few medium-sized trees growing here, and the spring is even strong enough to have created a small stream that runs for a hundred yards over the bedrock before vanishing again through a deep crack in the stones.

A cardinal is calling for its mate from the top of the tallest of the cottonwoods, and I can hear insects singing in the grasses and brush closest to the spring and its brief rippling brook. The angles of the hill have made this a shady place. It's so comfortable here that it would be tempting to stay the night. But not wise. We need a place with the security of something over our heads and at our backs. We'll have to keep going.

But not right away.

I'm sitting by myself on the shelf of rock above the spring, the only solitary one at the moment. The Dreamer and Lorelei, as always, are together by his cart. My mom, Victor, and Guy are downstream with their shoes off and their feet in the water. Guy is actually chuckling as they talk. The two who are closest to each other right now are my sister Ana and Luz. They are leaning against each other, smiling down at what they are holding between them in their laps. I'm trying not to listen to them, either with my super-keen hearing or my ability to grasp the thinking at the top of their minds, the things either about to say or barely holding back from speech.

I hear the whisper-soft scrape of a shoe on the stone above me, someone coming back downslope. I know who it is, of course. It's Hussein, who decided to climb up to the hilltop to both use that height to study the land we'd soon be crossing and to look back to make sure nothing dangerous is behind us.

"It is clear," he says as he lowers himself into a deep squatting position next to me. "No danger."

I already know that. I picked up that part of his thoughts even before I heard the sound of his feet approaching.

He gestures toward Ana and Luz.

"See?" he says. "This is good. She has found something that she did not know before. Someone like herself, almost another self. One of her own age who shares more with her than a brother or an older sister could ever share. She has found a friend. They can sit together and whisper small harmless secrets to each other before they sleep. Inshallah, it is a blessing."

I look over at Luz and Ana. Their heads are close together as they bend over the object held between them, big smiles on their faces as they discuss it. True to who they are and what our everyday lives are like, what they are talking about is not a piece of jewelry or a kitty or a new blouse. It's a sniper rifle they've just disassembled, cleaned, and put back together.

"Lozen," Hussein says.

His face is close to me now, so close I can feel his breath. "I am looking into your eyes. They are beautiful eyes, more beautiful than you know."

I start to say something. I'm not sure what. My breath is catching in my throat. But Hussein raises his hand.

"Wait," he says. "Listen. I see something in your eyes, behind your eyes. It is a darkness. And sometimes, those times when

154

my mind touches your thoughts, I sense that darkness, too. And I know what that darkness is. I know from where it comes."

How? I think.

"How do I know? I know because that darkness has been within me as well." He reaches down to lift up the bag of coins at his waist, shakes it so that I hear the jingle of metal against metal. "Each of these," he says, "each is a memory. Each is a life. A life that I took."

He lowers his head. "When you saw me, back at Haven, what did you see then?"

I don't reply, but "the most handsome man I'd ever seen" is what I am thinking hoping he's not hearing my thoughts.

"You saw a humble gardener," he says. "You saw a man who played his guitar and sang gentle songs. Is that not so?"

Again, my part of our conversation remains the same—no words at all.

Hussein raises his head. The look in his eyes surprises me. There is a fierceness there I haven't seen before. "It was my disguise," he says. "I would not let them see the one I had been, the one who had been trained in the ancient ways of the Hashishim, the assassins who served the Old Man of the Mountain. Trained and well able since I was half the age of your brother to kill in silence, in more ways than one can easily imagine. It was the life of my family for generations before me. We were Bedu, true, but more than that. At night our other selves came alive, and we did the work we were sent to accomplish for our Overlords. And it birthed something within me, a blackness that grew with each human life I ended, as my bag of coins grew heavier."

He pauses again. He is holding my hand now and I am not pulling away from him. I gently squeeze his hand.

Go on, I'm thinking. *Go on.*

He sighs. "The time came when the weight was too great for me to bear. It came after my family, all those close to me, were slain. Only I escaped. Ah, I made sure that the slayers of my family did not see many more sunsets. But in that revenge I took no satisfaction. I was lost, my spirit soiled by blood. I wandered then into the desert, ready to give up my miserable breath. But a djinn found me. One like your friend Hally. He took pity on me. He showed me how to find peace by putting my hands into the soil. By bringing forth life. And then—do not ask me how, for I do not know myself—he arranged for me to be brought here to your land, only days before the great Cloud came to obscure the eye of the sun. Thus it was that I found myself at Haven, accepted there because my hands had gained such power in aiding the growth of green things."

I nod. It explains so much about my friend, my true friend Hussein. I'd wondered at the abilities he'd shown since our escape, about the reason those seemingly useless coins were always on his belt.

He has also given me something. Knowing that he's felt something like the confusion within me is important. Though it does not lift my own darkness, it makes it easier to understand what I am feeling. More importantly, it is helping me to understand not just that that I need to be healed, but that healing is possible.

As I think that, I remember something my father told me.

"One who has to take other human lives may become sick," my father said. "It has always been that way, even for the Hero Twins. That is why Enemyway came into being."

My family's roots are not just Chiricahua. We also have Dine ancestors. Navajo as well as Apache. And Enemyway was a central Dine ceremony, an important one still being practiced until the Freedom from Religion laws were passed and all of our healers were either imprisoned or terminated.

That had happened before I was born. So what my father described was only a bare outline of what that ceremony used to be. But because he and Uncle Chatto had both gone through Enemyway, his words were charged with meaning.

"It came from the time of the Holy People, when the Hero Twins were born to White Painted Woman. Those boys were known as Child of Water and Killer of Enemies or Monster Slayer. They took it upon themselves to destroy the great monsters that threatened to end human life.

"But those mighty brothers discovered that killing, even killing merciless beings that might be seen as evil, lays a burden on your spirit. Even just touching the enemy can make you sick. So Enemyway was given to restore them to balance. It cleansed their hearts, cooled their insides, straightened their minds, and restored their strength."

Then my father described what the ceremony was like. He

157

said the healer made a beautiful painting on the earth using different colored sands and ground-up bits of dried bark. The painting depicted the Hero Twins, and my father was seated in the middle of that painting as the ceremony went on. It lasted for days. Not just the healer was there—his family and his friends were there as well, all joining their minds together to support him and pray for his healing.

And it worked.

"Our men who went to war all needed that," my father said. "War causes enemy sickness. Our white brothers understood that, too. They just called it by different names. Battle fatigue. Shell shock. Post-traumatic stress. But they did not know how to treat it the way our old people did. They did not have Enemyway."

So now I know what is wrong with me. I am suffering from enemy sickness. That is what has been filling me with a feeling of hopelessness about as deep as a tunnel to the center of the earth. But how can I treat it? Like those white men my father mentioned, like all of us now, there is no longer such a ceremony. I do not have Enemyway.

"Lozen?" Hussein says.

I open my eyes. I hadn't realized that I'd closed them.

"Something shall come," he says. "I am certain of that."

Then he releases my hands, stands, and walks down to the spring, leaving me alone with my thoughts.

CHAPTER TWENTY-TWO

Strange Scent

With the wind in his face, Luther stood atop the rise. Smoke was still lifting from the place he was headed. It was farther away than he'd thought, beyond the high hills on the other side of a wide plain. He had left the clockwork cycle behind when he climbed up here to find a vantage point. Nothing would bother it while he was gone. A certainty because of the measures he had set in place around the machine: traps involving trip wires and small, highly effective explosive charges.

Better safe than sorry. Another of his mottos.

Not as eloquent as the lessons of Miyamoto Musashi, whose *Book of Five Rings* had been the bible of the elderly Japanese ninja who had been his second teacher, Master Ito. His specialty had been the skills of small hidden weapons, of poison and stealth, and not being seen—emphasized in his lessons with blows across his student's back.

You must see and not be seen.
Whack!
Invisible!
Whack!
See and not be seen!

On days when there were many lessons the boy's back was welted and bleeding. Had it not been for Luther's powers of healing, it would have left wide white scars.

The old man proved not invisible enough to dodge the small, thin-bladed knife Luther drew on the day of their last lesson. It had pierced Master Ito's left eye, terminating both Ito and the second year of Luther's education.

Luther lifted his head. The small after-dawn wind still blowing in his direction brought him something different. What was he smelling? A rather pleasant aroma that seemed a mix of feline and anthropoid. Something large and living.

Which meant it could be killed.

Why miss an opportunity?

It took some time to traverse the distance he could have easily crossed in a matter of minutes. But his stealth was worth it when he peered out from behind a large stone and saw them. Three of them. And they had no idea they were being observed.

Alas for them.

Because Ito had been on his mind, Luther decided to honor his old master by using one of the skills he'd been taught so carefully. The throwing stars? Adequate for the small ones, true. But not for a creature as large and powerful-looking as the big one. The muscles rippled under its skin, moving as only large apex predators do. Its beauty brought a smile to Luther's face, a sincere smile. He deeply appreciated beautiful creatures.

It made killing them all the more meaningful.

But how? Not the gun. Ito had no respect for firearms. Unlike Luther, of course, who was totally unprejudiced about weaponry. As long as it killed what it was used against—that was all that counted.

No, to honor Master Ito, in whatever hell he now resided, Luther would use the most subtle of the deadly skills beaten into him by his cold-hearted first master.

Luther placed the red darts on a flat stone, taking time to admire their sleek shapes, the fine craftsmanship that went into their making to ensure that they flew straight and true. He took out the small wooden bottle, unscrewed the top, and carefully envenomed each tip. Prepare, prepare.

Prepare and you will not despair.
Whack!
Prepare and you will not despair.
Whack!

What a pity the old man could only be killed once, Luther thought.

Then, one after another, he placed a dart in the tube, lifted it to his lips, puffed out his cheeks, and blew.

Three times. Three perfect shots into the delicate skin of their ear openings.

The rictus of their limbs and the foam that dribbled from their mouths showed there was no need for a coup de grâce. It pleased him that the poison had been so swift and efficient. But one thing he noticed brought Luther regret. Tracks in the soft earth, larger and deeper than those made by the female, led away to the northwest.

Should he wait for the fourth one's return? No, he had other business to attend to.

Still, there was one more amusing thing that he could do. One that would likely bring the missing one to him eventually.

Pleasant work. Though it did take a bit of time. The skin proved unusually resistant, even in the small ones. Perhaps tough enough to prevent the penetration of a knife thrust, or even a bullet. But Luther was determined and, once through the epidermis, found it easy enough to saw through muscles, separate bones.

Perfect.

He took his machete from his belt and cut three stakes, one large and two small ones. He sharpened them at both ends, humming as he did so.

CHAPTER TWENTY-THREE

His Cart

We've crossed twenty more miles of barren country since my conversation with Hussein. I'm still trying to process it all. I feel as if I know him in a way I never did before, a way that has brought us closer together. And his words helped me. But not enough. It's become clearer to me that I need something, some ceremony, some way to bring my mind and spirit back into balance.

I need help. Those three words keep going through my mind as I plod along on the roadway that is only a little less hot and dry than it was at noon.

I need help. I need help. The sound of my feet as I walk echoes the rhythm of my thoughts. *I need help. I need help.*

But where will I find it? Maybe in our valley there will be an answer for me.

I'm feeling impatient about getting there. It would have been so much quicker if I'd just been alone. I could have cut across the hills, crossed the plain beyond, and scaled the small mountain that was its eastern boundary. Then I would have been looking down into the only place where my family ever knew peace.

But that kind of cross-country travel is not possible while you're leading eight other people and dragging a donkey cart. People who all expect me to help them, to lead them. And among those eight people the only two who have some understanding about what I am going through are Mom and Hussein.

But even they can't give me the final answer that I need. Maybe no one can.

I need to pull myself out of my despair, think of something else that will take my mind in another direction. But what? I pause, then step to the side to let the Dreamer and his cart roll past me.

His cart. I haven't complained, at least openly, about our having to keep to the open roads because of that cart. After all, it's certainly a useful addition, filled to the top as it is with various devices well designed to perforate, eviscerate, or just plain blow up any entity that might decide to view us as its daily entrée.

And, I'm not the one who's been pulling it. That task, of his own choosing, has fallen almost entirely to the One who was once bowed down to like a god and now has taken on the role of a beast of burden. Though even he has been affected by the noon heat and welcomed our recent break, pulling that cart has never appeared to be a difficult task for him. He hardly breaks a sweat when we go up a hill, and he easily holds the cart back from rolling over him as we descend the steep, winding grades we've been encountering on this two-lane track, which was seldom used even before lev-cars made highways unnecessary. Whenever we take breaks they are not for his benefit.

The road is level just now along this hilltop, the plain below visible for miles. All we need to do is go around a few more bends and we'll reach the place where we can take the side trail to Valley Where First Light Paints the Cliffs. Plenty of time for that. We still have at least another four hours of daylight.

There's a pull-off next to me, an area perhaps forty feet wide and sixty feet long shaded by the brow of a red-stoned hill flecked with mica. Hussein is about to go around that bend. The Dreamer and the donkey cart are twenty yards behind him. That cart. At this angle I am noticing something about it I didn't see before. Hmm.

I make a quick decision.

"Stop," I call out.

The Dreamer halts, as does everyone else in our line of travelers, including Hussein. I jerk my chin toward the pull-off. The Dreamer turns the cart effortlessly and pulls it back my way.

Soon we're all gathered together.

"Half an hour break, okay?" I say, looking at Hussein and Guy, who was the last to join us, coming up from his position at drag.

Guy and Hussein both nod their agreement. Though I am more or less in charge, it's usually the three of us together now who make such decisions about our journey as to when and where to pause or spend the night.

There's no spring here, but enough moisture has seeped from the rocks in the back of the pull-off for a few scraggly chamisas to take hold and bring forth yellow flowers. There are bees and other insects buzzing around them, life grasping at every opportunity it can to survive in the midst of all this barren land.

I sit next to Guy on a stone bench that must have been put in place more than a century ago to provide a spot for travelers to sit and look out over the vista below us. It's also possible from here for me to keep an eye on everyone in our party, which makes me feel a heck of a lot more secure. No one is being attacked at the present moment, which is a pleasant change.

Ana and Luz and Victor are a little farther down slope from us with Hussein, listening to him play his guitar, which he's retrieved from the Dreamer's interesting cart. Lorelei and my mother are sitting only a few yards away from them.

The only one still on the road, next to that two-wheeled wagon of course, is the Dreamer.

"He hardly ever goes far from your donkey cart, does he?" I say to Guy.

"Na," Guy agrees. "But it's not my cart, lass."

166

"What do you mean?"

"It's his. Showed up at the Armory with it in the midst of all the turmoil ye caused. Things blowing up and burning. But him as calm as a cucumber."

"His cart?"

"Aye. Said 'twas time for us to load it up and go."

Hmmm again.

I stand up and walk over to the Dreamer, who is standing on the far side of the wagon. His wagon. He's gazing out from the overlook. There's a bit of a smile on his lips, visible just below the mask that covers the rest of the face.

"Ah, wilderness," he says as I approach. "It is Paradise enow, is it not?"

"I suppose so," I say. I am not about to ask him what that word "enow" means.

"Indeed. And with our mellifluous friend down there singing like a Chinese nightingale, all that we lack is the proverbial loaf of bread and jug of wine."

Enough.

"I have a question for you."

"And why am I not surprised?"

"Why did you have this cart?"

"I did? Why use the past tense, my little assassin? Does not one have it still?"

"Stop it!" I chop the air with my hand. "Straight answer.

Guy said you showed up with this at the Armory. Was it just to pick up weapons or was there something else already in the cart? Something that you have not yet told us about?"

The Dreamer nods and leans back against the cart. "As always," he says, "you surprise me, Lozen. And you are indeed correct. There was and still is something else, something more precious than weapons. Do you know what that is?"

I think hard. In this new world of ours there's no longer any such thing as money. All the old objects and read-outs that meant wealth, from digi-credits to diamonds, are meaningless now. The real essentials are water, food, safe shelter, and weapons for self-defense. There is barter, yes, but only for useful things or actual services. Not tokens with no intrinsic worth of their own.

The Dreamer chuckles, knowing he has me confused.

"I could show you," he says. "But first, a test of your powers of observation. You must tell me what you have noticed about this wagon. What is unusual about it?"

I walk around the wagon. It's no small thing. It's fully twelve feet long and eight feet wide. Clearly it was made by hands that knew how to craft something strong and serviceable. It's banded with iron, and the metal wheels are circled by thick rubber, not tires with tubes that could be punctured and flattened. I look under it at the sturdy leaf springs, the heavy brackets on the bottom that hold firmly in place the twin bars by which it can be pulled.

What was it made for? It's serving the function of a munitions cart well enough, but what was its original purpose? Or *was* it meant for something else? What, as the Dreamer said, is unusual about it?

I look into the bed of the wagon, which is barely visible through the piled cartridge boxes and arms of various kinds.

Ah-ha! Just as I thought.

I step back and look again at the cart, noticing its height this time.

"I see it," I say.

"What do you see?"

"The bed of the cart is only halfway down. There's a false bottom."

The Dreamer claps his hands in barely audible applause.

"Excellent," he says. "Full points." He steps forward, presses two rivets in the side of the cart and then pulls out a wide, heavy drawer.

"Behold," he says with a theatrical flourish of his hands. "Step forward and see what is worth more to me than all the wealth of Araby—nay, more than my life itself."

CHAPTER TWENTY-FOUR

Black Black

Tahhr looked down into the valley. It had once been pretty, but not now.

Wisps of smoke were rising, but nothing else was moving. And the smells were bad.

Tahrr climbed down the cliffside, stepped onto the blackened grass that crunched under his feet. Grass black, trees black. No leaves, no birds. No insect sound.

Tahhr walked farther, remembering how it had looked when he had watched the humans who had lived here, seen they were not bad people, left without their seeing him.

There were still humans here, but not living ones.

His throat was dry. He paused where the water ran down from the cliff, water that was still clean before reaching the small stream below that was grey and flecked with ash. He drank deeply, then dipped water over his head. That was better, but the bad smoke smell was still there. On him, on everything.

What was it that made the smell so bad, worse even than the sick, sweet odor of burned flesh? Then he remembered gasoline—that was what it was called.

He growled at that memory, the memory of bodies like his soaked with gasoline and then burned while bad men watched.

He rose to two legs and walked farther, wiping the black from his paws as he went. Ahead were the shelters where the humans who were not bad had lived. Broken and burned now. And within the shelters were humans. Broken and burned.

The smell of guns was also in the air. Guns fired many times. Tahhr touched his arm as he remembered the bad humans firing their guns, aiming at Derrha. But Tahhr had stepped in front of her, taking the bullets that barely pierced his thick skin. He had taken the guns from the two bad humans who fired them. He could have killed both of them with one blow from his clawed hand.

No. He broke the guns.

Run, he said. Then he and Derrha ran. And the bad men did not follow.

Why did bad humans kill all these people? Why kill other than to eat? Why just kill to kill?

Tahhr shook his head and walked farther. Then he stopped, looked down.

A small one was there, as small as Tahhr's cubs. Not burned, quiet as if sleeping.

Tahhr dropped to all fours. Slid his hand beneath the small human with yellow fur on its head. He held it up close to his face.

No. No breath, its life was gone.

Tahhr reached up for one of the white flowers Derrha had placed in his hair.

CHAPTER TWENTY-FIVE

Books

Books.

That is what fills the drawer the Dreamer's just pulled from his cart. They had been concealed behind the curtains of his rooms at Haven. People thought those curtains hid devices of torture. Instead, they protected his library.

He strokes the binding of the closest book. "Milton," he says. He touches another. "The Romantics. Shelley, Byron, Wordsworth, Keats." Another. "Shakespeare." His hand continues tracing the names embossed on each book. "Great classics of western literature. Even dear old Dodgson and his little Alice—a bit like you, my dear. A lost girl wandering a strange land."

I've hardly understood a word since he opened that drawer,

but I do recognize the real emotion in his voice, the veneration as he speaks each name—that of some long-dead author, I assume—with such care.

"A collection," he says, "like no other. Books became such an archaic thing after everything was digitized. All those mega-trigs of data that vanished—poof—like smoke from the caterpillar's hookah as soon as the power went off. True, some libraries remained, but only briefly. The No-Nothings saw to that, mobs burning every book they could find as if knowledge was the cause of our downfall. They ravaged the libraries here—and, I must assume, everywhere around the globe, since human mob madness is a disease that spreads beyond reason. The idea of burning all those old books had been put forward well before the coming of the Cloud, you know."

The Dreamer puts his hands up to his face, touching his forehead under his mask. "I hope, pray, there are others like me. Ones who used what power they had to preserve the best of the true heart of humanity. And not just of the West."

He pushes that shelf back in, presses two more studs, and another shelf comes out. Some of the titles there are ones I remember seeing in his rooms. "Books of your peoples. Myths, legends, histories, such writers as Momaday, Silko, Harjo, Alexie." He shoves that shelf back in, and a third one emerges.

"And here are classics of the East. The haiku poets—Issa, Wang Wei, Basho, and the others. *The Ramayana*, the poets of the T'ang dynasty, *Gilgamesh*, the Talmud, *The Thousand*

and One Nights . . . even—in both Arabic and English—the Koran."

I hold up my hand before he can close that shelf and bring out another one.

"Wait," I say. "What was that last book?"

The Dreamer cocks his head at me. "The Noble Koran, the most holy book of the Muslim faith," he says. "Why do you ask? Did I miss something? Did your Apaches become Mohammedans?"

"Can I have it?" I ask.

"Why would you . . . ah, wait. It is not for you. Yes, I see by the way your face is growing redder than usual that my surmise is correct."

"Never mind that," I growl. "Can I have it?" I bite my lip. "If I can have it I promise to help you protect your books."

The Dreamer cocks his head first to the right and then to the left on his long, supple neck. For a moment I feel like breaking that neck of his and barely hold back a second growl.

But then he chuckles. "Ah, me. As fate would have it, I have not one but two copies. And I suspect our mutual . . . friend will take excellent care of this."

He removes the book with his left hand and holds out his right.

"Have we a deal?" he asks. "This book for your special protection of my priceless collection? Shake on it?"

"A deal," I reply, taking his hand.

We set out again exactly half an hour later. An hour's walk and we are almost there. And I am worried. What I thought were clouds on the horizon were something else entirely. I can see that now. As they gradually stopped forming and grew thinner, I realized they were not lowering themselves from the silvered sky. They were coming up from the ground. They were smoke.

Cooking fires? No, too much smoke. If it were any of our people, such campfires would have been small, carefully made with the right sort of wood to give off little smoke. Our fires were never made to give off so much smoke unless to send some sort of message.

I'd hoped that we would find people, Chiricahua people, in Valley Where First Light Paints the Cliffs—people who'd been in the valley with us and escaped when those heavily armed men from Haven killed my father and uncle and took my remaining family and me captive.

Haven was far enough away, the lands around it so difficult to travel because of the dangers that lurked by day and night around it, that I'd hoped no one other than our people had been back to our valley since we were dragged from it.

I look at the four tall rock spires. They reach up like the pillars of a giant lodge whose ceiling is the sky. Shaped by wind and time, carved smooth by countless years, they're circled in sandy layers of red and gray, yellow and black. Uncle Chatto referred to them as the Guardian Rocks because they stood at the place where the entrance of our valley was first visible from the trail.

Not that the entrance is easily seen, even from there. It's a narrow path, almost too narrow for the Dreamer's cart to negotiate. It can only be found by someone who knows it's here or stumbles on it by chance. There are other steeper ways to come into the valley, but unless someone or something is sure-footed as a desert bighorn sheep, those ways are almost impossible to follow.

There's a very faint odor on the air beyond that of the smoke. But I can't quite place it.

"Dead end?" asks the Dreamer, pointing at what seems to be nothing more than another ridge rising up a thousand feet beyond the Guardian Rocks.

"For your cart," I reply, unable to resist the urge to see if I can shake his usual superior self-assurance.

He almost does look perturbed, but only briefly.

"Oh, do tell," he says, his voice as smooth as butter.

I sigh. "No, there's a trail. It's just hidden around the next bend."

"Lead on, Macduff," he says.

Macduff? Who the heck is that? Another one of those weird remarks of his that I suppose I'll only understand after I read some of those books he treasures.

I look around at our little party. Guy, as always, is calm. Luz, who once again is standing right next to my sister Ana, has a sparkle in her eyes I haven't noticed before. Not only that, her hair is brushed and shining, and her face is clean. She and Ana might be two carefree teenagers off together on a walk, if it weren't for the M-16 rifles—lighter and easier to carry than a 30.06—they each have over their shoulders. And Victor, also armed with an M-16, is staring right now at Luz with a transfixed look on his face.

For the first time I realize that Luz is a rather pretty girl. Considering the fate that was always in store for pretty girls back at Haven—where the mercenaries serving the Ones always had first pick—it becomes even more obvious to me why her father, Guy, had her hide her light under a layer of grime and loose, shabby clothing. No doubt that my little brother has developed a crush on her.

My mother looks thoughtful. Though she does not have the powers that have somehow chosen me, she is a very insightful person and senses my disquiet.

Lorelei is sitting on the back of the wagon next to the Dreamer.

All of those people, every one of them, even Guy, are waiting for me to tell them what to do.

Me, as if I knew.

I turn to Hussein, who's come up to my right. Quietly waiting. His rifle is unslung from his shoulder. I jerk my head in the direction of the trail and lift my rifle. He nods, raising his rifle up in front of him. The two of us will go in to the valley and reconnoiter.

"Everyone else," I say, "wait here."

We start walking. I'm counting out steps in my mind. One and one pony, two and one pony. Fifty paces, a hundred. I feel the heat building in my palms, and do not have to lift them to know where the awful thing is that my power is warning me about. It's inside Valley Where First Light Paints the Cliffs.

As soon as we go around the bend it hits me—*it* being a small swirl of wind coming out of the valley's nearly hidden entrance and the scent it carries. It's the rank smell of the sort of smoke that never came from a cooking fire.

I say "nearly hidden" for a reason. The brush and trunks of fallen trees that had always been placed to conceal the little roadway leading into the valley have been moved aside and not replaced. The ground shows the tracks of booted men. Ten or more of them. Some of those tracks lead into the valley and equally as many tracks—from those same boots—lead out.

Their boot tracks head off due east from the entrance, back toward the wide, deserted interstate highway that we've avoided, taking a safer, more roundabout way to get here. If we'd come that way, we might have met them on their way back—back to Haven. I have no doubt about that.

If they did what I am afraid they did inside our valley, that meeting would not have gone well for them. Not well at all.

Someone sent them here who knew the location of our valley. It had to have been the Jester or Lady Time. I'm squeezing my left hand into a fist, pressing it against my forehead. No healing is waiting for me in here.

I should have known. I should have known.

"Lozen?" Hussein whispers.

I open my eyes and look at him, read the same anger and despair in his dark eyes, as well as the same kind of grim determination that has kept me going for so long.

He's just smelled what I've smelled on the wind: the sick-sweet odors of gasoline and burnt flesh.

I nod at him, and we enter the valley of death together.

The highest parts of the cliffs that flank the valley are visible, glowing gold and blue in the light that is touching them from the west. That's all we can see at first. It's briefly reassuring. Those high cliffs look just as they always looked during the sweet, quiet years my family and I lived here.

Hussein and I still have a small rise to climb before we can look down into the valley. I'd been looking forward to this for so long, hoping for the day when I could again breathe in its beauty. That was what I had been looking forward to until today. But now I just dread what I know deep in my gut I am about to view.

Butterflies should be lifting up from flowers, grass moving in the small wind, birds chirping as they flutter from the junipers and the pines. Small animals should be moving about in the brush. But all I can hear ahead of us is silence. And when we reach the top of that little ridge, silence is all that lies before us.

There's no grass to move in the wind, only flakes of ash rising from the charred floor of the valley. The trees are blackened skeletons, the birds and insects and animals gone—killed or fled before the conflagration. The smell of smoke and gasoline is heavy now, as well as another scent even more awful.

The dried black stubble that was once tall grass crunches under our feet as we walk forward. I'm stunned by how thorough the burning was. It must have been like a furnace in here. How did they do it? How could they?

There were people here, those of our people who had escaped, I'm certain. How many? I stare into the remains of the shelters we pass as we continue on. The valley is a quarter mile wide, half a mile long. Outcrops of stone reach into it like arms, and it is against those outcrops, sheltered from weather, that people made their homes.

And every home has been burned, as well as the people within them.

I'm counting them under my breath. One, two, three, four, five. They might have been people whose names I'd remember. But now there's no knowing who they were.

Other than my soft counting, neither Hussein nor I say anything as we walk on. I've now reached twenty dead bodies, twenty people whose lives were wiped out so brutally. From the wounds we've seen, visible even despite the burning, most of them were shot before the fires consumed their homes.

It's such an old story, a story that was repeated again and again for my people as they fought to remain in their homelands. First against the Mexicans who took them as slaves, then the Americans they'd tried to befriend in those battles where my namesake Lozen and her brother Victorio fought so hard. More than once the white eyes believed they'd wiped us out. We no longer existed as a people. We even started calling ourselves Indeh, rather than Tinneh. The Dead, rather than the People. But somehow we survived, even after our children were taken to their schools and told to forget all our ways. We even survived the brutal, impersonal rule of New America. And when the Cloud came and the power vanished, we remembered enough of our old ways to find places such as Valley Where First Light Paints the Cliffs.

But now? Now, when every point on this journey has been along a trail of death?

I can't give up, no matter how sick, how uncertain, how lost I feel.

"You still haven't beaten us," I whisper. "Even now."

I know Hussein heard me whisper that. The fact that he nods but remains silent shows me how much he understands my words.

There's just one more outcrop ahead. As we start to walk

around it, I feel a wave of awareness from my power wash through me.

Something is ahead of us around there, something living. I motion for Hussein to get low as I drop down myself to crawl forward across the blackened earth. I place my hand on the rock outcrop, lean forward to look around it. What I see is something totally unexpected.

Below me is a huge creature, something that looks like a giant cat. It is crouching in front of the remains of a burned shelter. A gemod. It has to be. But the scent of it coming to me on the light wind is not unpleasant. It is actually almost human. In fact, its two upper limbs look more like those of a human or a giant ape than any sort of feline beast.

I move closer, my rifle held up to my shoulder, looking over the sights, trying to see what it is doing. As I do so, a small twig hidden in the blackened stub of grass cracks.

The creature turns, and I see what it's holding. It's the body of a baby, held close to its gaping, sharp-fanged mouth as if about to bite its head off.

"NO!" I yell, and almost of its own accord, my finger pulls the trigger and my rifle fires.

It strikes the creature. I hear the thud of my bullet hitting it in the upper chest.

But it doesn't fall back. It just raises its head further, and its eyes look into mine—its eyes that are so human. Not at all fierce but filled with a very human emotion. Filled with sorrow.

It puts down the body of the baby, quickly but gently. And as it does so I see the flowers woven into the huge being's hair. I see the one white flower that it has dropped on the chest of that tiny dead child.

And its silent voice touches me, speaks mind to mind.

Why hurt Tahhr?

Then it leaps, not at me, but away in one huge bound.

Hussein is next to me, raising his weapon as the creature leaps again, up the almost vertical wall of the cliff, scaling it as if it was weightless and not three times the size of a tiger.

"No!" I push the barrel of his gun down.

I stand up, my rifle slung back over my shoulder. I cup my hands around my mouth,

"I'M SORRY," I shout. I hope it hears me, but it just keeps climbing, reaches the top, goes out of sight.

I'm sorry.

You should be.

The voice that intrudes into my head is the one I've been listening for. But why now, why when I feel as if I've just done something terribly wrong?

Hally? I think.

No, it's the Spanish Inquisition!

Huh?

Never mind, Little Food.

"Stop that!"

"Stop what?" Hussein says. That's when I realize I just spoke those last two words out loud.

Hussein is looking at me, waiting for me to explain not just what he should stop, but also why I just stopped him from shooting at a creature I just shot. While I am standing here, knee deep in what feels like mental quicksand engaged in silent dialogue with a Bigfoot.

I lift my hand to tap my head by way of explaining to Hussein just what I'm doing right now. But I forget it's the hand that is still holding my rifle and I bonk myself in the temple with the barrel.

Ooh, I bet that hurt, Little Food.

I almost say something but I hold it back because Hussein would probably assume it was his ancestry I was questioning with that remark. Instead, exercising the utmost self-control, I rub my forehead—with my free hand—and say through gritted teeth, "It's Hally."

"Oh," Hussein says. Then he moves a respectful distance away, leaving me space to continue my soundless communication with the person, if you can call a ten-foot hairy giant a person, who's chosen to help me in the past.

Hally, my currently unseen sasquatch ally who—after all we have been through—still keeps addressing me like I was hors d'oevres.

Why can't my life be less confusing for a change?

Because.

If it is possible to mentally scream, that is what I feel like doing now. But I try to calm myself down.

Be logical, Lozen. Ask questions.

Hally, where have you been?

Around.

What have you been doing?

Stuff.

Aaargghh.

Are you going to ask me who's on first?

What?

He's on second.

Here I am, standing in the midst of a scene of death and desolation, and I'm engaging with an abominable snowman in what I recognize as a silly routine between two corny actors in a viddy that was about ten times as old as I was when my father brought it up for me on our outmoded holoscreen. It's all so ridiculous that I have to smile and shake my head.

And, though I doubt he can see me right now—unless he's hiding somewhere underground nearby and looking out through a peephole—Hally seems to have sensed that smile.

That's better, his mental voice says in a tone that is much less joking. **You were in need of a touch of comic relief.**

More questions that I have words for are flooding my mind. What has he been doing? Is he back to help us? Can he explain what happened here in this place of refuge now transformed into the valley of death? Can he tell me about that creature with such sad human eyes that I deeply regret having shot? I want to ask those questions and more all at the same time. And, in a funny way, I can sense that Hally knows that, is hearing that jumble of uncertainty in my head, but is maintaining a calm, mental silence.

Hally?

Yes.

Thank you for coming back.

Don't mention it.

What can I ask you?

Whatever you want.

But what will you answer?

Whatever I want.

I can see what this conversation is going to be like unless I frame my questions better.

Could you just tell me some things?

Things you need to know?

Things I need to know? Why does that sound familiar? Then I remember.

You sound like Coyote.

Ah, Coyote. Now there is a creature after my own heart. But I am not about to give it to him. He will just eat it.

This time I do not phrase, if you could call it that, another question. I simply wait. I've been too impatient. Keeping silence is always the best way to hear something. I sense something like approval from Hally's end.

Good. You are listening. And there are things you need to know, or at least be prepared for. As well as things you know already.

There's a mental pause. He's waiting for a reply.

I know that I'm sick, I think back at him. *I know that this valley*—I look around—*has been lost to us. I know that I need help.*

Good. Three correct answers out of three.

Can you help me, help us?

There's a long pause. I look around, wondering if I am going to see him pop up out of the ground from a hidden tunnel. But the only thing moving is high in the sky above us. Turkey buzzards are starting to circle, having smelled or seen the death below that simply means food to them. I don't resent them, but I also am not going to leave this place without making sure that we have first properly buried the bodies of those who were murdered here.

As I think that, I sense Hally's presence again. First there's a general feeling, not anything put into words, of his sympathy, his approval. Then he mentally speaks.

I am busy now with . . . other things. So you will not see me now. But soon, very soon, you will see others. They can help you—unless you kill them first. Please do not do that. So, when you leave here, head north. And now, sadly, our tête-à-tête must cease. Toodle-oo, Little Food. Hello, goodbye. I must be going.

I sense his presence withdrawing. But there's another question I want to have answered.

That creature I just shot? You said I should be sorry. What was it?

There's a moment when I think I've lost our connection. But then Hally's voice touches me one more time, faintly as if withdrawing at great speed, but clear enough for me to understand.

You can ask your tall masked traveling companion about him.

And this time, swift as a shadow, short as any dream, he's gone. I still don't feel fully myself. How could I in the midst of this carnage? But for the first time in a long time, even though I have no idea exactly where we are going to go—aside from north—I feel a renewed sense of purpose.

Hussein is patiently waiting, his back turned, his eyes focused on the cliffs. There, high above the blackened devastation of what had been such a peaceful place, the light of the silvered sun is painting changing patterns on the ancient stones.

He lowers his gaze to look at my face. "It was good?" he says. "Your talk with the djinn?"

I nod.

"I am glad," Hussein says. "Inshallah. It is a good omen that he's returned to you."

I nod again and we begin to walk back toward the entrance to our lost valley. Hally is back and seems to be helping me, in his typical enigmatic way, once more. I should just accept that and be glad of it.

But my brain, as usual, is not about to totally let go of doubt. I'm remembering that crazy dream of mine in which Hally's purpose in serving humanity turned out to be directly related to the culinary arts.

As well as Coyote's words that Hally was more than he said he was, that he was not . . . from around here.

CHAPTER TWENTY-SIX

Flowers

Tahhr ran onward, swifter than any human could run, swifter than most of those others that human beings call animals. As fast as he ran, he felt it was not fast enough.

He ran straight, leaping over boulders, crashing through branches rather than going around the bushes and trees in his path. All of his strength and all of his simple, clear thoughts focused on one goal. Reach Derhha and the cubs. Move them safe—away from all humans, all humans.

But as his long strides and leaps ate the distance, something came to him. A terrible foreboding, the start of a sense of loss that could not be explained, an ache of something absent from the world. Nothing that he could express in words, but something felt like the earth under his feet, the breaking of branches, the wind in his face as he crossed the plain.

And then, on that wind, he smelled blood.

He reached the base of the high place, looked up and saw the faces of Derhha and the cubs looking down over the edge of that ledge where they made their shelter. But their eyes were blank as they looked down, not at him, not at anything.

A final grasp of stone, a great leap, and he stood there on the ledge. Seeing what he saw. Seeing what he sees.

Tahhr raised his head toward the silvered sky, opens his mouth, and shattered the air with a roar, a scream, a cry of such intense agony that if anyone were close enough to hear, it might have burst their eardrums, sounded as the world was being torn.

Like Tahhr's heart when he saw the severed heads of Derrha and the cubs impaled on stakes and placed so that they seemed to be looking out over a world as empty as his life had now become.

Tahhr lowered his head, arms out, sniffing the air, catching the human smell. A growl came from him, as deep as thunder rolling.

He found the bodies of Derrha and the small ones, placed his hands, his claws retracted, on their chests, and felt something come into his heart, a part of them that could not be stolen, that had waited to join him.

Where the earth was soft enough, he began to dig. He made the grave deep, gently lowered Derrha into the hole, piled flowers around her neck, her eyes closed now. He placed the cubs in each of her arms. The three of them sleeping together. Flowers all around them. He gathered branches from the yellow flower bushes to cover them before he began to push in the earth. When all the earth was in the grave he began to bring heavy stones, fitting them carefully together as if making a wall that would last a thousand years.

Then he stood. The light in the sky vanished and he remained there in the dark, unmoving. All through the night Tahhr stood, unmoving as the stones on the grave, the heavier stone in his heart. At last, when the light began to show itself again from the other side of the sky, he moved. He lifted one paw hand, the claw of his longest finger extended. He pressed it to the left side of his head, drew it down to cut into the skin, blood flowing as he drew a long line from his eye to his chin. Then, next to it, he cut two shorter lines.

The human scent of the one who killed his family was strong. It would be easy to follow. He would find the bad human who did this, and he would end his breath.

And if any other humans got in his way, he would end them, too.

Tahhr turned his face away from the mound of stones and all he loved. He leapt down the cliff face, ran following the trail, a trail that told Tahhr more about the one he was tracking. It was the trail of one who did not seek to hide his tracks, the arrogant trail of one sure of himself and his power.

Take care, the trail told him. The one you follow is strong.

So Tahhr made use of cover as he ran, staying on all fours, close to the ground. Swift as the flow of water among stones, he wound his way around juniper trees and pines, past great stones sparkling with bright colors. Once Tahhr would have stopped to listen to the small birds in those trees, to look at such sparkling stones, delighting in their beauty. But not now. No room any longer for sweet things in his thoughts. Only this trail, this trail he had follow. It led him down, down until it reached a wide road.

The trail of tracks on the earth ended. It ended where there were marks in the softer earth and sand. Tahhr had seen such marks before, marks he had not seen in many seasons. Those even, parallel lines could be only be from one thing.

A machine. A machine with wheels. A machine that carried the human away, carried him onto the hard black road where no trail of feet was left behind.

Tahhr stood up on his hind legs, arms dangling, opening and closing his fists, extending and then retracting his long claws, aching to tear at the flesh of the one whose trail ended here. The deep thunder growl rumbled up from his chest.

The trail on the ground had ended. But not the trail on the wind. The machine had its own scent, as did the killer who rode it. Tahhr would follow that wind trail of human and machine.

Follow until breath ended.

Something fell from the hair on the side of his head above his right ear. It fluttered down to land on the black road. A white flower. The last of those Derrha had placed in his hair.

Tahhr bent, retracting his claws. He picked up the flower from the black road where the heat would wither it, looked at its six white petals, the delicate yellow of its heart. He walked back off the road, placed it in the shade at the base of a glittering stone, touched it. Once, twice, three times.

Then he turned back to the road, dropped to all fours, and began to run.

CHAPTER TWENTY-SEVEN

Road of Stars

Twenty-six. That is how many we buried before we left the valley. At first, I'd thought that only some of us would take part in it, but I was wrong. Even the Dreamer and Lorelei helped dig the graves. It was the hardest work I've ever done, and I am sure it was that way for all of us.

It made it physically easier that we found a large, unburned storage shed back near the entrance to the valley, which held shovels and other tools—tools meant for gardening in our valley's fertile soil. But we would not be planting seeds now. We also found rolls of canvas meant as covering for wickiups and lean-tos. That canvas was used to wrap the bodies of those we pulled from the burned remains of their homes.

I'd wanted to keep my sister Ana and my little brother Victor out of it, but they would not hear of it. Ana just grabbed a spade and walked off with it before I could say anything.

"I can dig, too," Victor said, his hands wrapped tightly around another of the shovels.

In this world of ours, this world of so many uncertainties that death seems to be the only sure thing to be found on our trail, how could I refuse him?

Even with all of us working, it took a full day, a full summer day when the silvered light from the sky shines longest. Then the darkness settled in as suddenly as a blanket pulled over a face.

I'm standing alone now at the narrow neck that is the opening into the Valley Where First Light Paints the Cliffs. Aside from Hussein, who is also standing watch, everyone else is taking shelter in or around the storage shed where we found the tools and canvas. It's just about a hundred feet behind me. Though we will not be staying here, it's the safest thing to do just for tonight before we move on. The cliffs that rise high on either side are so high that it is only when you fly like a bird or walk to the very edge that you see our valley is here. Those cliffs are just gray shadows now. The only light to be seen comes from the sky. There's no moon tonight, so even though the cloud that never leaves is casting its thin haze across the night sky, many of the brightest stars can still be seen, especially those that make patterns that tell stories.

One of our oldest is about how Coyote got involved in putting the stars into the sky.

Back in the before time, before we humans were here, the

story goes that one of the Holy People had the job of putting the stars into the sky. All those stars were in a bag, and that Holy Person carried them to the top of the highest mountain. Then the Holy Person began placing them carefully, one by one, creating shapes that held great meanings.

Coyote came up to that highest mountain to watch.

"My friend," Coyote said, "I would like to help you. Can I help, yes?"

"No, my friend," the Holy Person said. "This has to be done with care. You are too impatient, Coyote. Just watch."

So Coyote watched for a while as the Holy Person made the shapes in the sky with those bright stars. It was taking a long, long time.

"Can I help you?" Coyote asked again. "This is taking way too long."

"No, my friend," the Holy Person said. "I told you, this has to be done with care."

But Coyote kept asking. He was refused each time, but each time he edged a little closer. Finally he was right next to that bag filled with stars.

"Look!" Coyote said. "What's that over there?"

The Holy Person looked. There was nothing there. But when that Holy Person turned away to look, Coyote grabbed the bag of stars. He opened that bag wide and hurled all those stars into the sky. Some just scattered here and there, but many of them fell together, making what looks like a wide trail all across the sky. That sky road has been called the Milky Way by white people.

That is why only a few of the stars in the sky make shapes, because of what Coyote did. I've heard it said that the story shows how bad things result when you get impatient. But you never know about Coyote. Sometimes when it seems as if all he is doing is bringing chaos, his actions produce something that's good. After all, his tossing that bag of stars into the heavens made that trail of stars.

I can see some of that sky trail tonight. Although the Silver Cloud is always there like a thin fog across the whole of the night, tonight that swathe of distant lights seems brighter than usual. I can see why some people used to believe it was the road that our spirits travel after we die, a path that leads to a better place, a home in the sky land where there is peace and abundance and happiness.

Uncle Chatto told me about the sky trail. He'd heard the story about it being a spirit road from someone he worked with, back in the old days when he and my father were warriors for the state. Though there were no longer any big wars of one nation against another, there were always people who tried to rebel, and it was the job of those like my father and Uncle Chatto to "pacify" them.

Pacify. Whenever Uncle Chatto spoke that word, their word, he would shake his head and say a little "Huh!" under his breath. And then he would usually say, "We did it because we didn't know any better. We were young and foolish and strong—and expendable. That is why they chose us."

The person, the other warrior who told Uncle Chatto his story about the sky trail, was also an Indian, but he was a Lakota from up north named Lenard. Those Lakotas, Uncle Chatto said, were more stubborn than some about giving up their old ways. Even after the FFR laws, they held onto stories and ceremonies in secret. Lenard said that the Milky Way was actually the footprints made by an old wolf who was the leader of his people. When he died, his spirit made those footprints so that the spirits of his people could follow him and be reunited after death, adding their tracks as they passed from the earth. Then when the human people came, the spirits of the wolves allowed them to use that same trail, and those people, too, left their prints across the sky.

Does that Sky Trail look brighter tonight because the spirits of those we just buried are following it?

I don't know.

But what I do know is that I am not ready for my spirit to follow that trail. I still want to do everything I can to protect those with me and keep their feet on this earth.

I hear someone's feet approaching now and recognize the sound. Every person walks a little differently, and if your ears are as keen as mine have become, you may be able to identify who it is before you see them.

"Victor," I say, without turning around.

He comes up next to me, then he wraps both arms around

me and rests his head against my shoulder. He's gotten much bigger over the past few months but has still not reached my height. I may even have grown a little myself during this past year. I'm not as tall as the Dreamer's towering height or Hally's massive stature, but I am taller than everyone else in our group of refugees.

"Lozen," he says.

That's all, but I don't have to read his mind to know what he's thinking.

"Yes," I say. "It was hard."

"But we had to do it," he says. The certainty in his voice surprises me. What he says next surprises me more.

"Are you all right?" he asks. "It's been so tough for you for so long."

I turn to look down at the shadowed profile of his face. My little brother has not come to me to be comforted. He's concerned about me, trying to lend me his support. Maybe I haven't done as good a job as I thought of hiding my anxiety from him and his sister. Maybe he has grown up even more than I realized over these past months.

He tightens his grip around me, and I squeeze his shoulder, feeling how much muscle is there.

"You're right." I admit. "It has been tough for me—for all of us. But I think we are going to get through it. Especially if we stick together."

I feel him nod. Then he unwraps his arms and looks up at me. "I better see how the others are doing," he says.

"Good idea," I agree.

The area of the storage shed where we are spending the night is protected by an overhang of cliff and screened on the other side by thick pines. It's the only place where the vegetation was not wiped out by the burning, and now that the wind has changed the awful scent of that burning can barely be smelled there. It's well enough hidden that no approaching enemy would see us until they were very close.

I located two places outside the valley entrance where sentries could best be posted to guard the valley entrance. Hussein is already at the first of those places. I'll soon make my way to the second one. The two of us will keep watch half the night. Then Guy and Ana will take the next watch till dawn.

I doubt that I will sleep at all tonight, not even after my watch is over. My mind is racing so much that it makes my feet want to start running.

But where can my feet run now, where can I lead everyone who depends on me, now that this valley so clearly can never be our home again? And what will we be running toward other than enemies—both those with sharp teeth and hungry mouths and those who carry weapons and walk on two legs?

I look up at those stars one more time and then turn my eyes back to the earth and its perilous roads that we still have to walk.

CHAPTER TWENTY-EIGHT

Four Deaths

The first death was the hardest.

His own death, that is.

Not his first kill. That was easy.

The look of surprise in the man's eyes when he realized that the boy he was fighting was stronger and quicker than he'd anticipated. Strong enough to break the man's left wrist and take his blade. Then the feeling and sound of the knife sinking in, the thud of its hilt against his ribs.

His knife teacher had not been pleased by Luther's success. He'd expected the man (one of his better pupils) to win. Not kill the arrogant boy, but control him, pin him to the ground, cut off just one ear. He told Luther that.

Which made it so much more pleasurable for Luther six months later when he opened his knife instructor's throat with one simple passing back stroke.

Luther's own first death was not from a blade, but a bullet. It was a stroke of bad luck. The gun that fell from the man's dead hand discharged as it struck the ground. And that steel-jacketed round pierced Luther's cheek and left eye. It missed most of his brain, but the shock stopped his heart. Darkness filled him.

When he woke from the cryo-chamber, though, he could see through both eyes. One was his, the other transplanted from the man who'd killed him. Since he'd killed the other man first, Luther had shown how valuable he might prove to be in the future and earned the right of revivication.

His body had proven easy to revive, the brain damage so minimal from the grazing of the right temporal lobe that it could barely be detected in scans. The only lasting result was that it left Luther with a bit less empathy.

It was a great relief that the surgeons chose not to add anything inorganic. Something in him made the thought of electronic implantation anathema, so much so that when the opportunity of such enhancement was offered in future years, he refused in no uncertain terms.

"Put anything more in other than flesh and blood," he growled to the med techs, who grew pale and quickly nodded, "and I'll tear your hearts out and eat them."

So it went with Luther's future repairs—the regrown lungs that replaced those destroyed by the acidic gas that led to his third death, the spinal column replaced after the fall killed him the fourth time—all were of real flesh and bone. No metals, no microtech devices.

Luckily for him, considering what happened with the advent of the Cloud.

He did appreciate that his replacements that were upgrades, though. The heart received after his second death—when his chest was pierced by a lance-sized piece of metal after the explosion he caused went off a bit prematurely—was much stronger and more durable. After all, it was grown expressly for him, expertly designed and created in a matter of minutes from stem cell–grown tissue on the med staff's tri-dee printer.

Luther braked the clockwork cycle. He ran his right hand back through his hair.

There was a prickling on the back of his neck. His hair stood up. He'd had that feeling before and knew to trust it.

He looked behind him down the road, straight for a dozen miles before bending around those bluffs. Another twenty miles back beyond that bend was where his cycle had been parked while he dispatched those cat-like beings.

Something, Luther thought, *is following me.*

He smiled. Of course. The mate of the big female creature he'd killed. He was not surprised. It was just what he expected, considering the little message he'd left for it. Luther's smile turned into a grin.

Heads on stakes. That was how it was done in the old days after destroying an enemy's village. Frighten the survivors from seeking revenge or make them foolhardy in their pursuit.

"You want to kill me?" Luther said. "Me? Kill me."

He thumped his chest with one fist. "Me?" he shouted, his voice echoing back off the face of a nearby cliff.

Then he laughed. "Get in line, kola. Take a number."

He pressed his foot down to engage the gears. "And catch me if you can."

The warm wind in his face, the heat of the sun on his face, Luther continued on eastward on old Route 10, as a rusted road sign read. No scent or sign of the ones he was hunting. He might catch their trail faster if he left the road and went on foot. But he liked this machine he was riding.

Keeping to the highway might delay his eventual meeting with that enemy killer he'd been sent by Lady Time to terminate. But why deny himself this pleasure, this feeling of near flight? He pictured how he looked as he drove, just like that viddy character—unstoppable, unbeatable.

Hours passed. He halted only once to rewind the mechanism, a procedure that required only a bit of time.

Then, as he came to a place where another road led due north, he stopped. He thought he'd seen, out of the corner of his keen right eye, something moving in the distance. That northern road was not one he had planned to take. It led up through an area where military weapons were once tested and army exercises had taken place.

He shaded his eyes. Yes. There was something there. He turned onto that road. Heavy fencing was still intact to either side. What he'd seen, miles away, was moving away from him up that road, running at a speed almost matching that of his cycle. But not quite. He was gaining on it little by little. Still too far to see all that clearly, but not a machine. An animal on four legs, running. And was there something on its back? Before he could be sure, whatever it was veered off to the left, leapt high, leaving the road and moving into the rougher ground within the fenced area. Then it dropped from sight.

Luther drove on another three miles. He came to the place where whatever he'd seen had left the road. The earth was hardened, but there was one large nearly round print to be seen where a hoof had dug into the earth as that big creature leaped off the road and over the eight-foot-tall fence.

No opening he could fit his cycle through. The ground beyond was rough, hilly, cut by coulees. The speed of that creature's travel meant he could not catch it on foot.

He cursed loudly. He'd wanted to catch whatever it was. See what it was before he killed it.

Another time.

He turned back to Route 10 to continue his original mission.

CHAPTER TWENTY-NINE

A Gentle Monster

I've done as Hally suggested and continued north. I've led us up from our camping place in the entrance to our lost valley to the larger road, Route 10, that leads north. Because of the Dreamer's cart we could not just cut cross-country, the way I would do if I was on my own. I'm keeping my promise to him, helping him guard his priceless cargo, especially since that cart holds a hoard of death-dealing devices just as precious to me as his books and much more immediately lifesaving.

Not that he agrees with me about that.

Just this morning we had another one of those discussions that makes my head ache. It started because—and this is ironic—I needed his help in deciding which way to go. It turns out the Dreamer also has a book in his collection that contains images of the land around us. I know because he chose to show it to me.

It's an ancient volume he calls a Road Atlas. It is filled with detailed charts of the entire continent. Maps—at least insofar as you could call something a map that is just lines and shape and colors on a simple 2D page, and not a holopic. But they do show mountains and rivers and roads, where towns and cities are or used to be.

He can read it much better than I can and thus offer advice on what he thinks may be the best ways to follow as we travel north, and what we'll find there. Such as, for example, that if we go far enough northwest we'll come to a giant hole in the ground. It's a place that I know nothing about other than it was called the Grand Canyon and it stretches for miles from east to west with no direct way over it. So we'd have to steer ourselves either northeast or northwest to go around one end of it or the other.

I know, I know. I'm supposed to be the one who knows this part of the world because it was the land of my ancient people and so on and so forth. But my own experience has been limited to the places around our valley of refuge and then maybe a fifty-mile radius—at most—around Haven. And we are going to soon be well beyond the trails where my own feet have trod.

I'm not my dad or Uncle Chatto. They truly did know this land as well as they knew the lines in their own hands. They're the ones who traveled, who met interesting people of all sorts—some of whom it was their job to kill, until they'd had enough of that.

By the time the Cloud came, in point of fact, Uncle Chatto and my father were on more than one list for termination. It was only by hiding themselves in plain sight, so to speak, that they'd managed to avoid being caught. Both of them had so much expertise not just in direct battle, but in the sort of cyber warfare that was once part of our world, that they'd been able to sort of confuse the computer nets about who and where they were.

Getting back to my little conversation with the Dreamer, it began when I asked him a simple question as he sat on the ground with his back against his cart.

"Can you look at a map for me?"

He looked up from the book he was reading, a book of philosophy by someone named Bertrand Russell.

"I can indeed."

He turned his attention back to his book. But I could tell he was just waiting for my next question. I flexed my fingers, took a slow breath.

"Will you look at a map for me?" I said.

"Ah, that possibility certainly does exist," he replied. Without even looking up.

He's enjoying this, I thought. And I would enjoy strangling him. But I kept my cool on the outside.

"Please," I said, "take out your Road Atlas."

"But of course," he said, putting the book he was reading

back into the open drawer, closing it, and touching a hidden catch to open another drawer. "Since you ask so nicely."

He extracted the volume in question. "And now?" he said.

"Please," I say, trying to be as precise as possible, "show me the page that relates to our present location."

"How well put," he said, opening the book with a graceful flick of his wrist. "One is glad to be of service."

And so it went. Well enough that I was able to get a sense of the land beyond what I could see with my eyes and make a plan as to which way we should go during this day. In addition to assisting me in charting that course, he was also able to provide advice on where we all might, just *might*, find shelter later tonight. It's an abandoned museum. (A museum is a place where people used to go to look at old stuff from the past instead of just viewing their viddys on stick-ons and holo-screens.) The walls, as the Dreamer recalls—having been there many decades ago (did I ever mention that he is over 140 years old?)—are quite thick, and the doors should be easy to barricade shut, assuming the place still has doors.

Though we might have to do a bit of, ah, pest removal first seeing as how such structures are often the haunts of unpleasant lurking things.

Great.

But before we started up, I did ask him a couple of other things, being careful how I worded my queries.

"Will you give me that book I asked for now? The Koran."

"Of course."

A careful pressing of the side of his cart in yet another area, and a new drawer slid out. He ran his fingers delicately across the spines of the volumes within.

"No, not this one, nor this one. Too precious, Ah, indeed. A more modern printing—only a century ago. With an adequate English translation addended, to boot. Not as deep or as well as some, but 'twill serve, 'twill serve."

I took the book from him with both hands, feeling that since it was something Hussein would probably treasure, I should show it that sort of reverence. I stowed it carefully in my pack.

"One more thing," I said.

"Oh, only one? What a surprise, my little Inquisitor. But then no one ever expects the Spanish Inquisition, do they?" He raised an eyebrow.

"One thing," I repeated.

"*Do* go on." He settled back against the cart again and steepled his fingers.

"Yesterday," I said. "I shot a gemod."

"Oh my, what a surprise. Nothing like *that* has ever occurred before."

I held up my hand. "Wait, I'm not finished. I shot it, but the shot didn't seem to bother it that much. I did not kill it."

"My, my, there is something new under the sun, Horatio. Might one inquire why?"

I felt troubled by what I was about to say, by the memory it brought back to me.

"It looked like some sort of cross between a tiger and an ape. I mean, it was huge and dangerous looking. But after I shot it, it just looked at me. Its eyes were so human and that look—it made me feel that I was wrong to have done what I did." I paused. "I even said I was sorry as it ran away."

"Hmmmm." The Dreamer had placed his steepled hands against his mouth. "Quite interesting, indeed. By why recount this to moi?"

"I thought you might know something about a creature like that. Do you?"

The Dreamer nodded. "I was never one to engage in certain of the pastimes so popular among my peers. By that I mean the transmutation of species to produce the sort of horrendous results that spelled their own dooms and now trouble us at every turn. But I was always curious." He chuckled. "The disease of the librarian, I suppose. So I did keep track of the various permutations, mutations, and genetic combinations being brewed up—a witches' brew of toil and trouble—in our quadrant of this continent. In our immediate environs certain things were popular, but not the intermixing of homo sapiens with the lower orders. Such, alas, was not the case to the north and west of here."

I got it. "You mean some of the creatures made there were part human."

The Dreamer clapped his hands together. "Indeed. Full points. And being human in part meant certain human traits, intelligence in particular, made them even more dangerous. Or, in the case of the one you encountered, not."

"Not dangerous?"

"Well, not exactly. After all, a creature made up of the tweaked DNA of a human, a giant feline, and a massive ape, when properly constructed, might have immense strength and more than the intelligence of the average non-human monster. That could always be dangerous. But unlike most of the deranged creatures created by my Frankensteinian colleagues, the one you describe—one I have indeed heard about—also was possessed of such human qualities as empathy, thoughtfulness, and a tendency toward preferring to observe other life appreciatively rather than crushing it out of existence. Harkening to the songs of the birds at sunrise. Pausing to breathe in the sweet scent of a flower in bloom."

The memory of the flowers in the creature's hair came back to me and the regret inside me at my hasty actions became even stronger. And I suddenly realized what its unspoken words must have indicated.

Why hurt Tahhr?

Its name was Tahhr.

"A gentle monster?" I said, my voice soft.

"Quite. And thus it, and its female counterpart, were seen as quite the disappointment by the One who made them. They

214

were so well made, their skins so thick as to make them virtually bulletproof, their musculature absolutely extraordinary. But they refused to fight, simply evading any creature that was set against them or, if cornered, merely rendering it immobile or unconscious. I found that all rather charming. However, the One who was their creator was deeply, deeply chagrined."

The Dreamer dropped one hand down low. "Quite deeply. So much so that I'm rather surprised that one of them survived. The last I heard, the One who owned them had decided to, shall we say, remove them from his inventory. Mind you it was but a week before the advent of . . . "—he gestured at the sky—"that. So mayhap they had not yet been reduced to their component organic elements."

We're making good time as we travel, despite my mental turmoil. Guy and I are taking the lead. Hussein is behind everyone else, taking the drag position.

We're all going at what my Uncle Chatto called a wolf-trot pace, less than a run, more than a walk. Aside from Lorelei, who takes breaks now and then to ride on the Dreamer's cart, no one is having trouble keeping up, including Ana and Victor. Both of them have continued their training with Hussein, and it shows in their increased stamina these days.

We've gone at least twenty miles thus far today. Our breakfast of oatmeal and preserved meat from the two javelinas was enough to give us plenty of energy for traveling. Maybe, in the town we're heading for, where that museum building the Dreamer spoke about is located, we'll find some other provisions. Maybe even some other real human beings.

I know we're not the only ones surviving on our own. My power has told me that. Now and then I get the feel of others like ourselves, not nearby perhaps, but out there on their own and not held in walled and guarded communities as we were at Haven. For now, we'll have to be careful to avoid walled places that are ruled by crazed and maimed former Overlords. Not a good idea to come to their attention, with so few of us.

The Dreamer has also pointed out several of those fortified strongholds on one of the maps. One is near the city of Phoenix to the west of us, another is located in a mine near Bisbee to the south, and so on. No. And no again. The feel of those places, when I reached out and felt each them, was just plain wrong. Twisted. Nothing for us but the likelihood of conflict and death.

I turn my power to the north. Somewhere there I feel the faint touch of distant, seemingly normal minds. Ordinary people who are trying to care for each other. But how far away are they? Dozen of miles away, hundreds? I have no doubt now that somewhere ahead of us to the north there are people we'll meet up with sooner or later. But the way that darkness sits inside me, confusing me, and the fact that I am still new to this part of my perceptions, seems to mean that I am not totally

216

in control of my power. I can't focus it the way I can focus my eyes or hearing on something. It comes and goes, like my mind-reading ability, almost on its own accord. So far it has shown up when I've needed it, but it is not with me all the time.

With one exception. Lately I seem to be aware every waking moment that there is a very strong and dangerous presence behind us. One that is gradually getting closer. That awareness is so strong that it isn't easy for me to concentrate my power elsewhere. The soundless voice in the back of my mind keeps warning me about it, making my hands tingle slightly when-ever I turn back that way. Another reason for us to press ahead at a trot on this trail of the dead.

There's a slight rise a hundred yards ahead of us. The road is climbing a small hill, and we slow our pace a little. There's an arroyo off to either side, and a big culvert makes enough space under the road ahead of us to handle the rush of flood-waters during the rainy season without the roadbed being washed out.

Am I sensing something? I signal to Guy that he should stop. He turns and waves back at the rest of our party, and they halt, all of us short of crossing the culvert over the wide sandy gully. I stand there, trying to clear my mind from the jumble of thoughts going through it. There's danger somewhere. Behind? For sure. That presence is still there. But where else? I wish I could focus my power better. I also wish I could magically transport us all from here to someplace safe.

I look ahead at the top of a distant peak. It reminds me of a story my dad said he learned from Jicarilla Apaches. Their homeland is further to the east, but us Chiricahuas know the Jicarillas very well. Back in the late nineteenth century when Geronimo, the last great leader to resist the Americans, was finally forced to surrender, all of our Chiricahuas were taken away. Even the Chiricahua men who had served with the American army as scouts and who had been able to find Geronimo and his little band when no one else could were loaded on trains under armed guard. Our whole Chiricahua nation was taken from our homes to POW camps far to the east by the salt water that goes on forever. Many died there. Then they were sent to other camps where more died of disease and sorrow.

One of those who died and was buried in that distant place was the first Lozen, my namesake. Years and years went by, and still our people were kept in exile in the south. Then they were all shipped to another place in the middle of the continent, the place that used to be called Oklahoma. More died there. Including Geronimo, who was now a very old man.

Finally, decades later, about half of those who survived were allowed to come back to the southwest, but not to our own homeland. The Jicarillas, our cousins, said they would take us. And that is why the father of my father and my Uncle Chatto grew up among those Jicarillas.

Anyhow, that Jicarilla story was about the people in the old times who had Eye Power. With Eye Power, they could just look. And any place they saw, no matter how far it was, they could just look and see themselves there and then they would be there in no time at all. Just like that. But that power was lost long ago.

It would be good to have that kind of power, I think as I look at that distant mountain peak. *Could I get that power, too?*

I think real hard about that, harder and harder until I feel a sort of trembling inside myself. I think about it so hard that I almost don't notice two things.

Numero Uno is that my hands are feeling very warm and twitching upward. Directing my attention not in front or back or to either side but above us. Above us!

Numero Dos is the whistling sound coming toward me fast from that direction.

"LOOK OUT!" I scream, throwing myself against Guy and pushing him off to the right as the rock, twice the size of my head, brushes my left wrist and thuds down so hard that it digs itself into the pavement of the road. Another rock lands where Guy had been a half second before.

"GET OFF THE ROAD," Hussein is shouting behind me. "UNDER THE CULVERT!"

Everyone is running, even the Dreamer, who has not

abandoned his wagon, but has turned it around and is pushing it down the slope. Lorelei, who was at the wagon's back when it was being pulled and now is at its front since it's been reversed, is holding on to the wagon with one hand and the Dreamer's right arm with the other. I can see why he turned the wagon around. Its weight is pulling it down that slope so fast that even the Dreamer's immense strength and long legs might not have been enough to keep him from being run over as it picked up speed.

He manages somehow, though, to steer its massive bulk and turn it so that it enters the culvert and disappears from sight. But not from sound—because I hear a big *THUD!* right after that, which means he must have run into something. Maybe a tree trunk that was washed in there by the last flood.

Hussein has his rifle in his left hand and has grabbed Victor's shoulder with his right hand. He's pulling Victor along, entering the culvert a second or so after the Dreamer. Mom and Luz are right behind them, followed by Ana. All of a sudden, though, Ana stops, turns, looks up, raises her M-16 and starts shooting into the sky.

BAM! BAM! BAM!

One rock and then another and another land splotting into the soft sand of the arroyo, each one closer to her than the last.

"GET UNDER THERE," I'm screaming at her as Guy

and I come charging down the slope, kicking up sand as we do so. I try to wave at Ana with my left hand, the one grazed by the stone, and realize my wrist is limp—broken or sprained.

BAMMMMM! BAMMMMM!

Gunshots echo out from *inside* the culvert. Hussein and Luz must be shooting at something—something inside the culvert. We're being attacked on two fronts. Ana turns, charges into the culvert, gun leveled.

Then a volley of more shots, from her M-16 and Luz's and Hussein's, the echoes almost deafening us as Guy and I reach the mouth of the culvert ourselves.

BAMMM! B-BAMMM! B-BAMMM-B-BAMMM B-BAMMM!

All of this has been happening in the time it would have taken me to count One Pony, Two Pony, Three Ponies, Four Ponies. If I'd been counting. And as I try to look up and see what Ana saw up there, more rocks start landing next to us.

SPLAT! SPLAT! SPLAT! SPLAT!

Guy pushes me forward in the culvert's dark mouth—where the shooting has finally stopped. And as my eyes adjust to the darkness I finally see what everyone was shooting at.

Something that is not at all a gentle monster.

CHAPTER THIRTY

Trolls

O r rather, what they *were* shooting at. The creature Hussein and Luz and my sister shot is quite dead.

As my eyes adjust to the darkness I realize another revision is necessary. Not creature. Creatures.

Holding my .357 in my good right hand, which I somehow seem to have managed to draw from its holster during our mad dash down the slope, I step a little closer—but not too close—to the bulky dead beings sprawled against the wall of the culvert.

Their enormous fat-bellied bodies and their big gaping mouths with rows of scimitar-shaped teeth make them look like the sharks I used to see in the viddys. Or at least they look the way sharks would look if they had long arms with hooked claws and short, massive back legs like those of an elephant. Their backs are dark gray, their bellies, upturned in death, are pale white. They look thick-skinned, but fortunately for us their skins, aesthetically decorated with bullet wounds, were not thick enough to resist fire from high-powered rifles loaded with armor-piercing rounds.

"There's two of them," I say out loud.

"One begs to differ," says a voice from farther within the culvert.

It's the Dreamer, who is examining the undamaged back of his cart some thirty feet from the third and largest of the three defunct horrors, its skull terminally crushed when his cart struck it head-on.

He pries something from between two of the metal bands on the cart and holds it up. It's a single tooth, half as long as one of my hands.

"Unique dentition, no?" he says in a calm voice. "Are you that land shark?" Another of those strange remarks that only have meaning for him—and, in this case, Lorelei, who giggles and then laughs even harder when he appends that reference to something from his abundant past with yet another. "Not the UPS man at all, eh? A land shark indeed."

I try to reach out to touch the big tooth. But when I lift my hand, a pain as sharp as that tooth looks shoots all the way up my arm.

I bite my lip and shake my head. Crap!

Lorelei is looking at me, no longer laughing. She hops off the cart.

"Let me see your wrist," she says.

"It's nothing," I say, but I let her take my arm. There's something about her manner, more assured than the usual way she presents herself.

"I was a nurse in another lifetime," she says. "And this appears to be a broken wrist. May I?"

I nod and she grasps my hand and forearm. She turns it, nods. Then she pulls quickly in opposite directions. Aggh! I bite my lip, but don't cry out. THAT hurt—but no more than having a red-hot knife thrust through my wrist and then twisted.

"My kit," she says, in such an entirely competent way that it's not that much of a surprise to see the Dreamer turn quickly to the cart, reach into it, and come out with a bag.

"Simple fracture," Lorelei says, " just above the wrist. Should heal straight, be good as new in a few weeks." She holds her hand back without looking. "Splints." The Dreamer places two flat, thin pieces of wood in her outstretched palm. "Now gauze."

In a remarkably short time she's done. I can't say that my arm feels totally fixed or that it doesn't hurt, but the way she's done her job—with such brisk efficiency—means that I can move that arm in almost a normal way. Slowly and with a bit of care, but almost normal. And my hand, which was only temporarily paralyzed by the impact of the plummeting stone, is working again. I wiggle my fingers, flex my hand. Shooting pain through my forearm, but who cares about that?

"Well done," the Dreamer says.

"What else did you expect?" Lorelei replies. "Now be a dear and put away my kit."

Yes, there is a lot more to her than I've been realizing.

I look around. My little company of fellow travelers have done just what I would have told them to do if my mind had not been temporarily on other things. Ana and Hussein have remained on guard at the culvert entrance where we entered. Guy and Luz have reconnoitered to where the culvert opens out on the other side. My mother and Victor have stayed near me, but both of them have now armed themselves, and they are standing back to back. Victor seems to have learned quite well from Hussein how to use an M-16, which is a light enough weapon for even a boy smaller than him to handle.

Interesting how being attacked on a nearly daily basis by beings wishing to add you to their menu can turn one into a warrior at an early age. But it's nothing new. That's the way it was for our people centuries ago when we were hunted by the Mexicans as if we were nothing but mindless animals to be exterminated or forced into their mines as slaves. Our children fought better than most of their Rurale soldiers.

I scan the culvert. Not exactly a scenic view unless you have a liking for interior decorating that places an emphasis on skeletal remains. Our trio of land sharks appears to have been in business here for sometime. The remains of a whole variety of creatures are scattered here and there, including those of humans.

Luz comes walking back to me while Guy remains at the

other end of the culvert. When she reaches me she motions upward with her gun barrel.

"My father says to look up. See what the trolls made."

Trolls, I think. Monsters out of European stories from their far north. Troll? Well, that fits them as much as land sharks. Trolls were big monsters that ate people and lived under bridges.

Then I look up as I was asked to do.

Oh my. How nice. What looked like solid pavement from a distance as we approached the part of the road that led over the arroyo is not solid at all. Instead, it is nothing less than a trap. As soon as enough weight is on it, a wide section of the roof of the culvert will fall open, spilling whatever was trying to pass overhead down into the place where open, eager jaws were waiting.

I'd been so preoccupied with the idea of Eye Travel that I had missed the warning my power had tried to give me. It was only because those falling stones drove us off the road that we avoided the same fate.

I shake my head again.

Crap, Lozen! You have got to concentrate or you are going to get everyone killed!

But what about those falling stones? Though they served the purpose of preventing us from falling into the Trolls' trap, they were certainly not meant to warn us. They were meant to end us.

I walk over to my brother. He's standing just inside the culvert, but out of view from anything directly overhead. That's probably why no more stones are falling.

"They're still up there," he says, pointing with his chin.

I look in that direction. At first they're hard to see and then I can pick them out. Birds. A dozen of them circling back and forth half a mile above us. They're not as huge as the pair of monster birds I destroyed along with their ugly offspring. I think I can judge how big they are by the stones they are holding, assuming those stones are similar to the ones they dropped, all about the same size—twice as big as the human heads those stones would have splattered like eggs. That would mean their wingspans and bodies are about three times larger than the biggest old-fashioned pre-gemod eagle.

The rifle Ana is holding has a high-powered scope on it. It's from the weapons that were on the cart, and not a gun I've used before.

"May I?"

Ana hands me the rifle.

"Let me use your shoulder," I say. Then, both of us kneeling, I use her as a rest and look through the scope. The enlargement combined with my own visual acuity allows me to make out what I was not able to see before.

These birds are unlike any bird I've ever seen before. They are holding stones not in claws, but in hind paws! And their heads are much more mammalian than avian. At the upward bend in their wings I can make out hands that I'd guess would come into play when their wings were folded.

"Flying monkeys?"

"Ah, but of course."

I turn my head back to look up at the Dreamer.

"Of course? You know what those things are?"

"One does believe so," he replies, placing his hands together in that prayer-like position which indicates he is about to share his superior knowledge.

He drops his hands, extends them palms up.

"Might one, as they say, take a look?"

He wants me to give him the rifle? That's a surprise. Somehow, even when he was pretending back at Haven to be nothing less than an evil torturer, I never pictured him using firearms. He and the other Ones always left that to their hired hands. But we've come a long way since then, and as the last few days of this journey have been in his company and we'll be with him for the foreseeable future, I guess I should trust him.

But no farther than I can throw him. So when I hand him the rifle I am careful to step behind him and stay close to him, my .357 back in my right hand.

The Dreamer holds the long gun with surprising competence, even though because of his height, his long arms and big hands, it looks more like a child's toy as he lifts it to his shoulder and tilts his masked face to peer through the scope with his one right eye.

He moves it about, following the circling of the distant simian aviators, humming under his breath as he does so. I can catch a few of the words. It's some ancient song I've never heard before.

"Hey, hey, we're the monkeys . . . of yess, indeedy do."

He lowers the gun, gives it to Ana, who is holding out her hands for it.

"Well?" I ask.

"Your surmise was correct," he replies. "Flying monkeys, *certainement*. Nasty creatures, indeed. In the absence of rocks, they will shower you with feces." He pauses and shakes his head, brushing his shoulder with one hand as if remembering something.

"How do you know this?" I ask. "Wait, you knew the One who designed those things, right?"

"*Corretto ragazza,*" he says. "One had the misfortune of being ushered into his aviary to observe his most prized creations. Alas, the heavy overhead netting did little to protect one from being bombarded from above."

He walks back to his cart, opens a drawer, and retrieves a book with a colorfully illustrated cover. "Not a literary masterpiece by any standards, but a book beloved in my youth. Before I outgrew its fantasy world and learned just how perverse the mind of its jingoistic creator."

"Perverse?"

The Dreamer taps the cover of the book. "Aside from spinning worlds of wonder for the callow young, the man who wrote this was the editor of a newspaper in what was once the state of South Dakota. In addition to referring to Indians as 'whining curs' and 'miserable wretches,' he called on numerous occasions for their total extermination. But you might say that he was rather egalitarian in his racist views, since he was in favor of similar subjugation and annihilation for persons of African ancestry and all those following an ancient faith known as Judaism."

I holster my .357 and he places the book in my hand.

"Do be careful," he says. "It's a rare volume." Then he chuckles to himself in bitter amusement. "Though that might be said of any book in these latter days, one supposes."

I leaf through its pages, stopping at a picture showing the creatures that resemble those that were so intent on spattering our brains on the sand. They are improbably designed, though. Their wings are simply stuck onto their backs with no connection to the massive pectoral muscles needed to sustain such creatures in flight. Then I turn back to the book's cover and read the title aloud.

"The Wizard of Oz."

The Dreamer nods. "One supposes that it might be said that, like the ones for whom the book is named, I too hid the secret of my impotence behind a curtain. The best metaphor in the entire volume, one that, lamentably, was followed by further tomes chronicling the history of that imagined land. One in which all Indians were absent, replaced by flying monkeys, considered by the author to be similarly savage beings that needed to be subdued into servitude."

I give the book back to him.

"No wish to explore the wonderful land of Oz, trot along a yellow brick road, accompanied by mindless and heartless compeers?"

He's lost me again, but I shake my head anyway, and he replaces the book in the drawer and slides it closed.

"Excellent judgment," he says. "Unlike the One who crafted these soaring simians. He was quite madly attached to that story, you know. I will not bore you with a description of the grounds of his estate. Terrible, terrible taste. And, as we all have now seen, he was especially enamored of the concept of flying monkeys. *Baumy* about the idea, you might say."

None of that information has been especially useful. Time to cut to the chase.

"What can you tell me that's *helpful?*" I ask.

"Just these few facts," the Dreamer answers. He holds up his right hand in a fist and then extends his thumb.

"First of all, they are absolutely voracious and constantly in search of prey. Secondly,"—he sticks out his index finger—

"they are terribly determined, and once they have sighted potential victims will not retire from the field of battle until they have achieved their goal."

"Of killing and eating us?"

"Precisely, which does make that a chink in their armor. And I say that metaphorically, for they are not possessed of impenetrable skin. Like the birds that are a part of their genetically modified make-up, they are surprisingly light for their bulky size, hollow-boned and unarmored. "

"Which means we can kill them with a bullet?"

"To put it bluntly. And such termination should be an even more attainable goal because of their last major trait."

He pauses, waiting for me to say something. So I play along. "Which is?"

"Like Hollywood Indians in an ancient videodrama—quite unlike any actual real-life aboriginals, in their propensity for whooping idiotically and riding wildly in circles about barricaded wagons while offering ample opportunity for the embattled white folks to pick them off—these soaring simians seeking our flesh are simply not that intellectually gifted."

"And if you translated that into simple English?"

"With properly sighted firearms, you can pick them off one by one because they're too stupid to fly away."

"Thank you," I say.

"De nada," he replies.

I walk to the other end of our place of refuge to Guy, who's still standing guard at the far end of the culvert. It doesn't take long to relay my conversation with the Dreamer to him. Or at least that part of it which both makes sense and is useful.

"The Dreamer has seen those flying monkeys before. He says we can shoot them and they won't fly away while we're doing it."

"Good," he replies, looking around the culvert. "This place reeks like a slaughterhouse, lass. Glad I'll be to get out in the fresh air again."

The two of us take a bit of time selecting the right rifles.

Of course I take the Winchester I've been using since I liberated it from Diablita Loca's men. Always go with the gun you know. Guy opts for an SC76 Thunderbolt from the long-gone United Kingdom. Both of them, of course, fire the standard 7.62 x 51 mm .308 cartridges. Ana is keeping the one she's been using.

Hussein takes a third scoped .308, and the last one is for Luz, who Guy assures me is nearly as good a shot as he is.

"Need to make sure they'll be on target," Guy says as he looks up toward our circling adversaries. "You'd say they're how far above us now?"

"They're closer than before. Two hundred yards."

"Excellent. Just what I set them up for. Aim high, allowing of the pull of gravity. Now we just need a steady rest."

"Will this do?" It's the Dreamer, pulling his cart behind him.

"Fine and dandy," Guy says.

We place the cart just inside the mouth of the culvert. By squatting down behind it and resting the barrels on one side of the cart, padded along the top with folded blankets, we're looking up and out. If directly overhead is at noon, we are pointing at one o'clock.

I'm at the farthest left, my rifle barrel resting on one of the yokes of the cart. Hussein is five feet to my right, then Ana, Luz, and Guy. It's not going to be easy to do this. Not only do we have to secure the targets in our sights, we have to account for their motion, leading them slightly. It helps that they are steadily circling and that there's no wind. And the sun is now off to the west and not so close or bright that it would blind us.

Even so, we'll be lucky if we actually hit more than one or two in our first salvo. Back when Ana was firing at them, she missed with every shot. But we're also counting on another thing about these creatures that the Dreamer mentioned while Guy and I were selecting the weapons to use. They not only bone-headedly stupid but also determinedly savage. If you attack them and injure one, the scent of their own blood drives them berserk. And they will swarm toward whoever injured them.

Whoopee!

CHAPTER THIRTY-ONE

Flying Monkeys

Through the sights of my rifle, the flying monkeys look way less cute than they did in the improbable illustration in the book that inspired their genesis. I can see the feral redness of their eyes, the thick matted fur on their bodies, the impressive teeth in their open mouths, their large bat-like ears. They're not wearing clothes like viddy critters or carrying spears, but the hands on the bends of their wings have long claws and every single one of those twelve nightmares in flight is clutching a rock in its feet. Apparently they have stashes of stones somewhere in the hills below them to have so quickly replenished their payloads.

They've actually circled a bit higher while we were getting ready. Nearer three hundred yards than two.

We've discussed how best to do this. Since they are flying around in circles, it means they're crossing each other's paths, making picking out a different one for each of us to aim at a difficult proposition. They are not sitting ducks.

Shooting fish in a barrel it's not—unless you are talking about a barrel as big as the sky.

So what we've decided is this: at my signal we'll all fire our first shots at the same time, me trying for the one farthest to the left and Guy for the one that ends up farthest right. The other three will just aim for the middle of the flock. From then on we'll just shoot at whatever we think we can hit. If we wound one or two of them, it may get progressively easier since the survivors may then be diving straight at us.

Easier, yeah. If you define easier as being neck deep in homicidal winged apes.

Guy has earplugs in his gear, and we've all availed ourselves of them. Five high-powered rifles all going off together is going to be deafening inside an echoing metal tunnel. So my command to start shooting is not verbal. I hold up my right hand, keeping my rifle in place by pressing the butt between my shoulder and my chin.

I hold up my little finger and drop it to start the agreed-upon three count as I slip my hand down into position, index finger on the trigger, safety clicked off. Breathe in, breathe out.

One and one pony, two and one pony, three and one pony. B-B-B-BAMM, BAM, BAM.

To my utter surprise, the flying ape farthest to the left, the one I was aiming to hit, drops its stone, folds one wing, and starts to fall. I look over my sights and see that the one most in the middle is also plummeting down, still clutching its rock in what I assume to be dead feet. I don't see either of them hit the ground because I am squinting back through the telescopic sight, trying to attain another target. It's not easy to do because they're moving.

What makes it harder is that I'm now hearing something very distracting inside my head. It started coming from the flying horrors as soon as my first shot hit home, a single thought that they all are having at the same time. The silent scream is hitting me like a searing tongue of fire, so filled with rage that I feel as if my forehead is being splashed by acid.

Killkilllkillkillkillkillkillkill!

BAM!

The gun bucks back against my shoulder. I've fired more out of instinct than design and I see the burst of red from the neck of the second ape-bird I've tried for. Two out of two.

I can hear everyone else shooting to my right. That familiar feeling as if time has slowed is with me. I'm putting down the rifle because it's not going to be fast enough now. Because all the remaining winged monkeys, six of them at least, are plummeting toward us like red-furred missiles, letting go of the stones they're carrying as they dive in.

My .357 is in my hand and I'm crouching. A stone thuds in front of me, rolls fast toward me. I lift my leg just in time to keep it from being broken like my left wrist.

Apparently I've just fired my gun because the body of a flying monkey crashes into the ground right behind the rock it dropped. If my left hand were working right I'd have my knife in it. Which would be helpful, since the winged ape I shot was only wounded. It's picking itself up now on my left, close enough to touch me.

It looms over me, blood oozing from the side of its head where my bullet only grazed it.

Crap! The thing is seven feet tall. It's going to swipe at me with those clawed wings before I can get another shot off.

WHUMP! That's the sound of a shotgun being fired over my shoulder. A shotgun that makes the winged ape an ex-winged ape as the double-0 buckshot hits its center mass and it crumples to the sandy floor of the culvert. A shotgun held in the hands of my mother.

In addition to the various rifles in the hands of us five, closer-range weapons and earplugs had been issued to the rest of our party just in case, including my mother and my brother Victor.

I nod at my mother, who nods back at me.

No more show of emotion than that, at least right now. We Chiricahua didn't survive nearly six centuries of attempted genocide to waste any time in the middle of battles with high-fiving or hugging each other.

I turn toward Hussein. No problem with his left hand. Or the long, slightly curved dagger in it that is buried in the throat of the definitively deceased adversary. He plants one foot on its chest, yanks the knife free, cleans it by wiping it once, twice across the beast's body, and sheathes it with a somewhat showy backward spin of the blade. Then he grins at me—maybe a little sheepishly because he knows he was showing off—makes a circle with his other hand, and then draws the edge of his hand across his throat.

All dead.

After scanning the sky for a few minutes and making sure it's clear, we venture out. I begin counting them. More than we first thought. Fourteen, all told. Only two—the one Mom shot and the one Hussein so efficiently performed a tracheotomy on—made it close to us. The others lay scattered over a half-mile radius. Guy finishes off the three that are still weakly moving by bashing them in the head with a heavy club he's pulled from his weapons cache. No need now to waste ammunition.

"Na much meat on them a-tall," he says, kicking one of the inert bodies. "Stringy at best. Nae worth the trouble."

I feel a tingling in my hands, turn, and shade my eyes with my right hand to look out over the wide plain north in the direction of the distant mountains. Dust rising.

Crap. Just when I thought things could not get more complicated.

"No worries, Guy," I say. "Looks like a lot of meat there. Coming our way fast."

CHAPTER THIRTY-TWO

Being The Good Samaritan

Luther had always had a sort of sixth sense that let him know things like that. It didn't surprise him when he had such feelings. All of his martial arts teachers had believed in those sorts of abilities—though they had tried to feed him mumbo jumbo that the way to perfect it was through meditation, fasting, all that stuff. It sounded like the same crap he'd heard around Pine Ridge. Purification, smudging with sage and sweet grass to remove evil influences and invite in good ones.

He'd never minded the physical discipline needed to attain the skills that had served him so well thus far in his lethal existence. And training the mind made plenty of sense, too. But the idea of purifying your spirit? That truly did seem like a load of crap to him. A purified spirit didn't protect his

Buddha-babbling wu shu teacher when Luther slipped up behind him and stuck a K-bar knife into his liver.

But feeling your target before seeing it or hearing it or smelling it? Now that made sense to Luther. What he had discovered was that, for him at least, the best way to strengthen that sixth sense of his was by doing what he did best—killing. The more deaths, the more he felt his power grow, as if he took a little of the life force from each person whose existence he terminated.

Yeah, his sixth sense was tweaking his mind, alerting him that he was closing in. But it was not precise enough to tell him more than that. What he wouldn't give just to have one of those DragonflyRs he used back BC, when tracking was made so much easier by those little drones.

Just as he was feeling a wave of nostalgia for some of the electronic tools of the past, something grey-furred and long-tailed dashed across the road in front of him, so close and sudden that it made him swerve and nearly lose control of the clockwork cycle.

He turned into the skid, braked the bike, looked back. All he could see to either side was sagebrush, chaparral, a few tall saguaros. Then a wide stretch of plain and hills rising into mountains. Nothing moving. Not even a freaking bird he could throw a shuriken at.

"Coyote," he said. "A damn coyote. That's what it was."

He thought for a moment about getting off the bike, looking for the coyote. Finding its tracks and following them till he got close enough to see it, then taking control of its mind just enough to slow it down. He couldn't do that for long. His ability worked best on birds. Bigger animals resisted too much for him to fully control them, though he was able to weaken them with that knife thrust of his thoughts. It would make it easier for him to just walk up and shoot the damn coyote while it was struggling, its body trembling as it tried to shake his presence out of its head. Bang! Then he could cut its head off, peel off its skin. Ah, yes. Hang its red naked body on one of those cactuses and its mangy grey skin on another. Pleasant thoughts, indeed.

Luther shook his head as he combed his hair back with the fingers of his right hand. What was he thinking about? He needed to keep going, not waste his time on a little diversion like that, satisfying as it might be.

But what was that? What was he hearing? He cupped one ear and turned his head to listen. Distant popping sounds.

Pow pow pow! Pow! Pow!

Coming from far away, farther along in the direction he'd been heading. Far away, but Luther recognized it for what it was. Gunfire. His sixth sense had been right. He was close, no more than five miles.

His mind began running through options about what to do now. Gunfire meant that some sort of fight was taking place. Probably an attack from something big and dangerous. Lots of somethings like that around these days. So it might be best not to rush in.

But he didn't want any "something" to take his kills. Maybe he should rush in, act the part of a rescuer, and save their bacon.

He smiled at that thought.

Yeah. Be the hero. Be welcomed as a newfound friend.

And then when the night came, silently slit their throats. He'd done that sort of thing before, played the part of the modest, helpful good guy. Black as his heart might be, Luther knew he had what was sometimes called an honest face. He was good-looking, sort of like one of those characters in the Western viddys that he used to watch. The ones who won the gun fights against the bad guys—and this always made Luther smile, being a Lakota Indian himself—who rode in to save the wagon train from the attacking red-skinned savages at the last minute.

A last minute rescuer. He'd enjoyed playing that role a few times. That had led to him being called a "good Samaritan," whatever the hell a Samaritan was, by that one party of five escapees from the buried site ruled by his Primaries. He'd shown up just in time to annihilate the half dozen Bloodless that had surrounded the five men and women, who had only makeshift spears for weapons.

Our hero, they'd gushed.

Aw shucks, Ma'am.

And when those escapees slept, confident that the tall, dark handsome man who'd saved them would protect their dreams, he'd choked them to death one by one and then brought their heads back to his Primaries as proof of his success.

Luther nodded. Rescuer it would be.

"Hey!"

The voice was so close that it actually made Luther jump.

He turned his head to the left. An old grey-haired Indian man was standing there, no more than ten feet away, leaning on a crooked walking stick. His face was dirty. His clothing was torn and patched, and his feet were bare, his unclipped toenails so long and gnarled that they looked like claws.

"What?" Luther growled

"Didn't mean t' scare you," the old man said in a whiny voice, showing his teeth as he cowered back. "No, no. I just need help, me."

How the hell did he get that close without me hearing him? Luther thought.

It ticked him off almost as much as having that coyote run across in front of him. If the old man had been standing in front of him, he would have just run him over.

The grey-haired old man took a few limping steps backward and held up one hand.

"Don't be mad at me. I just got a problem. Neeeed help. Pleeeeease?"

I could shoot him, Luther thought. *That would solve all his problems.*

As if he could hear Luther's thoughts, the old man moved again. A little quicker than Luther had expected. Now he was standing behind a tree.

"Not just me, no. My granddaughter, she needs help. She's a pretty young woman. Very pretty. Hurt her foot. You help us, pleeease?"

A pretty granddaughter? That does sound more interesting.

Luther swung off the bike.

The old man stuck his head out from behind the tree.

"Goood," he whined. "Goood, goood. You come now?"

Luther nodded, his left hand feeling the comforting shape of his knife on his hip. "Yeah. I'm coming."

The old man's head disappeared back behind the tree. "This way, this way," his voice whined. "Come on now, you come on."

Luther walked down off the road toward the tree. As he walked there was something in the back of his mind that he was trying to remember, but it was not coming to him. All he could think of right now was that old man, how pleasant it would be to see the look on his dirty face when Luther unsheathed his knife. And that pretty granddaughter. Her, too.

Alas for both of them.

Luther smiled.

"Over here, here, over here."

The old man was almost out of sight, but Luther caught a quick glimpse of his grey hair as he disappeared behind some tall bushes and he followed.

"Almost there, almost there."

It was a little surprising that the limping old man could move as fast as he did. Luther picked up his own pace to a trot as he rounded a bend, went up and over one hill and then a next, then began to descend into a little valley. At its far end was a small shack, little more than boards roughly nailed together with a rusted corrugated iron roof. The old man was already there, inside the shack, reaching out with one hand to gesture at Luther.

"Come on, here. Come on, here."

Luther reached the door and looked inside. The place had a musky animal smell about it, like poorly tanned skins, perhaps. No windows. No furniture other than a rickety table, two chairs, and a bed in one corner. And where was that pretty granddaughter?

"She went to get water," the old man said, patting Luther's shoulder. "Come soon. Now you sit, sit down. Let me give you food. Good food."

Luther sat, part of him unsure why he was being so compliant. Why not kill this old bastard now? No, wait till the granddaughter gets back. Don't want to scare her away. Plus a bowl was being placed in front of him, and the food in it smelled good.

"Eat. This is good food. Eat, eat." The old man's voice was more commanding than whining now. Luther hardly noticed that with the bowl of food in front of him. Good food.

Luther began to eat. No spoon or fork. He just used both hands, shoving the food into his mouth, hardly chewing. Swallowing, shoving in more.

Ah!

He pushed the last into his mouth, dropped the bowl and then closed his eyes, savoring the taste.

When he opened them again, it was dark all around him. He was lying on his side. How long had he been sleeping? He sat up and looked around. Where was the shack? He was sitting at the end of a dry arroyo in the midst of a tangle of old, dry branches and cottonwood bark. And what was that in his mouth? It was soft and moist and tasted like . . .

He retched, opening his mouth wide to retch again and again, trying to cough up the smelly filth that he had packed into his mouth and his throat. He wiped his hands in the sand to clean the sickening odor of feces off them.

Damn that old man. I'm going to skin him alive when I catch him.

As he pushed himself up, his legs feeling shaky, he felt for his knife. The sheath was empty.

The moonlight was bright enough for him to see his way. But it took him longer than he'd expected to get back to the road. Dawn was just breaking when the highway came in sight. What seemed like no more than a few hundred yards as he followed that deceitful old bastard had been miles and miles.

And what he found there did not please him. His clockwork motorcycle was there, but every part of it, gears, wheels, cogs and springs, had been stuffed full of dirt and leaves and twigs. It would take hours to clean out. And, to make it worse, that sandy soil, those leaves, twigs, and every inch of the entire machine had been soaked with coyote urine.

As Luther set to work, he kept mumbling under his breath these words:

"Not kill, no. Skin 'em alive. Every coyote, every old Indian man I catch."

CHAPTER THIRTY-THREE

Friends

What I can see through the scope looks like a monster approaching us from the north. It's a gemod for sure, some sort of strange creature that is part human and part four-footed beast. And not just one of them. There's another coming up over the rise behind it, then another and another.

We've My first impulse is to defend my family. I can get off a shot from this distance with this rifle. I have the lead creature in my crosshairs and I know I can make this shot, even from this distance of a mile away.

But is my first impulse right? I remember that cat-creature that seemed part human, remember the touch of its mind against mine, the flowers in its hair, the gentle way it put down the body of that murdered child, a child I now am certain it neither meant to eat nor had harmed in the first place.

Why Hurt Tahhr?

I made a mistake. I won't make that mistake again.

I lower the rifle.

"Lass?" Guy says. I look to my right and see that he is holding his rifle to his shoulder, has it resting like mine on the blanket-padded rim of the cart. If I fired, his shot would be close behind mine, and not one but two of those beings—which have all halted their advance and are standing silhouetted against the sky—would be dead.

And I remember something else. What Coyote said about others coming from the north, others who can help us—unless we kill them first.

"Lower your gun," I say to Guy. "And you, too," I say to my sister and Hussein, both of whom had followed my lead and trained their weapons on the approaching creatures.

They all do as I say, look at me with a "What's next?" look on all of their faces.

"Let me try something," I say. "Can I use that staff I saw in the cart, Guy?"

A little smile appears on his face as he pulls the staff from the weapons cart. "Aye, lass, but let me show you a wee bit of something about it, first."

When he does so, a similar smile comes to my own face. Interesting. I accept it from him, carefully.

"It's fine as long as I don't . . . "

"Press there, or twist here," Guy says.

I fasten a white towel to Guy's more-interesting-than-I-first-realized staff and then step out onto the plain. I walk a dozen paces, raise it over my head. I'm not sure if a white flag of truce means anything to those half-human, half-animal beings, but it doesn't hurt to try. Then I try something I have never done in any of my encounters with gemods before. I reach out with my mind.

Friend, I think at them. *Friend*.

The answer comes back to me so quickly, so eagerly that it makes me step back half a pace.

Friend? You are a friend?

The thought is so clearly formed, so familiar that it shocks me. It's not fierce or strange, like that of a gemod. Nor is it like Hally's thoughts, which though clear and I suppose friendly, have always had an edge of something deeply alien to them. It seems so human, like the thoughts I've picked up now and then from Hussein or Guy or the Dreamer or my family members.

Yes, I reply. *Yes. Who are you?*

Rose, the answer comes.

A gemod with a human name?

Rose?

Yes, Rose Eagle. I'm Lakota, and so are the people with me. Can we approach?

Okay.

Cool.

Cool? A gemod that says cool? A gemod that says it's a Lakota Indian?

But those friendly—I hope—beings are already trotting to us. Fast. I need to tell the others what is up.

I turn to everyone back in the culvert. From the looks on everyone's faces, from the way they're all staring at me, they are for sure wondering what's up now. Maybe they all know enough about me by now to know I've been engaged in silent conversation with our new arrivals.

"It's okay," I say. "They say they're friends. But just in case, everyone else stay back."

They're now only a few hundred yards away. And just as my mother says the words—says them with something like a combination or awe and delight in her voice—I see what they really are and realize how dumb I've been not to have seen it already.

"Horses," my Mom says. "Riders on horses!"

CHAPTER THIRTY-FOUR

Riders

I stare at them. They're only a few yards away and they've stopped. They're so close that I can smell them. It's a sweaty odor, one I've never smelled before, but it smells so good. So very good. So right. It's the smell of horses.

Horses. Riders on horses.

My mother's words are echoing in my ears. Everyone behind me has been silent since she spoke those words, spoke them like the first words of a prayer.

People on horseback! It's a sight I thought I would never see again except in my dreams, now that we no longer have viddys. It's even more beautiful than I imagined, and I feel my eyes growing moist. Horses. They are almost exactly as I imagined they'd look after hearing my father and Uncle Chatto talk about them, after seeing them in those old viddys and in books.

Except they look a little different somehow. For one, their heads look broader, and overall they are quite a bit bigger than I'd imagined they would look. They make the large dark-haired woman on the horse closest to me look as small as a child. She's at least as tall as I am, and her shoulders and chest are more bulky, her bare arms and legs more muscular.

But it doesn't matter if these beautiful animals do look a little different than I expected. They're horses, real horses!

I am so glad to see you, I think.

My thought is immediately answered. But not by that big dark-haired woman who I am sure is Rose, the one whose thoughts reached me.

We are glad you welcome us.

It's the horse speaking to me, though it's not in words that I hear it translated to me by my mind. It's more in the way of emotion, deep emotion that moves me.

"That's no ordinary horse," Guy says. He's come up to stand next to Mom, actually a little in front of her as if he's looking to protect her. There's a bit of that same reverent tone in his voice that I heard in my Mom's.

As for me, I'm feeling what my father told me that our old people felt when they composed Horse Songs, praising this creature that changed their lives for the better. I remember how he told me they described their horses—as embodiments of such forces of nature as the whirlwind with their swiftness and the thunder with the rumbling of their hooves across the land.

I've just heard and felt that thunder as this herd of horses came thudding up to us. It's stirred something deep inside me. Yes, they are gemod. But so what? I can tell there's nothing evil or twisted about them. I can feel that. My power is assuring me of that. Whoever created these beings from the DNA of various creatures must have had the vision in mind of something far different from a monster, of bringing back our lost horses as something new and probably immune to the virus that killed off their forebears.

There's a dozen of those new horses. Four have riders on their backs. One of those riders, on the jet-black horse that is closest to the shell-white one being ridden by Rose Eagle, is a very good-looking guy who is probably her age, and also her something else from the way he's looking at her. He's a little old for me but still worth looking at. He is also big—looks to be probably almost as tall as Rose.

The other two riders are also big people. They're a man and a woman who look to be about Guy's age. The older woman's horse is red, while the broad-shouldered older man is on a dappled grey.

Every horse of the remaining eight is just as perfectly formed and just as distinctive as the first four that are being ridden. I wonder what it would be like to see the world from their backs, to thunder over the land and race with the wind. I feel as if the only thing I want to do right now is climb up on one of those incredible beings.

You are all so beautiful!

Thank you, little sister.

It's a thought that comes not just from one of them, but from more than one. Maybe all twelve of them.

The woman named Rose smiles down at me.

"Awesome, aren't they? I love it when they communicate with us like that. That means they've accepted you, by the way."

"You heard it?" I said.

She shakes her head. "No, but from the look on your face right now I'm betting that's what happened. Am I right?"

I nod, feeling a bit at a loss for words.

"And you heard me talking to you that same way, right?"

I nod again. "Rose," I say. "Rose Eagle."

"Good. It sort of comes and goes with me—this mind talking."

Is it that way with you? she thinks at me.

Yes, I think back. *But it's been getting stronger.*

She presses her lips together and nods down at me. Then she taps the big animal she's riding on its shoulder. It bends one of its front legs, lowering its back, and she slides off to land next to me.

"Hau kola," she says, extending her hand. "Hello, friend."

I take her hand, hold it as lightly as she holds mine. She's taller and broader than me, and I can feel her strength. A good person to have as a friend.

She turns and looks back toward her companions. "Our

256

allies here," she says, "don't use names to identify themselves, though you can tell whoever's touching your mind—or if it is all of them at once. They're herd creatures, after all, and sharing their feelings comes naturally to them. I think they are doing it all the time with each other, talking that way. But when we humans are speaking out loud, we just call them by their colors. Black Horse is the one who chose me." She nods back toward the biggest of those huge animals, a black horse with a bald face.

"White Horse chose Phil—who's my . . . " she continues, smiling up at the tall good-looking man who nods back with a similar smile " . . . friend. Red Horse chose Aunt Mary, and Grey Horse chose Uncle Lenard."

The older man trots forward on the grey horse that is his partner.

"Hey, hey," the man, Uncle Lenard as Rose named him, says to Guy, "Is that you, lawman?"

Lawman? I look hard at Guy. He looks back at me and then, as if reading my mind, shrugs his shoulders. Yet another part of Guy's past I did not know about. Then he turns back toward the man on the grey horse.

"Lenard Crazy Dog," Guy says, amusement in his voice. "You're not dead yet."

"Nope, here I am still alive and twice as ugly." Uncle Lenard leans down to look at Guy's scarred face. "Been keeping an eye out for me, Lawman?"

The woman called Aunt Mary groans loudly at that taste-less pun, but Guy ignores it.

"Na," Guy says, his face impassive. "I had enough of that."

The Lawmen were the enforcers of justice for our planetary overlords back in the days BC. Being a Lawman certainly explains Guy's unusual competence with weaponry, but I have a hard time imagining him as one of those ominous rule enforcers, women and men who were hard as stone and just as emotionless. They were the ones who ran the detention camps and were charged with either eliminating or bringing in—to what was called justice—those who tried to go against the system.

Uncle Lenard chuckles. "Not all that surprised by that, kola."

He turns toward Rose, who has been listening, like me, to the tête-à-tête between the two middle-aged men with a com-bination of interest and surprise. "This fella here"—he jerks his head back down toward Guy, who now is stroking the cheek of Grey Horse—"he's the main reason I survived that last time they caught me and sent me off to Distant Detention. This lawman here, it seems, unlike most of the others there, still had a soul in him. The two of us, we'd talk and got to know each other some. Though it might surprise you to know it was me usually done most of the talking."

When he says that the middle-aged woman on the red horse, Aunt Mary, sighs audibly and rolls her eyes up toward the sky.

Uncle Lenard pays that no mind. "Ain't no friendship like the one sometimes forms 'tween a prisoner and his guard. More'n once, he turned a blind eye—pardon the pun, eh? When he was on the torture crew, he'd accidentally forget to connect one of the leads so that the current didn't go into me and fry my brain like it was supposed to do. Couldn't do that much about the beatings except get in the way of the others accidental-like when they were putting the boot to me, but he'd do what he could after, sneaking in medicine to me. And when the power went, Lawman here just stepped aside, unlike some, and let me go my merry way."

"Ach, and if I hadn't stepped aside you'd likely've gone through me, Crazy Dog," Guy says. He's smiling now. "But dinna call me Lawman. Just Guy now. That's all."

Uncle Lenard Crazy Dog reaches down a hand. "Guy it is, kola," he grins as the two of them shake.

Then Guy turns toward my mother. "Lenard," he says, putting his hand on my Mom's shoulder as she steps forward, "this is Louise Whiteshell." The way Guy speaks my Mom's first name is so . . . affectionate that it surprises me. "She's the mother of our Lozen here. Louise, meet the Crazy Dog."

Uncle Lenard Crazy Dog kicks his left leg high in the air over the head of Grey Horse, vaulting himself off the big gemod's back to land lightly on the ground. It's a move more like one done by a dancer or a trained athlete than a man in late middle age. I'm a little surprised, but what he does next surprises me more.

259

He reaches out to take my Mom's hand in both of his. "Louise Whiteshell?" he says, in a voice that is no longer joking. He looks around as if expecting to see someone among us. Then he turns his eyes back to Mom, who has drawn her lower lip in and is biting it softly. Most people would not notice that, but most people are not my Mom's daughter. Mom only does that when she is thinking of my dad.

"Blanco," Uncle Lenard says, "your husband, right? And Chatto, your brother."

Mom nods.

Uncle Lenard shakes his head. "Hoo-wee," he says in a way that makes that word full of respect. "We was in the same unit before I turned reb," he says. "Two best men I ever knew who weren't Lakota. Are they . . ."

Mom nods again, lifting her chin as she does so, saying more with that little gesture than you could with a thousand words about how much she misses them, how much she loved them, how proud she will always be of both her husband and her brother.

Uncle Lenard lets go of her hand and steps back. "It was an honor to know 'em," he says. "An honor to meet you and . . ." his eyes take in Victor and Ana and then me ". . . your family."

"Thank you," Mom says, her voice soft, but full of so much strength that once again I remember it's her, as much as my dad and my uncle, who passed warrior ways down to me.

I'm moved by what has just transpired. It's great just how well we are getting along together. However, as Lenard shakes my hand and then Victor's and Ana's, the fourth person in their party, the old woman introduced as Aunt Mary, has said almost nothing so far. She's a handsome woman and it's pretty clear that she and Uncle Lenard are, if not married, then a couple. I feel drawn to her, but I also sense something about her that is different. Not bad, but it's as if there's more to her than just the kindly smile she is showing to everyone.

As she takes my hand, she suddenly shifts her gaze straight into my face in a way that might seem rude or intrusive. But it's not that. It's something else. Her dark black eyes are looking into mine, piercing mine, in a way that is so deep, so intimate, so questioning that I have to turn away.

"Hunh," she says, as if deciding something. Then she spins on her heels and walks off, leaving me with a feeling of disquiet, as if something has begun and I have no idea what it is.

I turn my thoughts back to how very interesting it is that our two groups of rebels have so much in common.

Talk about coincidence. In fact, I wonder just how much their turning up this way is a coincidence, especially considering the messages I got—first from Coyote and then from my oversized, overly-furry enigmatic buddy.

Hally, did you set this up?

No reply, just as I expected.

I turn back to the big woman, Rose, who's towering over me with her giant black horse looking over her shoulder at me, its head turned so that it is looking directly into my eyes with its big left eye.

I can almost hear it saying "Hau, little human."

Hanging around them too much may give me an inferiority complex.

"How did you find us?" I ask her.

Rose Eagle points with her chin at the flying monkeys that are still scattered around us on what was recently a battlefield. Then she smiles at me and raises an eyebrow.

Okay, I get it. The sound of a bunch of high-powered rifles all going off could be heard for miles around. Maybe they even saw the simian horrors circling over us from far away. All they had to do was follow their ears and eyes. That answers the how. But not the why, aside from their being naturally helpful, being—what was that term from the old story in the Bible? It was a parable my Dad liked, about a guy who just assists someone injured out of the kindness in his heart. The Good Samgamgee? Anyhow, I have the feeling that it has to be more than that.

So I phrase my next question really directly.

"Are you here because you were looking for us?"

"Bingo," Rose Eagle replies.

She's looking over my shoulder. I turn and see the rest of our little gaggle of pilgrims peering out, all of them gathered in the road culvert's shadowed mouth. I can understand why. Reason Numero Uno is just plain curiosity, now that it appears our new hooved and mounted arrivals bear us no ill will. Numero Dos is that they are probably in need of some fresh air. The stench of the dead trolls and the charnel house they made of the place is getting worse as the heat of the day increases and makes its way even into the slightly cooler culvert.

I gesture for them to lower their weapons and come out, and they do just that. The first to reach us is Hussein. His entire attention is focused on a brown gemod horse with a white star on its forehead. The way he nods and then walks right past me, almost as if in a trance, tells me that the two of them are in the sort of silent communication I've just experienced. The brown horse bends its head to him, and he presses his cheek against it, his hands raised as if in prayer. He's speaking to it in a language I don't understand in words but do understand in emotion. It's the way I felt when I first saw these beings, first touched them.

Hussein looks back at me. His eyes light up. "Lozen," he says, his voice filled with wonder. "This one has chosen me. By the grace of God, my life will never be the same again. Do you know what horses meant to us, to the Bedu?"

And to the Chiricahuas.

"I do," I say.

That brings a smile to his face as bright as the sun used to be pre-C.

"Come here."

He grasps my left hand gently. As usual, that touch of his fingers sends a current of warmth through me. I try not to show it as he draws me closer to Brown Star. "Here," he says as he places my hand on the giant horse's neck. "She wants you to touch her."

Yes, I think, hoping he is not hearing my thought right now. *She does.*

Uncle Lenard, who has mounted Grey Horse again, is now approaching the culvert mouth, ignoring the Dreamer, who looks askance at him. The Dreamer and Lorelei are the only ones who've hung back, avoiding the round of introductions, staying close to his cart filled with the weapons that hide the cargo my tall, imperious confederate values so deeply. After a brief moment inside, Uncle Lenard comes trotting back out. Uncle Lenard is holding his nose, and the way Grey Horse keeps snorting tells me he found the smell in there just as displeasing.

"Man," Uncle Lenard says. "You bumped off those big stinky things, too? You folks really made a killing, eh?"

"We aimed to please," Guy replies.

This time I groan along with Aunt Mary.

"Now who would that be?" Guy says.

What is he talking about? He's looking at Rose Eagle's shoulder, which is partially covered by her thick black hair. I move away from Hussein and Brown Star to look there myself. Two small bright eyes peer out between the long strands.

Guy lifts up his hand. "May I?"

"If it's all right with him," Rose says.

Guy holds his hand out. As he does so, the head of a little creature, a mouse of some kind, pokes out, its tiny hand-like paws parting the curtain of Rose's hair

"Come and make me acquaintance," Guys says, his voice soft. "I'll nae hurt ye."

The jumping mouse makes a chirruping noise and then vaults out onto Guy's calloused palm. It turns around twice, then sits up on its haunches, moving its front paws together as if washing them.

"Lovely," Guy says. "And what does it think as it looks up at us? Ah, to see ourselves as others see us."

He strokes its back with one of his rough, bent fingers, lifts it back toward Rose's shoulder, and lets it hop back into the concealment of her hair.

A simple enough moment, but one that everyone watched and one that, to me, more than anything else that has just happened, seems to have made our two parties feel even more like one.

By mutual agreement, pretty much unspoken, everyone seems to have accepted that Rose and I are sharing the leadership. We walk off together away from the others.

"Where?" I ask.

Rose points with her chin up the road. North.

I nod. It's the direction we were headed already. And the opposite direction from that inimical presence I am still sensing behind us to the south.

"When? Now, right?"

Rose nods. With all the noise we made battling those flying nightmares, it is time, maybe even past time, for us all to vaminos, hit the road, get out of Dodge, and just plain depart.

"What's up there?" I already have a general idea of that. The Dreamer's map showed me that Old Route 10 passes through the ruins of a ghost town that was actually named for Geronimo. Then it continues on through the dry lands of the former San Carlos reservation, where some of my ancestors were herded by the army, heading for the tree-green heights of the Sierra Ancha and the Maztzal Mountains.

Rose smiles. "You'll like it," she says. "Two days' ride and we'll be in the White Mountains. It's a beautiful place—not like all this desert land. That's where the main body of our people have camped. The four of us humans and our twelve four-legged friends are just the scouting party."

"Sent to look for us?"

"Yes," Rose says.

"How did you know about us?" I ask, already feeling I know the answer.

"We had a little help," Rose smiles.

"You mean big help? Big hairy help?"

Rose giggles, and I find myself liking the sound of that little laugh of hers so much that I can't help laughing myself.

But we've talked long enough now, almost too long. We need to get going.

"We'll talk more later, right?" I ask.

"Try and stop me," Rose says, lightly punching my arm.

It's the kind of thing sisters do, and it brings a warm feeling to me. But at that very moment something else washes over me. It's that aura of dark despair, that feeling of being punched in the gut by depression. Maybe it's the letdown finally hitting me after the fight, after the rush of adrenalin that sped through me.

I know that it shown in my face, because Rose is now grasping my arms, leaning close.

"Are you all right?" she asks.

I intend to say yes. Say I'm fine as I usually do. But that's not what comes out of my mouth.

"No," I say.

Rose nods. "We need to get you together with Aunt Mary." She lets go of my arms. "Okay for now?" she says, her voice much like mine when I walk with Ana. That thought brings a smile to my face, a weak one, but a smile nonetheless. Me as the little sister?

"For now," I say.

Something about the way I say that makes Rose laugh, and for no logical reason I can understand, that laugh actually lifts my spirits and I laugh with her. Maybe, a part of me thinks, I actually can find healing among these new friends.

"There's a good place for us to camp tonight," Rose says. "We checked it out on our way here. Then we locked its doors so that nothing would get in there while we were gone. An abandoned hangar. Plenty big enough for all of us, horses and humans alike."

"Good," I say. And it really is good. Not just that we'll have a secure place to pass the night, but also that for once the responsibility for finding such a place hasn't fallen on my shoulders alone. This partnership with these Lakota horse people is starting off well.

By the time we walk back to rejoin the others, I can see that partnership has gone even further. Everyone has found a horse—or maybe I should say that a horse has chosen one of them. Mom, Ana, Victor, Luz, Guy, and Mom are all mounted and ready to go. As is Hussein, who is, of course, on the back of Brown Star.

Ana and Victor appear more pleased than I can remember either of them looking in days—no, weeks or months. Maybe even years.

One horse is standing apart from the others, its head turned our way as Rose and I approach. Its marking are unlike those of any other. It's a grey and white mare, the white aligned in stripes from her chest and shoulders halfway back along her body, almost like an extinct African animal I saw once in a viddy. I am pretty sure it was called a zebra.

She walks straight up to me, bows her head to me. Then she speaks, not with words, but with a wave of another sort of communication that passes into me. It's so strong and so gentle that for a moment it takes my breath away. I understand what she is telling me. She feels my spirit and is pleased by what she feels. She is choosing me, or rather is offering herself to me if I choose her.

Of course, I think to her. *Of course.*

I am glad.

She places her nose close to my face and breathes with me as I place my hands on either side of her cheeks.

I don't remember climbing up on her back, but somehow that is where I am now. And the view from up here is amazing. The whole world looks different when you are on a horse. I look around at everyone else in our party and from the looks on their faces, it seems as if they are feeling some of that same wonder and delight.

Rose comes up next to me.

"Striped Horse is really something else," I say.

Rose nods. "The first horses the Spanish brought were

striped like that. So were the ones that were here ten thousand years ago."

How does she know that? No time to ask, because she raises her hand in a signal and we are on our way, walking, trotting, and then at full gallop along the road—with the exception of the Dreamer and Lorelei, who are sitting in his beloved cart that is now harnessed to a brown and white dappled mare who seems to not even notice the load she's hauling.

The wind is in my face, my hair is whipping back, my hands holding tight to the mane of Striped Horse, whose back is as comfortable and easy to sit as a padded chair.

Yes!

How can I explain what I am feeling now? I lean my forehead against the back of Striped Horse's neck. Her warmth is so comforting. And her smell, the clean, tangy smell of horses! How have I lived without it?

Every inch of her seems to be connected to me. I think I could fall asleep on her back and no matter how hard or fast she ran, I wouldn't fall off.

In a way I also sense much of what she senses. The way she's connected to all the other horses—and so am I. She's connected to the land, to the wind, the thunder, the lightning—and so am I!

I wish I knew one of the horse songs my people composed when the horses came to us the first time, hundreds of years ago. We saw them not just as gifts from the Creator, but as a part of ourselves that had been missing.

Killer of Enemies made them, according to one old story that my father told me. He formed horses of different colors from the earth and then life was breathed into them. At first they were wild and ran away. But then he made it rain, a heavy rain. In that rain those first horses bunched together and he was able to rope them with yellow ropes made from the rays of the sun and black ropes made from the sun's shadow.

As I think about that story, words start coming to me. Are they words I heard my father or my Uncle Chatto chant when I was little? Or are they older than that, words that were kept by the wind and waiting to find me?

My horse's hooves are made of dark agate.
Her legs are swift as the lightning.
Her body is a thundercloud.
Her spine is made of a stalk of corn,
Her tail is a trail of smoke.
Her mane is made of streaks of rain.
Her eyes are made of stars.
Her lips are made of black beads
Her teeth are made of white shell.
She never knows thirst.
My horse never tires.

And then I can't help it. I have to do it. I open my mouth and let the words of that Horse Song come out. It can barely be heard, I know, over the thunder of hooves all around me. But that doesn't matter. I feel that song as I ride and so does Striped Horse.

"WAAAAAH-HEYYYY!"

CHAPTER THIRTY-FIVE

In This White Room

I open my eyes. White. White all around me, even the comfortable gown I'm wearing that feels like soft cotton.

I sit up and look around. The room I'm in is all white. If you can call it a room.

It's more like being inside an eggshell that's empty of everything except me and what I've been asleep on. No lights in here, but the walls glow as if they are translucent and letting in a light so evenly distributed in this white room that I cast no shadow.

I stand up from the bed. If you could call it that. It's a featureless tray that conformed to the shape of my body when I was on it and now is totally flat. And now it is totally gone as it recedes back into the wall, leaving no trace that it was ever there.

My bladder feels as if it's about to burst.

As soon as I notice that, something else materializes out of the wall. A seat with a hole in it. I pull up my gown, sit on it, and relieve myself. As soon as I'm done and stand again, the seat does the same vanishing act as the bed, gone, absorbed back into the curved, glowing white wall.

Where am I?

Here.

What?

Or not.

Hally!

The wall in front of me either dissipates or recedes—it's hard to tell which—and there he is. It's Hally, all right, surrounded by control panels and monitors and sitting in something like a captain's chair in one of the old space viddys. Except instead of his usual naked hirsute state he has a goofy helmet on his head, big boots on his feet, and a frigging quadruple extra-large T-shirt that reads COMMANDER CODY AND THE LOST PLANET AIRMEN.

I stare at him, shaking my head.

He sweeps one of his giant hands down from his head to his feet.

Too Buck Rogers for you? he says.

"Huh?"

Never mind, too esoteric a reference, I suppose. He chuckles and raises his right hand in a strange sort of V-shaped salute. ***Live long and prosper. I come in peace, Earthling. Nanu, nanu.***

"Stop it!"

Hally grins, showing his huge teeth, his long fangs glistening in the strange effulgent light all around us. Dressed as he is, that open-mouthed grin of his looks more sinister than usual. He stands up and takes a step forward. As soon as he does that, the clothing he was wearing is gone and so is the spaceship seat and everything that appeared to be around him. It's just Hally, standing in front of me in this white room with his hands on his hips. The smile he beams down at me is positively benevolent as I glare up at him.

Wait a minute!

"This is a dream."

Hally nods. *You could say that. In fact, you just did.*

"So am I really here in this . . . egg? Or is this all just going on while I'm sound asleep?"

Two quite interesting questions, those, Hally replies, his mind voice professorial, as he steeples his hands just like the Dreamer does. *Verrry interesting. Like the ancient emperor who dreamed he was a butterfly that was dreaming it was an emperor who . . .*

"Just stop it, please?"

Hally reaches out his right hand. *Let me see your arm.*

I hold out my left arm. Even though this is probably a dream—and I am not a Monarch butterfly—my bruised arm still has the splints and wrappings on it that Lorelei applied two days ago.

Hally's big hands take hold of it with surprising delicacy.

He strips off the bandages and the splints and tosses them over his shoulder.

Hmm, broken but competently immobilized. He twists it slightly. *Does this hurt?*

"Ow! Yes."

I thought it would.

I want to snatch my arm back from him before he does something else painful—can you feel pain like that in a dream? But he is holding it too firmly now, near the elbow and well above the broken bones that grated when he torqued my hand. He extends his other hand palm-down over the broken place, and I feel a sudden flow of intense warmth, like a wave of hot water washing up from my fingers all the way to my shoulder.

Hally gives me back my arm.

So, he says, *how are things going now?*

"Don't you know?" I ask. "You always seem to know everything, even before it happens."

He shakes his big head. *Do not mistake me for more than I am*, he says—in a manner that seems quite serious. Then a smile comes back to his face, and his voice spoken mind to mind falls back to its usual maddeningly ironic tone. *I know what I know but I would never state, in the manner of Popeye and Jehovah, that I am what I am.*

He spreads both hands out, palms up, and shrugs his shoulders. *So how are things by you, already?*

I sigh. I have to answer him, I guess. What else can one do when confronted by an esoteric, corny sasquatch who constantly uses you as his straight man?

How are things? Where to start?

I think, knowing Hally is sharing my thoughts, about all that has happened, about the way my little brother and sister have been growing, about the Dreamer and his library, about my relationship with Hussein, which means more to me every day even if I can't seem to tell him that. I think about our journey along what I've begun seeing as a trail of the dead, especially after reaching the ruins of the valley that had once been my home. I think about the tragic murders of all those innocent people who lived there and the anger it brought into me—and that makes me think about the shame I felt after shooting at that cat-creature. I think about the gemod monsters we've had to kill. The giant gila monsters, the scorpions, the trolls and flying monkeys. Will there ever be an end to the enemies that want to destroy us?

Then another thought comes to me, the thought that in the midst of all this bleakness, I still have my family and my friends. I have Guy and Luz, and even the Dreamer and Lorelei have shown themselves to be far deeper and better people than I'd expected. And then there's Hussein. He's always there beside me, patient and helpful, and I get a warm feeling when I remember him holding my hand and . . . And I know, I know,

I'm thinking about him again. I can hear something like a mental chuckle from Hally right now.

I don't just have my family and my old friends. I have new ones now, too—Rose Eagle and her people and the gemod horses they brought to us. Or rather the horses that brought themselves our way and have chosen to accept us.

Those horses. That thought brings a smile to my face. True, I still have this blackness inside me that threatens at any second to drag me down into the depths of despair. And I have this continual sense of a deadly determined presence getting closer and closer. My crazy life is this continuous mixture of peril and possibility.

So what else is new?

"Pretty good," I reply. "'Better than before, at least."

Good, Hally's voice rumbles in my mind. **Now keep it going that way**.

CHAPTER THIRTY-SIX

The Book

I don't remember closing my eyes, but when I open them again I am no longer inside the eggshell room. I'm lying in my blankets on the floor of the flyer hangar where we bedded down last night. I'm sleeping fully dressed, aside from my boots and my aviator glasses, which are right next to me alongside my bowie knife and the gun belt with my .357, a finger's width from my right hand.

I push myself up to a sitting position. The nearly unbreakable translucent material that covers the dome is glowing from the early sunlight. Almost like an eggshell.

So it was just a dream.

Then I realize something. I just pushed myself up with my left arm and there was no answering twinge of pain from the fractured radius and ulna bones. I look at my bare forearm. My bare, unbruised forearm. The splints and wrappings are gone. No sign of them anywhere. As I turn my wrist, open and close my fingers, rub my right hand along the place where the break was located, I realize that it feels as if it was never broken.

Okay, Hally. Thanks again.

I look to my right. Mom and Victor are sleeping peacefully. Victor's arms are thrown up over his head, and Mom's left hand rests on his chest. Guy, who is already awake, is sitting on his own blankets just a few feet beyond them, watching them sleep with a tender look on his rough, scarred face. He looks up and me and nods. I nod back. The bedrolls to my left, where Luz and my sister had been, are empty. So is the space a few arms' length beyond where Hussein spread his blankets.

It takes my frazzled brain a moment to process what I'm hearing because it's so different from the sounds and images that I've been obsessing over.

It's the soft drumming of a guitar. A voice is added, one that is as melodic as those perfectly tuned strings.

Hussein's voice, of course. The song he's singing, for some reason, sounds very old to me. I can't understand the words because they are in that language in which Hussein now and then speaks a few words—usually a quotation or proverb of some sort. But the rhythm of the song and its words suggest something to me—the sound of hooves—and I know it's a song about horses, a sort of praise song about them. It makes my own mind quiet for just a little while as I listen and feel myself on the back of Striped Horse.

I get up and walk over to where Hussein is sitting, playing his guitar and looking out through the just-opened hangar door over the land that is changing colors with the rising dawn.

Ana is not there. But I know where she is. She and Luz are sitting together on the other side of this big hangar. A shaft from the morning sun is falling on them, making it seem as if they are glowing from their own light. They are whispering something to each other and giggling. It makes me feel happy for both of them, but also a little jealous. I never had a friend like that when I was Ana's age. I could probably understand what they're talking about if I concentrate, but I respect their privacy.

As I approach, Hussein doesn't pause in his song. He's still singing as I sit down beside him, and he keeps singing as if I'd been there all along. When he's done, the silvery sun has lifted, and the land has been painted with its shimmering light. Then he looks over at me and gives me that shy smile of his, his head bent a little, looking up through those dark lashes of his.

"Here," I say. I hand him the book that was given me by the Dreamer.

He puts down his guitar and takes the Koran from me. As soon as his eyes register the title, he draws in a quick breath.

"Ah," he says. He holds the book in both hands, opens it carefully, runs a finger down one page and then another.

I can feel his happiness and excitement without having to hear any of the words that must be going through his mind right now. It's like a wave of warmth washing over me.

He lifts his eyes from the pages and finds mine.

"Habibi," he says, almost as if he's forgotten it's a language I do not know. Then he quickly switches to English. "My friend," he says, "my true friend, friend of my heart. Do you know what this means to me?"

It's not really a question, so I don't answer it.

Hussein places the book in his lap and reaches out to takes my hand, then lifts my hand to his mouth and kisses it. It's such a spontaneous gesture on his part that I do not snatch my hand back as I might have done only a few days ago. Instead of holding back how I feel, I allow the smile to come to my lips, allow the thought to come to my mind that I would like to have his arms around me, like to have him kissing more than just my hand.

"Thank you," he says, giving me back my hand.

Keep it, I'm thinking. But I just say, "You're welcome."

"This book," Hussein says, "it is the holiest book of the faith of my people. It is a good book. Long ago, a great man, the Prophet, blessed be his name, heard the word of Allah, of God, and wrote it down. Its poetry is so perfect. Its teachings are so profound. It teaches us to care for our families, to give to those who are poor, to cherish the gifts of nature."

Hussein pauses and shakes his head. "My father spoke to me

about the Koran, but it was only from memory. Until now I have never held a copy of the Book. How did you come by it?"

"The Dreamer," I say. "He gave it to me in return for a favor."

Hussein chuckles. "Of course. Who else would it be? You know, I always knew there was more to him behind that mask. Of the Ones who ruled us at Haven, it was only the Dreamer who would pause to listen when I played my guitar and sang. Unlike the others, it seemed to me, he still had a heart within his breast."

Hussein's words are a surprise to me. It makes me realize something I've felt but not ever consciously expressed to myself before, that he has a way of seeing into people that's just as deep as the ability I have, now and then, to hear their thoughts.

He turns his gaze back down to the Koran, opens it, reads silently for a moment. Then looks up at me.

"Inshallah," he says. "A blessing to be treasured. Indeed, I thought all were gone, destroyed by our masters who said all ways of worship were worthless."

I nod my head. It was that way for my people, too.

"It is sad how men who have power treat others they see as different, others who do not have power. In fact,"—he caresses the book in his lap—"there have even been those in the past who have used this sacred book as a pretext for doing evil. They said it told them it was right to kill those who did not follow their way of worshipping Allah." Hussein sighs. "Is it not tragic how we human beings can fool ourselves? How we can justify doing awful things to each other? Is that not so, my friend?"

"Yes," I say. I am touched by Hussein's words, but I am also feeling as if he could be saying anything, even just reciting the alphabet, and I would still be enjoying this moment with him. We're sitting so close that our knees are touching and the way he is sharing his heart with me makes me realize how much more I want to know about him, how I want him—even as damaged as I am—to be a much larger part of my life.

Hussein shakes his head. "But who am I to speak? A man who was an assassin, a man who is not worthy of this book, of your friendship?"

"No." I say. And this time I am the one who reaches out to take his hand, something I've never done before. I grasp his hand tightly, my heartbeat throbbing in my clasped fingers. " You are worthy. I couldn't ask for a better friend. Really."

That radiant smile comes over his face. "I must tell you," he starts to say. Then he pauses and looks down at my hand, my unbandaged hand that is grasping his so tightly . . . my magically healed left hand.

"How?" he says.

I'd forgotten. I suddenly feel self-conscious. I let go of his hand, hold my own hand up, wiggle my fingers.

"Hally," I say. "Or maybe not. I dreamed I was with him and that he did something and made it better."

"Dre-e-e-eeeam, dream, dream dream. All I have to do is dream-e-e-e-eeam."

A voice nearly as melodious as Hussein's croons those words from behind us. I'd sensed him approaching, so I'm not surprised, aside from the fact that he has such a beautiful singing voice. It's the Dreamer, of course. And I would like right now to punch him for disturbing us. Worse still, I think he knows just how I feel right now because he steps back out of my reach. He's enjoying having interrupted our all-too-brief moment of intimacy.

That maddening half-smile curls the Dreamer's lips below his mask, and he makes one of those graceful, semi-dismissive gestures of his with his hands.

"So," he says, "your enormous ape man returned to bestow his blessings upon you?"

"I don't know. Maybe, maybe not. Maybe it was all just a dream."

"And mayhap all this about us is but a dream as well? And when we wake, will we cry to dream again?"

Huh?

He chuckles. "Likely not."

He turns his gaze on Hussein. "So, you now have the book. Or should I say The Book?"

Hussein nods. "Thank you," he says in a polite voice.

The Dreamer shakes his head. "Thank not this one, but our little killer here. It was her largesse, not mine own." He points his chin toward the direction of the rising sun. "Mecca,

I might add, is that way. Too far for us to hear the muzzein, assuming any still exist."

Both Hussein and I look at him, equally confused by that remark.

The Dreamer, as usual, doesn't explain his cryptic remark. He just wanders humming back toward his cart, a hundred feet away from us where Lorelei is holding up a bowl of the breakfast she's just prepared for all of us humans from a box of long-dry cereal grain and water sweetened with sugar—part of the food stores Rose Eagle and our other new friends are sharing with us.

I look around our little band of—what? Outlaws? Avengers?— it's a band that I was leading before Rose and the others showed up. Maybe it's all out of my hands now, right? Which means I can relax. Or not. I just don't know what to think or how to feel about it, even though our new allies—humans and gemod horses alike—all seem so darn likeable. It's almost as if they always were here with us. People and horses alike.

As we eat the food Lorelei prepared, which is surprisingly good, I notice how people are sort of all paired up, except for Victor, who is—thank the lucky stars—still too young, even though he does clearly have a crush on Luz. She and Ana are sitting so close together that their shoulders are touching, and

Ana's once again saying something to Luz that's making her smile.

Aunt Mary and Uncle Lenard are chuckling over what he just whispered in her ear. I didn't mean to listen in, but I heard quite clearly what he said. They are, by the way, not husband and wife. He is not Rose's real uncle. She just calls him that. And I am NOT going to repeat what he whispered because it is too embarrassing. I mean they are old people, for cramp's sake, and I hope my face is not getting red from what else he just said to follow up that first disgusting remark.

Then there are Lorelei and the Dreamer. He has been behaving ever more solicitous and courtly around her almost every day. Extending a graceful hand to help her off the cart, sweeping his arm across his body to gesture her to go ahead of him. The next thing he'll be doing is calling her "my lady," if it keeps up like this, as if he were a knight in some old-time story.

It doesn't take any imagination for me to note that Rose and Phil are very much a couple. I mean, they are not acting all goofy in love or saying inappropriate things like Uncle Lenard. But the looks they give each other when they think no one is looking? You could light a match off them. Every now and then I've seen them sort of drift off to where they assume no one else can see them. Right now, all matter of factly,

Rose is taking the cup of water from Phil's hand, drinking from it, handing it back to him.

And then, and maybe this is because my imagination is working overtime with all this stuff going on around me, there's my mom and Guy. They're sitting next to each other, and he just brought her another bowl of food. Mom smiled at him. He smiled back.

Now that I think about it, they've been talking a lot to each other lately. About the weather, about how beautiful the gemod horses are, about the sunset last night. Guy and Mom together? I'm not sure how I would feel about that. I'm probably just imagining it. I need to think about something else.

The horses. I can feel them in the field behind us, and they, too, have paired up. Striped Horse and Black Horse, for example, are standing next to each other, nuzzling each other head to tail.

Which leaves me and Hussein. Right now he seems to be trying not to intrude on my space by sitting way away from me. It's as if he senses what is going on in my head. Or maybe it is just that he has that book now. He's just been holding it, not looking through it again. Sort of as if he can't believe it's real. I'm so happy I was able to give it to him.

I am happy for him. After our talk, can I dare now to think about being happy with him? Especially when I can't be happy with myself for more than a few brief moments at a time before

I start spinning back into an uncertainty darker than midnight?

I could say my feelings for Hussein are complex, but they're really not. I know now for sure what I would like him to be. Like us to be. But is there space in my sick, crazy life for that? Not now. Maybe there never will be. This growing black hole inside me is threatening to engulf everything. It adds to my usual uncertainty about what to do next. I find myself seeing faces when I close my eyes. They are indistinct at first, and then they become human faces, the faces of people I killed. Edwin, Diabilita Loca, those whose deaths I caused when I attacked the barracks at Haven. All I have room for in my head—aside from the bats that keep bouncing around in there—is to try to focus on putting one foot in front of the other so that I can do whatever I can to keep the people I love safe.

That's why I rebelled against the Ones. That's why I helped them escape from Haven. It is all about my family and those closest to me.

Rose stands up and comes over to sit with me.

"We should talk before we hit the road again," she says. "Okay?"

I nod.

CHAPTER THIRTY-SEVEN

Taking it Back

What are your goals?" Rose asks.

It's the first thing she's said since she told me we needed to talk and came to sit by me. We've been sitting here without speaking, in a kind of companionable silence for at least half an hour, long enough for the morning sun to lift clear of the horizon and shine even more brightly through the wide-open doors of the hangar.

And that's been all right by me. I've never liked having to rush into a conversation. Sometimes people can say as much to each other through silence as they can through words. What Rose's silence has been saying to me is that she trusts me, cares about what I think. That she wants to talk with me about things that really mean something. Most things that happen really fast are not usually all that good. Real friendship and trust take time.

"My goals?" I reply, shaking my head. "Keep breathing."

Rose smiles at what I've said. "What about your long-term goals?"

Long-term goals. I haven't ever thought about the future that way. My plans have all been short term. How to kill a particular monster that has selected me as its entrée of the day. How to protect my family. How to get from one place to the next alive and relatively undamaged. How to avoid trouble if I can, and blast it out of existence if I cannot. The furthest ahead I've been able to think has only been getting from Haven to what I'd hoped might be a real haven, the Valley Where First Light Paints the Cliffs. But that turned out to be nothing more than a hope that was turned into ashes.

Long-terms goals for me now means making it alive from one sunrise to the next.

Rose nods at me. She's heard my thoughts.

"I can understand that," she says. Her voice and her broad friendly face are calm. "I want to keep the people I love safe from harm on a day to day basis, too. But that is just the start. And we can't do it all by ourselves, can we?"

I look over her shoulder.

Since we've been sitting together the other people in our party have started doing things. Right now the two closest to us are Guy and Uncle Lenard. They've spread a couple of deerskins on the ground and are busy disassembling, cleaning, and reassembling the rifles we recently used. As they work

291

they're talking quietly, reminiscing about the past when Uncle Lenard was the only one who was the renegade. Mom and Aunt Rose are standing by the entrance doors with their head together, talking about something . . . or someone. Me? Ana and Luz and Lorelei are all working together packing things to get ready to leave. My brother Victor is over by the Dreamer's cart, looking at a book he's just been handed by the lanky former Overlord.

The only ones I don't see are Hussein and Phil. They quietly slipped past us a few minutes ago, heading outside to take their turns at the sentry duty that was handled last night in shifts by both people and gemod horses. When Hussein left, his eyes catching mine briefly as he passed me, Brown Star was walking just as quietly beside him.

I turn my eyes back to Rose. The only one in our party who is still sleeping is her little mouse. The end of his tail is sticking out of the breast pocket of her jean jacket. Rose looks down at him and smiles, then she reaches up and runs her hand along the long braid that hangs down the side of her face. A braid like that has a certain meaning, Mom told me. It shows that you had given your heart to someone.

Rose nods again. It seems as if right now just about everything I am thinking is getting through to her, not just a few stray thoughts. Surprisingly, I'm, comfortable with that.

In the hazy sunlight, smiling the way she is, all the lines in

Rose Eagle's face are visible. She's lived more years than I have, and her tanned face shows that. Our old people sometimes said a woman should watch out and not smile or laugh too much because it would give her lines like that around her eyes and make her look old. Not much chance of my getting lines like that. But I don't think those lines made Rose look bad at all. As a matter of fact, she's still way prettier than me.

It's peaceful sitting like this. Or it should be peaceful. But my mind is not really at rest. It's never at rest anymore. It's at war with itself.

What next? I think. *What next?*

"We're taking it back," Rose said.

"What?" I asked.

"All of it, for all of us."

It was such a big idea delivered with such calm certainty that it took my breath away for a moment.

"All of it?"

"Not all at once," Rose says. "But bit by bit. That's what we've been doing for the last three years, ever since we left the Caves. Whenever we meet real people—people like you—we ally with them. We help them and show them how they can help themselves."

"Real people?"

"Yup," Rose shows her perfect teeth in that big grin of hers. "Doesn't matter whether they're Indian or white or brown or yellow. All that matter is that they're real people. And that includes real people with hooves and four legs. We are all going to do it together. No matter how long it takes."

My reaction to her explanation of what they are up to prompted two responses from me. Both are unvoiced and, I know, mentally heard as well.

Response Numero Uno: *Wow!*

Response Numero Dos: *Who are you kidding?*

I mean, I think, *do you have any idea about how big a task that is? How big this continent is?*

Yeah, I know. I'm one to talk, never having been more than a hundred miles away from either Haven or the Valley Where First Light Paints the Cliffs.

Rose looks at me and speaks her response in the same way I expressed my disbelief.

Yes, she says silently. **We know**.

The floor of the deserted hangar is covered with dust and sand that has been swept in over the years it's been left unused. Rose picks up a stick and leans over to her side to use its point to draw a rough map in the dust.

"Look." She outlines the shape of North America. I recognize it from the Dreamer's atlas that I've been studying. I have always had this ability to remember things clearly, even after seeing them just once, and I only have to search in my mind for a second to bring up the image there of any of the pages that I looked at in that book of maps.

"I see," I say.

Rose then sketches onto her rough map the divisions that were once the seven huge states that made up the continent, each ruled BC by one of the nearly omnipotent Overlords that governed this part of the planetary corporation. "Here's where we are." She stabs the stick down into the center of the southwest. "And here's where we were," she says, touching the center of the area that bore the name Great Plains on one of the Dreamer's maps.

She begins making dots in the sand. One, two, three . . . a dozen of them. They stretch from north to south, from her plains to our deserts.

"Those are the places we've liberated so far. Helped the people there take over their own lives, formed alliances with them. We've also been eliminating gemods as we go."

As she continues to talk, I'm listening in near disbelief. Just about everywhere, people have been glad to see them and ready to join their alliance. Everything has been done in our old Indian way—by consensus. Rose isn't the only leader, just one of those who work together to lead by doing what everyone agrees should be done. And there's a Women's Council—her Aunt Rose being one of the members of that—that approves whoever is chosen to be a leader. Nobody, so far at least, has been trying to make himself or herself more powerful or materially wealthy than anyone else. And if they did, they'd have their role as a leader taken from them by the Women's Council.

"A lot of it," Rose says, "is because of the Horse People. I think it's because of the way they communicate with us and with each other. It's made a kind of connection that dampens down the sort of ambition that ruled those people who reigned before the Cloud came."

A part of me really admires that whole grand idea. But another part of me is not listening. It's the part of me that is stained by despair, by the sickness of heart and spirit that I never can really shake now. I feel as if I am teetering on the edge of a deep well and that one wrong step will send me falling into it, falling forever. Despite the positive things that have been happening, the appearance of Rose and the Horse People, the growth I've seen in Ana and Victor, the way my relationship with Hussein is on the verge of becoming something more, the clouded part of me has not lessened. It has been getting stronger. I'm frightened by the cynicism that bubbles up from that darkness. It's telling me that nothing matters, nothing can be changed for the better. At times it's so powerful that I feel sick to my stomach.

That part of me is doubtful it can ever succeed. Sure, they've done pretty well thus far, but what will happen next?

So far so good—that is what the man who fell off a cliff yelled out when he was halfway to the ground!

What worries me the most—even when I manage to repress that dark cynicism that threatens to swallow me—is the sure knowledge that lots of other crippled but still-strong survivors of our former global ruling class exist. And they are not giving up.

In Haven alone, there were things being worked on in the shops of each of the Four that could be used to reestablish something of their vanished technological might. Sure, electricity is no longer an option. But gears still mesh together, and wheels still turn. Steam power and clockwork tech could produce machines that can run as fast as our Horse People. Or faster. I know for a fact that Lady Time's artisans were trying to craft at least one or two things like that and there were rumors that the Jester's people were working out ways to lift people up into the sky again. No way will those two crazy Ones give up without a fight.

Ours is also a world in which gunpowder still goes off. And there's a vision in my mind that won't go away of steam-powered tanks with huge cannons rumbling across the land. What can riders on horses do against things like that? And now the faces of the people whose lives I ended are coming back to me again. They deserved to die; they would have killed me. But that doesn't matter. I am the one who killed them. I took their lives. They're circling me, their dead mouths speaking my name, accusing me. I'm feeling sick, dizzy, as if I am about to collapse on the ground right in front of Rose.

"Lozen," Rose says, her voice sounding distant. "Lozen!"

The urgency in her tone forces me to look up, look into her dark, flashing eyes. "I know it's going to be hard." She reaches out and grasps my hand. "But with people like you, we can fight back. It won't all happen quickly. But we will keep at it." She smiles then, a smile that is meant for more than just herself and me because she is looking down at her stomach, and as she gently places her left palm there, I realize what has been causing this sort of glow I've been sensing around her. "And so will our children to come," she says.

"All right," I say, holding tightly to her right hand. "All right."

I'm gripping Rose's hand the way a drowning person grasps a life preserver thrown her way, feeling her drag me back from the abyss.

We sit there like that for a while before she lets go of my hand.

Better?

Yes.

"Now," she says, the tone of her voice changing, "I have something else to tell you. It's about the one who's following you. I know who he is. I saw him before we found you. He was riding some sort of machine. He chased me for a while but then we left the road and leaped a fence, and he couldn't follow."

A machine? I thought those things were all gone. That shocks me, but the fact that Rose actually saw the one who's after me shocks me more.

"You saw him?"

"Yes. And I know him. His name is Luther Little Wound. He is Lakota, like us, but not like us. His other name is Four Deaths."

She tells me the sad, skin-crawling story of how the one who is hunting me is both more and less than a man, how he was turned into an implacable, nearly unkillable monster.

Great. My luck just gets better and better.

CHAPTER THIRTY-EIGHT

Kill Something

Luther had to kill something. That was what he needed. And not something small. Nor should the killing be all that quick. Something that knew he was killing it while he took his own sweet time about it.

When he felt frustrated like this, killing was the only thing that would help.

First it was the birds. It had always been easy before. Just make eye contact with a bird and he had it, he was in its head, burning its little brain to a crisp while he controlled it, seeing through its eyes until the black curtain of its death came down and vision ended.

But ever since he'd met that old man, all the birds were avoiding Luther. Not one would allow him to get close enough. Soon as they sensed his presence, they would take flight, flying straight away, never turning back. Nor could he catch any bird circling overhead and looking down the way hawks and buzzards and eagles had done in the past. Instead they just soared up, up, and away.

It was as if someone had been going ahead of him and warning the birds to avoid him.

That thought, unlikely as it was, pissed him off even more.

All he'd been able to snare with his mind were small things that could not fly and thus scout far ahead for him. A skink, a few snakes, though none as big and tasty as that fat rattler. He'd also caught one unwary half-grown jackrabbit. He'd had a little fun with that one. Making it ram itself again and again into a rock until its head was nice and bloody while he made a fire. Then having it walk, slooooowwwly, into that blaze, while its fur and skin began to burn.

Perhaps it was just his imagination, but having an animal cook itself like that made the meat taste better.

But even the smoke from the fire that he'd fanned over his motorbike had not gotten rid of the rank urine odor soaked into it. That smell got worse as he rode farther. It made him feel even more pissed—literally.

When he'd come to the culvert, the stench of the bloated corpses inside the noisome space had been easier to take. Even the stinky bodies of the apes with wings—too bad none of them were alive and accessible to his mind—were nowhere near as bad as the smell of the machine in which he'd once taken such delight. No more rolling down the highway and feeling as if he'd been born to be wild. Now he was stuck on top of a mobile sewer.

He'd found many tracks. A dozen or so different humans and the hoof tracks of at least that many animals. And there had also been the parallel marks that could only be wheels bearing a heavy load, leading down into that culvert and then up and out onto the road toward the north.

But none of those tracks had been fresh. He was a day behind them.

Gritting his teeth, he'd gotten back on the bike. If it hadn't been faster than walking or running, if it hadn't been that the rack on the back had proven such a useful place to lash on the weaponry he'd collected from the Jester's inept crew, he would have just ditched the damn machine.

But he needed the speed and the guns and so pressed forward.

However, as the day went on, he pressed slower. Despite having cleaned the clockwork as carefully as he could, the gears were slipping, and a grinding noise was coming from somewhere deep inside its mechanism.

And then it stopped short, never to go again. He reached in to clean it further, grasped a flange.

SPROING!

Luther jumped back just in time to avoid being pierced by a thin piece of flat metal that shot out and then continued to extrude from the clockwork bike as the main spring unwound, yard after yard after yard.

It left him with an even deeper need to kill something.

He brushed his hand back through the thick hair that had fallen down over his eyes . . . and immediately regretted it. The rank odor from the bike had clung to his fingers and now been transferred to his hair. He cursed again.

It was starting to get dark. The flow of day into night was always swift at this time of year. He was not going to press on into the darkness. Not that the darkness frightened him in any way. Nor was he tired. He could go for days without sleep with little ill effect. But he needed time to think.

He had also begun to sense the presence of something, several somethings, that might assuage his need. He opened the storage box on the back of the dead machine.

Ah, yes, just what the doctor ordered. He took it out, then walked—upwind from the machine—to the steep embankment, a cliff really, that came down to the road. He looked around. Perfect. It took him only a few minutes to set things up. One here, one there, another there in a semicircle in front of him. The only way they could approach.

No doubt that they had his scent. He grimaced at that thought. Anything within two miles would scent him the way he reeked now.

He lowered himself with his back against the sheer cliff, stuck his unsheathed knife blade-first into the ground by his side, moistened his index finger, dipped it in the black soil, then used the dirt to draw a circle on his forehead.

Soon enough, he heard whispering voices coming closer. Alas for them.

When the sun rose, he was still sitting there. Or rather sitting there again. Luther had been kept busy that night. There'd been seven of the Bloodless. For some reason, there were never more than seven in any band of the creatures, their little troops at least twenty miles apart. Perhaps it was all that the land had the capacity to sustain.

Whatever. Luther didn't care. What he cared about was the pleasure ahead of him.

His snares had been effective. Four of them were well caught, struggling to free themselves from the wire loops that cut bone deep into the flesh of their legs. Easy for Luther to come up on them, knock them down and bind them further with loops of wire.

The three who evaded his traps made it necessary for him to terminate their existences more abruptly than he'd hoped. A skull split here, a head lopped off there, a chest crushed under his heavy boots.

In a way, what Luther was up to was a sort of experiment. He knew that the Bloodless were never seen in daylight. Was it just because they were nocturnal and stealthy, or was the sunlight lethal to them—as in the old stories of such blood-sucking semi-human creatures?

He'd taken care in the way he'd arranged things. He'd staked them to the ground so that the sun's rays would touch one after another. To make sure they would be fully aware and not miss any of the show, he had been kind enough to slice off their eyelids.

"Wakey, wakey, sleepy heads," he crooned as he strolled between them. "Daylight comes early!"

They hissed at him, at a loss for words, it seemed. Then, as the sun's beams began to touch their naked bodies, a few words did emerge. Or rather, one word repeated again and again at ever-increasing volume.

"No, no, NO, NOOOO . . . " Until it became a less intelligible shriek of agony.

It was pleasant, but a bit disappointing. Their bodies did not disintegrate into dust or even burst into flames. They merely reddened, quite readily and swiftly, as the silver sun's light caressed their flesh.

Their unblinkable eyes did steam, just a bit, before they became orbs as blank as the white of a fried egg. But there was nothing more spectacular. Within a matter of minutes and an equivalent amount of increasingly hoarse screaming, they were all quite dead.

And Luther was feeling much better. Now if he could just catch the eye of a bird, just one bird. He looked around, looked up at the sky. Empty. But wait!

Another presence was making itself felt.

It touched his mind, much in the way he had touched the minds of birds in the past. But that touch did not harm or control him in any way. Instead, it brought a smile to his lips because of the lovely simplicity of the message it was sending.

Death-Death-Death-Death.

Ah, a kindred spirit.

He turned to welcome it.

CHAPTER THIRTY-NINE

The Right Direction

I know this land we're crossing. I don't know it from ever having been here before, though. I know it from the stories I heard from Uncle Chatto. He was the one who spoke most often of the warrior woman whose name I carry and those who fought by her in those years. He spoke especially of her brother Victorio, and of the grim old medicine man his family called Goyathlay, the Yawner, the hard-to-kill guerilla fighter known to the Mexicans and then the Americans as Geronimo.

We just rode through what was once a reservation, one of the many places where, for a time, Geronimo lived before one of his "break-outs," which simply meant that he reclaimed the freedom that they kept trying to take from him. It's a place that is still as grim, as barren as it was during his time. San Carlos. The lake that sits near it looks sick, and we do not venture close to its waters.

We continue on, the hooves of our new friends eating the miles. We pass through the abandoned place where a road sign bears Geronimo's name. It's an irony he might have appreciated, a town named after the Apache the white settlers of our lands hated and feared more than any other. It's left quickly behind.

And, as we follow this trail of so many deaths in the past and, the black cynicism in me whispers, so many yet to come, we begin to gain elevation until we are at the edge of a place where the land dives down as swiftly as a hawk dropping out of the sky. The road winds and curves down into the canyon where the Salt River flows before rising up again in similar sinuous curves to climb out of it on the other side, clearly visible to us on this rim though miles away. I feel dizzy looking at what lies ahead. The only thing that is keeping me on its back are the wordless messages being sent to me by the four-legged ally I'm riding. I'm thankful for the concern and kindness emanating from my Horse Person friend. The support of Striped Horse is almost enough to counter my sickness, but not quite.

As I sit there atop him, trying to get my head together, Aunt Mary edges up next to me on Red Horse.

"How are you, honey?" she asks me.

There's something about her that makes it as easy for me to call her Aunt Mary as it is for Rose, who is her niece by blood and not by choice. That's why I answer her honestly rather than saying "Fine," as I would to most anyone else, even Hussein or Mom.

I turn and look into her eyes before I speak, though. There's such depth in her eyes, such a presence of something very ancient, and also very prone to laughter.

"Not good," I reply.

She nods.

"I feel it in you, sweetheart. You been carrying so much it's a wonder your back isn't bent like a bow."

"You can feel it?"

"Yup. Sort of like ghost sickness. Felt it and seen it in men mostly, after they come back from wherever they were sent back then, sent to kill other human beings without really knowing the reason why. Not that you haven't had your reasons."

"We call it enemy sickness," I say.

"Lots of names for it. There was PTSD, warrior's heart, but they was all the same. It just wasn't meant to be that we would kill each other without it twisting something in us. Unless we was like that one who's after you."

I know his name now from my conversation with Rose. Should I say it? Speaking the name of an enemy is supposed to be as bad luck as saying the word "snake" after dark instead of saying "stick."

But so what? Screw him.

"Luther Little Wound."

"Yup. Four Deaths. That is the one who is after your head. Now there's a person—if you can call him that—what doesn't have to worry about getting sick from killing. Because you got to have a soul to do that. He went so far in the wrong direction, right into that darkness, that whatever soul there might've been in him was drowned a long time ago. Or replaced by whatever took his heart over and just plain pushed out the human part of him."

I sigh. "I guess, sooner or later, I'll have to face him, won't I?"

"Make it later, honey. First thing we got to do is get you right."

I'm nodding. Why I am doing that? Why am I acting as if Aunt Mary is someone I've known and trusted all my life, someone who understands me better than I understand myself?

Something in me, my heart, my spirit, my power or whatever, does know her. Like maybe sometime long ago and in other lives we had a family relationship. There are connections between us that my people have always recognized. To the eye they seem as thin as spider webs in the wind, but to the eye of the heart, they are seen as strong bonds that are not easily broken by time or distance, that connect us to each other, to the past that is never gone, to the listening land.

That's the way it is with medicine. With good medicine. Which is what I realize, even as clouded by doubt as I am, that

Aunt Mary is offering me. It may not be the sort of healing that the Hero Twins were given, the healing that people in the time of my Dine grandfathers still knew, when paintings made of sand and bark and precious dust were drawn on the earth and the haatali would chant the healing prayers to restore the balance of one whose spirit had been twisted by war. But whatever is offered, I need to take it and hope it will work for me, hope it's not too late to bring me back from the shadow land whose edge I've been walking.

Is it too late for me?

Aunt Mary is patting Red Horse's neck. I can feel the pleasure that he feels as she does that. She's looking at me, and so is Red Horse. His big bright right eye and her two dark brown ones are making contact with mine in a way that shows they both heard my mental question.

"Nope," Aunt Mary says. "You have got it bad, honey. That is for sure. But I do believe it is not too late. You are heading in the right direction and we are all going to help you get there. Soon as we get linked back up with the rest of our folks, we're taking you to this place I've found, a good safe place. Then, just for starters, we're going to do a sweat."

"Like the one you did for me?" an amused voice says from behind us. It's Rose's voice. I wish she wouldn't do that—sneak up on me like that. No one else other than Hally has been able to do that until now.

I manage not to show my surprise by doing anything other than nearly falling off the back of Striped Horse, which is only prevented by the way she shifts her body to the side to avoid my overbalancing. I can sense her amusement as she does that.

Rose and Black Horse slip between me and Aunt Mary, who is shaking her head.

"Rose," Aunt Mary says, "now that's just not fair, sweetheart. That was a whole different thing."

Rose nods. "Yup," she agrees. "Sharing a sweat lodge with two gigantic gemod carnivores was the definition of different." But she's smiling as she says that, and even though I do not get the joke I am smiling, too.

Is it possible that, in spite of everything going on in me that I may have a chance of getting better? I wish I could believe that.

Aunt Mary looks around, her eyes taking in not just us humans, but the horse people. "We're not alone this time," she says to Rose. "It's us and them. They'll help us." She points with her lips toward the other side of the canyon, miles away across the Salt River. "And there's good medicine up over there. I can feel that."

Good medicine. I hope so.

CHAPTER FORTY

Offering

The man-sized red-scaled horror that stood before Luther was cradling something in its claws, something brown-furred that squirmed as it was displayed to him. A jackrabbit.

An offering?

That was what it seemed like to Luther, but he didn't move. Caution before action. Respond in some aggressive way? Time enough for that later if it came to that. Dangerous as this new thing looked, Luther trusted his own abilities.

He studied the creature, appreciating the cold intelligence in its eyes, the obvious strength in its tightly muscled limbs, the way it seemed designed for a purpose much like his own. He also noted, with some amusement, that it seemed to be responding in the same way to him. The touch of its mind to his seemed not to be hostile, even though it identified itself as a lover of death.

Chirrrg?

The first sound it had made. He interpreted it as a question.

Go ahead, Luther thought.

The creature opened its large beaked mouth, displaying a double row of curved knife-like teeth. It turned its head sideways, one eye still on Luther, leaned forward, and bit at the jackrabbit, which twisted and squealed in pain but could not escape. Blood sprayed from the place where the animal's right foot had been. Some of it struck Luther's face as the red-scaled thing nodded and held out the squirming jackrabbit.

Chirrrg?

Luther took the bleeding jackrabbit, lifted it, grinned, and then bit down hard to tear off its other front paw. The animal's squeals were even more agonized as he handed it back.

Chirrrg!

The creature bent its head again toward their shared living feast.

What a good start!

The only unfortunate thing about their exchange was that the jackrabbit's life lasted but another two bites. Then shock took over, its heart stopped pumping, and it went limp as a sock filled with sand. That took some of the fun out of it. But they continued passing its body back and forth until nothing was left of the bloody meal.

Luther picked a bit of fur from between his teeth as the creature lifted its own scimitar-clawed hands to lick the last traces of blood from them.

It looked at Luther with first one eye and then the other.

Chirrrrg.

A ritual of acceptance, Luther thought. Was there now some sort of bonding between them?

As if to prove the accuracy of Luther's assumption, the creature leaned forward, rubbed its head twice against Luther's chest, and then straightened.

Chirrrrrg!

Luther studied his new compatriot. Had it recognized him as a human, a human like those who had created it from a mixture of genetic materials?

It stood as tall as Luther. Stood on two legs—massive legs likely designed for leaping as much as running. Its heavy tail, meant no doubt to provide balance like the tail of a kangaroo, was covered with red reptilian scales. Its toothed beak was reminiscent of those of the long-dead thunder lizards. But though its shoulders were narrow, its arms were human shaped and long as a large man's. The intelligence Luther read in its startlingly blue eyes was more anthropoid than saurian.

Saurian? Ah!

Luther remembered now. He'd never seen this particular gemod before but had heard of it. A blending of homo sapiens and avian DNA enhanced through reverse engineering of a large bird—was it an emu?—back to something resembling the raptor dinosaurs remembered deep in its genetic code. The result had been unusually successful. A vicious, canny predator that loved nothing more than to hunt and kill, bred to be as intensely loyal as a dog to its master and the others in its flock or pack or whatever. Gang, perhaps.

Luther had seen a holo-viddy of them at work—six or eight of them set against a bear-like creature five times their size. They'd worked quite efficiently together, some leaping in and out to tear at its haunches, cutting its leg tendons with their razor teeth, while others attacked its front, blinding it with quick slashes of their long front claws. Then, when the monster bear was down, moaning in agony, all of them tore open its belly, gorging themselves on its entrails.

Pleasant and entertaining to watch a lethal team function with such admirable precision.

But this one was alone.

Or was it?

The gemod raptor was looking over Luther's shoulder now, bobbing its head up and down as if in some sort of signal.

Chirrrg. Chirrrg. Chirrrg. Chirrrg. Chirrrg. Chirrrg. Chirrrg.

Luther turned around. The smile on his face broadened into a toothy grin as, one after another, the seven other members of the gang of raptors that had accepted him as their new master hopped forward to rub scaled foreheads against his chest, offering their loyalty.

Ah, Luther thought, it's good to be king.

CHAPTER FORTY-ONE

Strange Tracks

Tahhr had been running, running hard and fast for a long time.

A full day had passed since he found the thing of metal that had carried the one he was following. Tahhr had circled it. A dead metal thing now. The sharp scent of coyote urine was even stronger than the bad smells of oil and metal.

Tracks had led away from it, footprints to follow.

Tahhr's chest hurt inside. So much running. His breath came hard as he paused and looked across the canyon below, the black road twisting like a snake with no head and no tail. Somewhere along that road the one he sought was ahead of him. Not far now, the fresh scent told him.

Thirsty, he tore open a barrel cactus, chewed the soft wet pulp inside. Enough to quench his thirst for now. Then he ran again on all fours, his strong legs carrying him faster than any human. The sun moved across the sky as he ran, following the tracks and the scent trail, getting closer and closer. Then he stopped. New scents had joined the scent of the bad man he was chasing. Strange scents. Not human or bird or snake, but all blended together, joining the scent of his enemy. And there were many tracks, the tracks of the one he was following and others like those of giant birds. They led toward a grey hill, its base littered with large stones, its higher slope marked with leafless trees with red scaly trunks.

One tree stood alone on the top of that hill, outlined against the silver sky. It was a long stone's throw away, and something seemed wrong about it. Tahhr stood up on his hind legs to study it.

Suddenly that tree moved, turned, and Tahhr realized it was no tree at all. It was his enemy, looking down at him. The man opened his mouth in a grin, lifted one hand and brushed it back across the top of his head. He waved at Tahhr and then, like a black spiderweb touching his face, the man's dark voice spoke inside Tahhr's head.

Come, kill me.

Tahhr shook his head, trying to clear that black web from inside it.

Come, kill me. Come on!

The man smiled even wider, his teeth glittering.

Come, Come on! Why are you waiting?

Tahhr growled, dropped to all fours to run up the slope.

"SAY HELLO TO MY LITTLE FRIENDS," the man shouted at him.

Chirrg. Chirrg. Chirrg. Chirrg.

The grey trees were not trees either. They turned toward him.

Tahhr saw them, their red-scaled bodies, their long claws and wide mouths. They were not as large as Tahhr, but they were many.

His enemy was laughing now.

"BETTER RUN AWAY," he shouted.

Tahhr did not run away. He ran toward them, growling deep in his throat. He knew that death was ahead of him. He did not care.

His feet sprayed up earth as he ran. Four more leaps and he would be among them.

But as he passed between two of those boulders at the base of the hill, the ground moved in front of him. It rose up, opening like a mouth. Two long arms reached out, wrapped around him, pulled him down as the earth closed above him, and he was plunged into the dark.

CHAPTER FORTY-TWO

Names

The Salt River Canyon is behind us now, and we're almost at the place that used to be called Fort Apache according to the Dreamer's atlas. It's in the high lands of the White Mountains, the place where the northern cousins of our Chiricahuas lived. Lived, though, is the wrong word because that is in the past tense. According to Rose, who passed through here on her way to the place where we met, they still live here. They've stayed with this land despite efforts made by hundreds of years of would-be conquerors.

My dad had talked about these Apaches, how it was among the White Mountain people that many of our people lived for a time. It was in 1885 when the white eyes soldier chief we called Grey Fox was in charge. Grey Fox had promised good land for growing corn and hunting if we surrendered, and that was what our people did. Even though Geronimo and Lozen and a handful of other fighters wanted to continue resisting, the children were hungry, and most of the other women longed for a peaceful life.

So they were herded up into these mountains. Though they were not sure they could trust the White Mountain Apaches—many of whom had been scouts for Grey Fox—it turned out that they were given a good place. It was along Creek Where Turkeys Come for Water. The creek had good water, and there were trees all around it. The nearby plain had lots of antelope and other game to hunt. Maybe life on this reservation would be different.

But then things happened as they always did. It was not just that the white eyes soldiers proved that they could not be trusted. It was also that our people had been herded together, confined, and kept in. And there were old disagreements that festered among them. There were quarrels and there was drinking. Finally, the decision was made to leave. Some blamed Geronimo, who was always happiest, it seemed, when there was fighting. He told the people that the Grey Fox had decided to hang him and the other leaders and that their only hope was to leave because the white eyes soldiers were coming to get them all. For whatever reason, the decision was made to break out, and so they did. Nana, an old and trusted leader, and Geronimo led them. They trusted Lozen's power to show them the way back to the Sierra Madre Mountains in Mexico.

"Not everyone agreed," my uncle Chatto had said as my father paused in his story.

My father had nodded at him. "The one your uncle is named for was a good man, but he chose to stay with the white eyes. He believed he could make them see reason."

"A lot of good that did him," Uncle Chatto said.

"So it was only a quarter of our people who left the reservation. About forty warriors and a hundred women and children. And Lozen worked her power and used what it gave her to lead them back to the Sierra Madres, back to those mountains. There was fighting along the way, and their journey took them two weeks, but they got there without losing even one person."

"But it was close to the end," Uncle Chatto said.

My father had nodded again at that. "Maybe they felt that it was better to die trying than live without hope. After all, so many of their friends and relatives had already gone before them to the Happy Place. That was why those last Chiricahuas to resist began to call themselves by a new name. They no longer called themselves Tinneh, the People. They called themselves Indeh, the Dead."

I feel like one of the dead right now as I look out over the land before me toward the place where we are heading—to the east of Fort Apache. I wonder if it would have been any different if Lozen and the others had stayed here. Maybe not. But despite that dark despair haunting me, some small part of

323

my spirit is saying that it can feel the call of this land. It's telling me that there are places here that remember us, that there are good people who will welcome us.

According to what Rose told me, when she and her horses arrived here they were met and welcomed by White Mountain Apache people. Somehow those Apaches had survived in small bands. Even during the reign of our planetary Overlords some had managed to find refuge in the forests and mountains and to avoid being culled or put into forced labor.

"They had help doing that," Rose said, without specifying what sort of help it was.

"Some of it was the land," my mother says. She's riding next to me. I am certain that she has been feeling what I've been feeling since we came up out of the canyon—feeling it without the dark cloak of confusion I cannot seem to fully cast off.

I've never been here before, but there's something hauntingly familiar about the sight of the tree-clad mountains. Am I seeing it through the first Lozen's eyes, through some part of her that is living in me? Why else would it seem as if I am remembering the sharp, fragrant smell of the evergreens that fills the cool air, air that is alive, air that is bracing after the arid plains around San Carlos, where it seemed there was nothing but dust piling layer upon layer.

Everything knows we are here.

That voice comes from within me. Not from someone else.

It's telling me to reach out, to accept the connection. But I can't. It's as if half of me is dead and the other half is struggling to keep from dying.

"The names know us," someone says next to me. It takes me a second to realize it's my mother.

"The names?"

My mother nods. "Our old people, such people as Lozen, remembered the names of these places. And those places helped them. I was taught that the names of places have always protected us, given us power, healed us."

Had my mother ever talked like this before? But then I remember she was the one who first called the place where we had lived Valley Where First Light Paints the Cliffs. But it was not a name she made up. She said it was a name that told itself to her.

All of a sudden, names are coming to me, names I know that I can't possibly have remembered all by myself.

I am Trail between Green Rocks.
I am Line of Red Along the Cliff.

They are making my head spin. I'm feeling that same kind of disorientation I felt when the Mountain Spirit, the gans, showed himself to me in that abandoned house.

I am One Cedar Standing Alone on the Ridge.

I am Water Lying on the Bottom of a Hill.

How? I think.

"How indeed," Hussein says.

Once again he has come up so quietly next to us that I didn't hear him. But I guess I have to get used to that happening. He's on the back of the stallion with the star that chose him and those horses can move so quietly. They also have a kind of something about them, almost like a field of energy, which makes it difficult for anyone to see them unless they wish to be seen. It is even hard for me to sense them with my power.

It also seemed to be true that whenever someone riding one of our new hooved allies gets within a few yards of me, they can read my mind, or at least whatever is at the top of my thoughts.

"What do you mean?" I ask Hussein.

"About this land," he says. "It is speaking to you, yes? I do not know how, but I am hearing it also."

"Oh," I say, looking down at my hands, but still watching him out of the corner of my eye.

My mother and her horse have moved away from us, as if to give us space. I'm not sure if I'm glad about that. Part of me, that dark confused part, wants to turn away, to tell Hussein to leave me alone. Another part wants to look into his eyes, wants him to be even closer. He nods at me as if he understands what is going on in my head, and he keeps talking, his voice gentle, reassuring.

"I think," he says, "it must have been like this for my old people in their deserts. The deserts loved us, you know. They gave us the space and time to think and to be peaceful. In those wadis, my father said, a man could clear his mind. It feels the same here to me."

What can I say to that? Or think? I'm in the middle of a dizzying whirlwind where any direction I turn is just more confusing.

If he does sense what I'm feeling, to his credit, Hussein doesn't respond. He looks away, over the plain in front of us that stretches below the purple mountains.

"You must still stay awake," he says. "There is this story about a man who was riding his camel at night. He felt so at peace as he rode along, so much in tune with the rhythm of his camel's strides, that he fell asleep. So it happened. And as he slept he relaxed. He relaxed so much that he fell off his camel. Ahhhh-ah! But that was not the worst of it. For when he fell it was not upon the ground. He fell onto a big animal. It was a sleeping hyena that woke when the man landed upon its back. That man was now as wide awake as the hyena. He grabbed hold of its ears as it leaped up and began to run."

Hussein lifts his hand to his mouth, covering a smile.

"What happened then?" I ask. His story, the way he's been

telling it with that melodic voice of his, has pulled me out of myself for a moment. I really do want to know.

"Ah, that is as far as my father went with that story. So I do not know. Maybe that man is still riding the back of that hyena. All that he said when he ended that tale was two words."

"Stay awake?"

"Yes."

Stay awake, I think.

Yes. I need to stay awake

Even in this place where the land is welcoming, I am still in a world of enemies. I may not be Indeh, but I am still following the trail of the dead, this road where the hill of death is ready to rise up and greet me at every bend. No matter what I do, all I will find is cold endless night and deep darkness.

"No," Hussein says.

"What?" I say, my voce harsher than I intend.

Our two horses move together, so close that Hussein's leg is pressed against mine. He takes hold of my arm with the same gentle firmness that is in his voice.

"It is not all darkness for you. You must not give up, habibi," he says. "You are needed . . . by all of us. This land is speaking to us. It is saying that there is healing for you here. You will see the dawn."

CHAPTER FORTY-THREE

Horse Ceremony

It's not yet dawn.

I've been taken along a narrow winding path to a place where a stream is flowing over mossy rocks before emptying into a deep pool of cool water that is shaded on one side by a single juniper tree. Jackrabbit grass, grama grass, mountain rice, and salt-weed are all growing around the clearing behind us. Plants that horses love to forage on. Ponderosa pine, piñon, and more junipers clothe the slopes above us. In this one sheltered spot, seven huge rocks rise around us. They lift like hands rising up from brown earth that is speckled with glittering stones—mica and quartz.

It's a safe place. That is what everyone keeps saying to me. But part of me doubts that.

The large house made of stone—a former armory—which is the center of this stronghold of the White Mountain people,

329

is two miles below us and out of sight from here. It's where the rest of Rose's Lakotas and the Horse People are camped, along with our new White Mountain Apache allies.

A little of the curtain of darkness that seems to cloud my eyes every moment now—waking or sleeping—lifted when they welcomed us two days ago. First came a group of two dozen men and women on horseback who thundered toward us across the wide plain spread between the mountains. The rhythm of those horses' hooves made my heart beat faster and almost brought a smile to my face to match the smiles on everyone else in our party. But not quite. By the time we rode into camp, all that was keeping me in the saddle was the way Striped Horse moved, as if each step beneath me was done in such a way that she prevented me from falling.

I could barely register what was going on around me as we were surrounded by talking, joking, welcoming people. Some of them looked to be the same age as Ana and Luz, and the two of them, despite their initial shyness, were soon drawn off into a group of girls. I just hoped some of those girls were as fond of weapons as my little sister and Luz, or their conversations might be a little strained.

If I'd felt better I would have chuckled at what I observed happening with Victor and the several boys who were eyeing him. Even half-drowned as my senses were, I could feel them appraising each other. Before the end of day there'd be wrestling matches and stone-throwing contests between them, and I had no doubt that before dark they'd all be bruised and acting like old friends.

I slid to the ground, grasping Striped Horse's mane to keep from falling, feeling the wave of concern from her mind as she let me lean against her. The sun, though hazy, was hot, and yet I was feeling cold inside, cold and more tired than I could ever remember.

"Come with me," a woman's voice said from behind me. Then Aunt Mary's two firm hands were grasping my shoulders. She led me to an arbor off to the side, a simple structure of upright stripped saplings with a flat roof thatched by evergreen boughs.

"You're worse off than I thought, honey," she said. "It's deep in you, darling. That power you have, that way of hearing with your mind and taking things into your heart, opened you up so much. You been a killer, but you never gave up any of your caring. That's kept you human, but it feels to me as if you've drawn more death into you than a dozen ordinary men could handle. We have got to get you back into balance. So you just sit now. Tomorrow we start the ceremony."

So that was what I did. I sat and watched, no one—not even those closest to me—coming close to me, politely leaving me alone in my own space. I watched as people got to know each other, as food was served out. Even the Dreamer and Lorelei seemed relaxed as they sat and ate with the others, the Dreamer's cart guarded by two Horse people.

No food was brought to me. I had to fast before my ceremony started.

But I listened with my ears and with the little thread of my power that I could still feel. All of the voices and stray bits of thought that I could catch were filled with welcome, with sharing, with the promise of friendship. Sure enough, just as I'd expected, Victor was back with that group of boys. There was a cut on his cheek and a satisfied look on his face, and it was clear from the way the other young men looked at him—and to him—that he had already established himself as someone they would choose to follow. Ana and Luz, meanwhile, were with an equally adoring circle of five other girls. The only thing that surprised me was what all seven of them were holding and intently talking about: not guns, but cloth dolls dressed in the sort of clothing our old people wore a century and a half ago.

As the night settled in, a bonfire was lit and stories were shared. Part of me really wanted to join the circle then, but I couldn't. I watched as if there was a wall between me and everyone else. There was laughing and a lot of the sort of teasing that our people do with each other. My father always said that people were meant to laugh—laugh with each other and also at ourselves and our own human foolishness. Two of the men who were laughing the hardest were Hussein and Phil, who were acting now as if they had been friends for ages, rather than just a few days.

Then one of the White Mountain men everyone called Dog asked Hussein if he had a story. Hussein turned to Phil, who nodded go-ahead. Then, first glancing over to where I sat alone in the shadows under that arbor, Hussein once again related his Bedu tale about the man riding the hyena—with even more details and hand gestures than when he shared it with me.

"You sure that man wasn't a Chiricahua?" one of the White Mountain women asked when he was done. It was an older white-haired woman sitting next to Aunt Mary. Emily Lewis was her name.

That made everyone just about fall down laughing. Even the four or five horses that had drifted in and placed themselves in a circle around the gathering stomped their feet in what I sensed meant they were just as amused.

The Horse People. I could feel them around us—and not just those who had come in to join the circle. The rest of the herd was ranged around us in a much greater circle. My power, weakened as it was, sensed what they were doing. They were our sentries, keeping watch for danger. I shared, too, how keen their night vision was, so much better than the original horses. By the faint silver glow from the sky of the half moon, they were seeing as well as if it was midday.

The herd here numbers over sixty horses. Only twenty of them had riders when they arrived here in White River. Most of them, horses and riders alike, had remained here while Rose and her smaller party went south to meet us. One of the reasons why the White Mountain people made Rose and her Lakotas so welcome—the main reason at first—was the horses. Just seeing them was so powerful.

And when they were told that some of those horses would remain as friends and allies here at White Mountain, stallions and mares that would bring more of their horse people into the world, the joy those White Mountain Apaches felt could hardy be expressed.

Four of those horses are here with us now, part of my healing ceremony. I hear them moving in the darkness around me. Their steps are deliberate, louder than usual. They sound like drums being beaten together in an old, old song. All four of them doing that slow dance are mares. So, too, are all of the human people who were chosen to be here by Aunt Mary and Emily Lewis, who are running the ceremony together. This is a woman's healing ceremony, not one for men.

My two days of fasting hasn't made me feel weak. It's made me feel a quivering in my chest, like a bird about to spread its wings.

Aunt Mary is sitting in front of the sweat lodge, outlined by the glow of the fire. She's the one who directed the building of the lodge, the placement of the fire. Rose was the one who gathered the stones that are now glowing white-hot in the fire's heart. My mother and Ana and Luz are the ones who gathered the firewood. Emily Lewis provided the sage and cedar. Aunt Mary brought the sweetgrass and tobacco that will be burned.

Emily Lewis is holding a pouch that is filled with pollen. She is the head woman elder here and will take things over after we've all done the sweat. She remembers things that most people have forgotten, and the language she'll chant is not English.

Aunt Mary is singing now, singing in time with the drum beat of the horses dancing around us. I'm hearing her words through my ears and in that deeper place within. Those words feel like a southern wind blowing through me, driving out the cold. Because this ceremony is mine, because it is sacred and being done in this way, I won't say much more about it other than it is beginning. And as I duck my head to crawl into the sweat lodge, its clean darkness is so different from the blackness that has been drowning my spirit that, for the first time in a long time, I am beginning to feel hope.

I t's perhaps six hours later.

Or maybe six centuries.

Time, in the whole Western sense of time, just went away. I'm sitting alone again, on a hill looking over the plain. I'm being watched from a respectful distance by those who did this for me and with me. I feel their presence, their minds still one with me.

I look at the pollen coating my arms and hands and legs. It's the same sort of coating of pollen that I would have been given if I'd been able to go through the rite of passage ceremony in which I would have taken on the role of White Painted Woman, the ancient holy person who was the mother of the Hero Twins.

That's not the ceremony I just experienced. What was done for me was something that was both old and new, a blending of ways to fit this new time, to fit what I needed to bring me back to balance.

I taste the pollen on my lips. I know what it is to feel new again, to let go of that darkness that was in my heart, to breathe in blessings and breathe them out again to share with everything that is alive and good. Yes!

Striped Horse is quietly grazing on the grama grass a spear's throw away from me. She was more than part of the ceremony, for at times I felt her as if she was part of me, a part that was becoming whole once again, restoring the coolness to the center of my being, connecting me once more to the circle that had felt broken.

After I came out of the sweat lodge and was placed in the circle where the rest of the ceremony was to happen, she came up to me, leaned forward and breathed into my face, touched my cheeks with her nose. I remember, when the ceremony was almost done, the way she circled me four times, pausing at the east and pawing the ground, then the south, the west, the north. Each time I felt the pain within me lessen, the sorrow and despair that had been hanging over me like a grey cloud, piercing me like a black poisoned arrow, leave me.

I take a deep breath, let it out slowly. I cannot stay here in this high place forever, cannot live here within this healing moment. But when I leave here, when the other women and I walk back down the mountain, I will take it with me.

And whatever battles I have to fight, I know I will be ready. I'm strong again. I'm clear again. I can work again for my power.

CHAPTER FORTY-FOUR

My Plan

Rose shakes her head.

"I don't like that plan," she says.

"It's not your plan," I reply. "But it is the way I do things."

"You're risking your life."

"So what else is new? And it's worked so far for me."

Rose shakes her head a second time. I almost say *you're not the boss of me*—which is something that my brother Victor used to say to me until after Dad and Uncle Chatto were killed and we ended up in Haven.

But even though those words would be more or less accurate, they would be rude. I don't want to be rude to Rose, of all people. She's shown herself to be a real ally and I think of her now as a true friend, someone I can trust. Her interests and mine may be a little different—mine being small and focused, and hers being about as broad as the horizon that stretches out before us as we stand together on this mesa we've climbed together, just the two of us, to get a better view looking south.

I look over at her, admiring what I see. She's good-looking, tall, straight-backed and wide-shouldered. Her long braided hair frames her broad face. Her arms are crossed, and as she stands there, one foot slightly in front of another, she seems like a statue of how a strong woman should look. She's more cautious than I am, but we are alike in so many other ways. We're both determined. We've both lost people we love and we both love people we wish to protect, even if we go about it in different ways.

Yes, our interests are different. But in more ways than one they are also the same interests.

To restore the balance, to help the people find a way back to peace. And to rid this land of monsters, which is where yours truly comes in.

It's in my job description.

Anyhow, I do not say anything either rude or conciliatory. I just cross my arms and turn my head to look south again, the direction from which the tingling of my palms tells me that danger is approaching.

Not following me as fast as before, my Power tells me, but still after me with just as much determination.

The one who wants to kill me is getting closer. The one whose name I now know to be Luther Little Wound. Four Deaths.

How do I know that he is close? It is not just my Power that has told me that.

When I woke yesterday morning, Rose was sitting next to me. The look her face was a combination of pain and anger.

"He's close," she said between her teeth. "Come with me." She strode outside, vaulted into the back of White Horse, waited a moment for Striped Horse and me, and then the two of us galloped to the south.

What I found waiting us was not pretty. A small group of Lakota and White Mountain men were gathered around something covered by a blanket. When it was removed I saw what was a man, what had been a man before he was pegged to the ground and killed—slowly, it seemed. He didn't look familiar.

"Who?" I asked.

"We don't know," Rose said. "An outlier."

Outlier. That was what the White Mountain people called those who remained hidden in the hills, trusting their ability to remain concealed, perhaps living in a cave, drinking from a spring, catching small game and foraging for food plants.

Half a dozen such outliers had come in to join the main body of people after Rose and the Horse People arrived.

Maybe this man had been caught while he was trying to do just that.

And now he was nothing more than a message, a message expressed by his death and by the note pinned into his chest.

SEND LOZEN SOUTH OR EXPECT
MORE OF THESE

HAVE A NICE DAY

I know what I have to do. Not just because of that callously evil message, but because of the dream I had last night. Though that dream did not seem at all like a dream at the time.

We had made our decision. We were headed together toward the south, toward my enemy and his allies.

We would meet them halfway after passing a deep canyon where a small river flowed far below.

Rose had explained to me how dangerous our adversary was, how he had died four times and returned to life. How he became even more deadly and determined and nearly invulnerable after each succeeding resurrection. His skin would shed bullets now as if they were raindrops.

341

But how could he defeat all of us? We had not just twenty well-armed humans, especially well-armed now that Guy had shared that store of weapons out among us, but also our gemod horses, our intelligent, powerful allies. We were prepared. We were sure of that.

"Let's go," Rose said as we rode out.

"Hoka hey!" Phil agreed. "We are ready."

Yet in that dream, which seemed to be reality at the time, we had been wrong. Our enemy ambushed our outriders and killed them and their horse companions silently.

We began riding past a grey hill and suddenly we were under fire. People were falling. Horses were falling. Armor-piercing rounds thudding into bodies. Hidden mines exploding.

And then screaming, unearthly screaming as things were leaping in from all sides and attacking us. In the dust and smoke, we couldn't make out what they were, aside from glimpses of red-scaled skin and the swift slashing of gore-dripping teeth.

Rose lay on the ground, creatures tearing at her flesh, her wide-open lifeless eyes staring at the silver sky. Rose's partner Phil was being lifted by a huge dark-haired bear of a man, who'd moved quicker than a cat as he attacked. Then Phil was thrust down with terrible force, his back broken over that man's bent knee. Guy was dead, Hussein was dead. The acrid smells of gunpowder and blood were filling my nostrils as I tried to stand but could not because the bullets that had struck me had paralyzed my legs.

Something had me by the back of my neck and was shaking me, shaking me as I tried to fight, to reach my knife, my gun, something, anything. A wide blade, more sword than knife, was being thrust toward my throat.

And then I woke up—on the floor, Hussein grasping one arm and Guy the other, my sister and brother with their arms wrapped around my legs. All of them were bruised, blood dripping from Guy's nose where I later learned my knee had struck him. Rose was a few feet away, also looking a bit battered and holding my belt with its still-holstered revolver and sheathed Bowie knife.

The Dreamer, standing farther back from the fray with his arms crossed, was the first to speak.

"Bad dream again, one assumes," he said.

I finally turn back to Rose and speak.

"I have to do it alone," I say.

"Because of the dream," Rose says.

"Because of that and also because it's who I am."

"I wish I had your courage," Rose says.

So do I, I think. But I don't say that.

CHAPTER FORTY-FIVE
Meeting People

There's this old story about Coyote. It has been going through my mind as I walk southward, having left my companions behind so I can embark on my solitary mission.

Long ago, they say, Coyote was out walking along when he met Badger. In those stories Coyote is always meeting people.

Badger was carrying a pack on his back. Right away Coyote wanted to know what was in it.

Nothing you would want, Badger said.

Of course that made Coyote even more curious.

Maybe there is food in there, Coyote thought. Coyote was always hungry.

Cousin, Coyote said, let me travel with you. Let me keep you company.

Badger agreed and so they traveled along together.

Cousin, Coyote said. Your pack must be heavy. Let me carry it for a time.

You can do so, Badger said. But do not open it. There is no food in there. You would not like what I have in my pack.

So Coyote took the pack, and they walked on for a while longer until they came to a hill.

Cousin, Coyote said, I have to urinate. I will go over here behind these bushes. You keep going and I will catch up to you.

Fine, Badger said. Just do not open my pack. Then, as Coyote went behind the bushes, Badger continued on and went over the hill.

As soon as Badger was out of sight, Coyote opened the pack. There was no food inside. All that pack held was darkness. That darkness came billowing out and everything around Coyote was dark.

Help me, Coyote said. I cannot see.

Badger came back.

A bad thing you have done, he said. He gathered the darkness and put it back into his pack. Then Badger continued on alone.

Coyote sat there for a while. He was angry at Badger. Then he continued on until he met Bobcat.

Hello, Cousin, Coyote said.

Hello, Cousin, Bobcat replied.

The two of them sat down to talk.

Shall we play a game? Coyote said.

Yes, Bobcat agreed. Let's scratch each other's back and see who has the strongest claws.

Coyote looked at Bobcat's feet. He could see no claws at all. He looked at his own feet and saw that his own claws looked long and strong.

That sounds like a good game, Coyote said. Who should go first?

You go first, Bobcat said.

So Coyote went first.

Sit up straight so I can scratch you from head to tail, Cousin, he said. He scratched Bobcat's back as hard as he could. He dug his claws in and raked them all the way down Bobcat's back.

Ey-yeh-yah! Bobcat said. You hurt me. But Bobcat was not really hurt.

Coyote felt pleased.

Now it is your turn, he said.

So Bobcat went. Bobcat extended his long sharp claws that had been hidden. He raked Coyote's back with his sharp claws so hard that he took skin and meat off Coyote's back.

Coyote jumped up. Ey-yeh-yah! he yelled. You have killed me, Cousin. He was really hurt.

Ever since then, the skin on Coyote's back has been tight, and there is very little meat there.

Why is that story going through my head, walking along with me as I walk?

I pause as I walk, leaning on the staff that Guy has insisted I take with me along with my usual weapons, the rifle slung over my shoulder and the other little surprises stowed in the heavy pack on my back.

I remember what my mother used to say when she told us Coyote stories during the winter, even we were kept in Haven.

"Don't be like Coyote," she said. "Be like Badger."

Coyote is a fool, but he is always a teacher.

I know that better since meeting him. Trickster though he may be, Coyote is part of our people and part of this land. Somehow, and I can't exactly say how I know this except through the inexplicable workings of my power, I feel that Coyote helped me in another way, that one reason my enemy Luther Little Wound has been delayed in reaching me was he also met Coyote. I need to pay attention to Coyote's lessons.

My enemy may think he knows who I am, may think he knows my weakness. But I'm like Badger, who got rid of the load of darkness he was carrying. I'm like Bobcat with hidden claws.

"Hold that thought," rumbles a deep, familiar voice to the left of me.

Of course I jump. And of course it is Hally, standing close enough to touch me.

"How do you do that?" I say, regretting my words as soon as they've left my mouth.

Jedi mind trick? Hally replies, this time speaking as he usually does to me, mind to mind.

Huh?

Scotty just beamed me down.

What?

Hally nods sadly.

Ah, of course. They never allowed you common folk to see any of those in the viddys you were allowed to view, did they? None of those good triumphing over evil against all odds. So it would mean nothing for me to make mention of the possibility of my having a Ring of Power that renders me invisible, eh?

No!

It has taken my large hairy mentor less than ten seconds to confuse and irritate me to the point that happy as I am to see him, I also am feeling the impulse to brain him with this staff.

Hi ho, he mindspeaks, *enough of obscure cinematic references, eh? So little to do and so much time. It's off to work we go.*

Hally raises his huge hand, steps a few long paces forward, extends one long finger toward a giant boulder covered with pictographs. He taps it and a door swings open.

Someone in there for you to meet. Or shall I say meet again?

All I can see is darkness.

Hally steps aside and gracefully gestures inside.

In we go. After you, Alphonse.

And what else can I do? I go in.

CHAPTER FORTY-SIX

In Focus

Luther was feeling irritated.

His new allies were lethal. That was good. And they were loyal. That was good, too. But they also had minds of their own and were not about to do exactly what Luther wished them to do.

They enjoyed killing so much that it was constantly distracting them. No matter what living, ambulant creature they encountered, be it large or small, they felt the compulsion to chase it, catch it, kill it (not that quickly), and finally greedily consume it.

Jackrabbit?

Chirrrg!

Chase, catch, torture to death, consume.

Deer?

Chirrrg!

Chase, catch, torture, consume.

Lizard, snake, scorpion, centipede, moth?

Chirrrg!

CCTC.

All the while their nasty little brains filled with that single humming refrain.

Death Death Death Death.

It was becoming boring. Especially when he had to wait while they wasted at least a full hour digging out every single insect in an anthill they delightedly encountered.

Luther buried the thought, lest his new friends sense it, but he was already looking forward to the time when the red-scaled raptors had outlived their usefulness and he could bestow his own bit of death on each of them in turn. Poison darts? He still had plenty of those. Decapitation? A round through the side of the head into the brain?

But enough of those thoughts for now, though his temporary allies seemed oblivious to them with their limited brain capacity.

They were also rather nearsighted physically. They seemed unable to see things more than a hundred or so yards away.

But they should still be of use in what he had planned. A simple enough strategy. Draw the humans and those horses they were riding into a trap. A place carefully booby-trapped with the small, effective mines he carried in his bag. Then attack from all sides at once.

He'd tried, just as an experiment, extending the control of his mind over the red-scaled pack. It had taken a bit of effort, holding them all in place, keeping them in focus, but it had worked. They'd all been a bit dazed after, but they had not died like the birds whose brains he'd burned out as he controlled their flight and took over their vision.

In the case of his rapacious new companions, his control had been light, a simple *just wait and then kill what I tell you to kill*, centering his attention on a cow elk that had been unfortunate enough to show itself to Luther's keen eyes at the distant edge of the evergreen-thick tree line just then.

There.

Their attention shifted.

Wait!

They waited.

Now!

And off they went, bounding and chirrging and death-death-deathing.

It had not impaired their killing ability at all, just left them a bit dazed and lethargic after they finished feasting, consuming every scrap of the elk, meat, blood, and bone.

It had worked well enough for him to be sure he could do it again, keep them in focus, at least once or twice.

But once should be enough.

CHAPTER FORTY-SEVEN

New Old Friends

It took me a moment for my eyes to adjust. Then I saw him and knew who he was, if not exactly what.

I drew in a sharp breath and my hand dropped toward my holstered .357.

Hally took hold of my wrist. Gently, but firmly.

No! Friend.

The being I'm looking at, the same giant gemod ape-cat that I shot not long ago, rises up from all fours to stand on its hind legs. It's almost man-like as it towers over me, nearly as large as Hally. I see the claws extended from its long fingers, the sharp fangs displayed in its open mouth.

Then it closes its mouth and those claws retract. And I see the look in its eyes, read what is there with both my eyes and my mind. Sorrow—deep, deep sorrow from wounds that go far deeper than those shown by any of the scars marked on its sinuously muscled body.

"Tahhhhrrrr," it growls. But there's no threat in that growl. "Tahhrrr," it growls again, placing its hand on its chest. And I realize what it's doing. It has a name. It's telling me its name.

I lift my own hand, place it over my heart.

"Lozen," I say. "Lozen."

"Looo-zzennn," it replies.

I nod, and it opens its mouth partway, showing its teeth in what I think must be meant as a smile.

"Loo-zzzennn," it says.

I extend my hand. But instead of taking it as a human would, Tahhrr drops to all fours and bends toward me, exposing the vulnerable back of his neck. I place my palm there, feeling the smoothness of Tahhrr's fur, the warmth of his skin beneath as I stroke it with my hand.

"Goood," Tahhrr purrs as he leans into me, almost knocking me off my feet, though I keep my balance, "Lozzennn good."

I look over at Hally, who is showing his own impressive dentition as he beams down at us.

Ah, this could be the beginning of a beautiful friendship.

Then, and I can't explain this except to describe it as a wash of communication and emotion that sweeps over me like a warm wave, Tahhrr gives his mind to me. His memories, all of them, are suddenly mine as well. How he was born and mistreated, how he found his mate, his other half—Derrhha. How they escaped, found a place where they felt safe, every detail of their lives together including the joy of their mating, the coming of their children and then . . . and it's so awful, so unendurable, that I would fall to my knees if my hand was not resting on him, the murder of his family, the red anger that consumed him and set him on the trail of the same person who has been seeking my life.

And now I am on my knees, my arms are wrapped around Tahhrr's neck. I am crying, for him and with him.

"I am so sorry, Tahhrr."

And my sorrow is not just for all that he's lost, all that I've briefly felt as if his loss was my own. I'm also sorry because I know that this happened because of me. If that implacable hunter had not been sent out on my trail, he would never have . . .

Stop.

I look up at Hally. His face is more serious than I've ever seen it before.

No guilt. Feel no guilt. What has happened has happened.

I stand, and so does Tahhrr. He has one of his big paws resting on my shoulder. I feel so natural about him doing that. It's as if I've known him all my life now. I wonder if something similar to what passed from him to me also went the other way.

Hally is right. Uncle Chatto told me about what one needs to do to move on after bad things have happened.

"If your cup is filled with bad water," he said, "water that you cannot drink, there's only one thing to do, my niece. You know what that is?"

"Pour it out and fill it again with good water?"

"So," I say to Hally. "Tahhrr is going to go into this fight with me?"

Hally nods.

"And you?"

Hally shakes his head.

"You mean it will just be the two of us?"

The grin comes back to Hally's face.

Since when did three plus one equal two, Little Food?

He turns back toward the wall of the cave where the door had closed behind us. He touches it and it swings open again to show the two people who are standing there and have clearly been following me since I left our camp—following me without my Power warning me they were there.

CHAPTER FORTY-EIGHT

A Plan

Kin we join this party?" Guy says. "Or is it by invitation only?'

Hussein doesn't say anything, he just looks down at his feet. But there's a smile at the edge of his mouth, despite the fact that Tahhr has risen up on two legs to loom defensively over my left shoulder. A deep growl issues from his open mouth.

"Tahhr fight?"

"No!"

I reach my hand out to reassure my huge best buddy that there's no threat. He settles back down at my touch, though he continues that warning growl at a softer volume.

No threat, but a lot of meddling behind my back. Like how come neither Guy nor Hussein reached back for the rifles slung over their shoulders but just stood there? Brave though I know them both to be, why was it they seemed unsurprised at the impressive sight of my new bodyguard? Seemed, in fact, to expect something like him? How exactly did they get here?

I look back over my shoulder at Hally.

"This was all your doing, wasn't it? You brought them here, right?"

He just rolls his eyes up toward the ceiling, his palms held out in a "who, me?" pose. Butter wouldn't melt in his mouth.

Guy and Hussein are waiting for me to say something to them.

I lift my shoulders and then drop them with a sigh.

"All right," I say. "You can come. But we do it my way."

What a surprise!

"Shut up, Hally!"

Guy winks his one eye at me. " 'Tis your party all the way, lass," he says, and Hussein nods his agreement.

Okay, I'll admit it. I'm pretending to be exasperated, but I am actually relieved.

I did have a plan to go it alone. It was my usual plan. Head straight for trouble and then see what happens next—and that was it. Not the greatest strategy, I suppose, but you tend to go with what has worked in the past. After all, I'm still here and a whole bunch of my past enemies are not.

But this time is different. I'm not going against a gemod

monster that doesn't expect me or know anything about me. This time my enemy is a human monster, one who knows a lot about me. One who has been pursuing me. One who is probably at least as well prepared for our confrontation as I am.

So he knows I am coming. But I know that he knows that I'm coming. And he does not know that I have already seen in my dream what might happen if I tried coming in force. So even though he knows that I know that he knows, he doesn't really know all that I now know.

Confusing enough for you yet?

I look at my two human friends, better friends than I deserve. One of whom I now realize, since my mind has been cleared of the darkness, I need to embrace as more than a friend.

Really embrace. Literally.

As I think that, Hussein raises one eyebrow. And this time, though my face does feel hot and I know it's getting redder than usual, I'm glad he's heard what I just thought. I nod to him and get a bright sunbeam of a smile in reply.

I have to turn my thoughts back to what's immediately ahead. Okay. The three of them will have my back. A new, slightly better plan, is beginning to take shape in my head.

Tahhr is still giving off that rumbling growl, so deep that it vibrates inside me. I reach out and hook my arm around his neck.

"This is Tahhr," I say. "He is with us."

Guy and Hussein nod, but remain at a respectful distance. Not that bad an idea.

I squeeze Tahhr's shoulder. "Tahhr, these are my friends. They are good."

"Good," Tahhr rumbles.

His voice is just short of a roar. But he stops growling and steps slowly forward on all fours. Guy and Hussein do not move as he stalks up to them, rises halfway to thrust his huge head next to Guy's face and then Hussein's.

"Frrrrieennnd? Frrrieennnd?"

He does not lower his head to expose the back of his neck as he did to me. Clearly he is not offering the kind of relationship that he and I have just established.

But both Guy and Hussein seem to know what to do. They each extend both of their right hands palm down in a gesture that someone—any guesses who that ten-foot-tall furry busybody might be?—must have taught them.

Tahhr bends his head, opens his mouth, and closes it on Guy's hand—which thankfully is still there and not bitten off at the wrist when Tahhr releases it, more or less unharmed aside from a line of shallow puncture wounds oozing a few drops of blood. Then he does the same to Hussein's relaxed hand.

"Good," Tahhr growls softly, acceptance in his tone. Then he holds out his own paw-hand to Guy, who makes no attempt to put it into his mouth—which would be like trying to fit a size fourteen foot into a size two boot. Instead Guy just bites down on the top of Tahhr's wrist, his teeth leaving no mark at all. Satisfactory enough, apparently, for Tahhr nods and then holds his paw-hand out to Hussein, who does the same as Guy.

I can feel Hally's approval of the way things are going. And I'm moved by what I've just witnessed. Meanwhile, my new plan has come together in my mind during this ritual of bonding and brotherhood.

"Okay," I say, dropping to one knee and beginning to draw on the soft earth of the cave with the stick that was conveniently placed there. "Here's what we are going to do."

When I've finished, I look around the small circle. The only one who looks slightly skeptical is Guy, but that's no surprise. If he didn't question at least a little bit of what I'm proposing, he wouldn't be Guy.

"So," I say, looking directly at him.

"Na, 'tis good enough, lass. Just one wee thing to add."

He shifts the pack from his back and opens it.

Oh. Good idea.

CHAPTER FORTY-NINE

Challenge

Luther was not feeling pleased.

He felt, he supposed, rather as a child does when the friends he expected failed to show up for his birthday party. Not that he knew or celebrated the exact date of his birth. Or, for that matter, had any friends. But the simile was close enough.

He expected, at the least, a good-sized contingent of would-be attackers. But what did he see but a single person approaching from the distance?

Perhaps he should have made his invitation even more inviting—but it had been hard enough to find that one victim. He'd searched quite a while before spying him out. Actually nosing him out. Only Luther's enhanced sense of smell had led him to the lone human whose concealment had been quite visually effective. Although, alas, it had not masked the scent of his sweat.

One person. Still two miles away. If only he could find a bird, even a sparrow, to give him a better look. But no. Just lizards and snakes . . . aside from one unfortunate roadrunner.

Luther looked over with some irritation at the nearest of the raptors, which was concealed behind a boulder, crouched down and picking bits of flesh and feather from its teeth. His command for it to stop had only come after he realized what it was pursuing and its jaws had snapped on the avian.

Moments after that, his eyes had caught sight of the distant movement on the place where the trail wound from due south toward the east to rise to that cliff top.

The silvered sun was behind that figure, that single person standing now on the edge of a canyon. Using the scope of his rifle directly into the sunlight would not be at all advisable. Painful if not blinding to his vision.

Whoever it was, he or she was still far from his carefully laid trap where the trail led by the grey hill, where he had been so certain the lay of the land would insure that any party of would-be attackers filled with righteous anger would pass.

What was wrong with those people? Didn't they have enough sense of moral outrage to come after him en masse, determined to bring the miscreant to rough justice?

Or was his message effective? Was the one he sought sent

out by consensus from the group in the faint hope—ha!—that she might somehow defeat him or that her sacrifice might assuage him?

Then he saw what he needed. An eagle circling high overhead, near that cliff top. Was it beyond his grasp? He reached out with his mind and gained a connection. Not deep enough one for him to take it over, bend it to his every wish until its small brain was burned to a cinder, but enough for him to briefly see what it saw before it dove out of sight and beyond his mental reach.

It was her. Lozen.

And she was alone. Using the eagle's acute vision, Luther had seen beyond her, a land empty of any motion, a broad land that could not conceal a party of riders on horses.

He looked again and saw with his own unaided eyes that Lozen was raising something over her head. A staff with a red cloth tied to it. Now she was waving back and forth, clearly to attract his attention.

Not a white cloth, the color of either parlay or surrender. A red cloth, the color of challenge and battle.

Come and get me. That was what it meant.

Of course, Luther thought. And come to get you I shall. Or rather *we* shall.

CHAPTER FIFTY

Attack

The eagle that agreed to help me lands a little behind me and perches on a branch of a scraggly ponderosa. It's shaking its head, as if it had flown through a spider's web and some of the sticky strands are still clinging.

I touch it gently with my mind. It suffered what would be a mild concussion in a human brain. An injury, but not one with crippling consequences.

Thank you, I think to it.

It chirps once, softly.

I can hear the insistent roar of the river from behind me, hundreds of feet below the cliff edge. It's been getting louder as I've stood here, a result of the storm that must have started dropping rain miles upriver a hour or so ago. But my attention is focused to the valley below, that valley we followed into a death trap in my dream. I lift my rifle, look through the scope.

It brings into focus the one who is standing there looking up at me. A large black-haired man with a hard face, close-set eyes under heavy brows, teeth showing in an unfriendly grin. He raises one hand, runs it back through his hair, then drops out of sight before I can get a firm bead on him and pull the trigger.

It's what I expected he'd do. If what Rose told me is true, I have not just lost an opportunity. Even if I had gotten off a shot, managed to actually hit him at this nearly impossible range, that bullet would not have penetrated his skin. She knew that because she was told so several days before they met us—when she and her allies attacked the Dakota territory stronghold that was his home base and overthrew its masters.

Bulletproof or not, I need to be closer to attack him.

But not to worry. He is certainly about to graciously answer my need.

Ah, good to feel my old sardonic sense of humor back in place where it belongs, rearing its head whenever someone or something wants me dead.

L uther looked to the north. The dark clouds over the mountain were dumping rain there. No rain here, but the effect of that storm was being felt in the river that curved around that peak to flow rapidly down just below him. Flood waters from the arroyos and small, once-dry streambeds were reaching here now, adding to the force and sound of the river's surge. What had been a whisper was now a roar. Luther looked at those waters and shook his head, a shiver going down his spine. Water like that was the one thing that worried him, the one danger still present in his dreams that seemed to have the power to take his life.

But enough of such thoughts.

He looked back toward the high point where his prey still stood waiting for him. Most would not know that. But Luther had scouted the ground well over the past two days. Several of the trails could only be traversed by something with the climbing ability of a mountain goat.

No problem there for his red-scaled cronies. They would reach Lozen before him, surrounding her in positions of concealment. And then wait for his arrival.

WAIT!

He repeated that command as powerfully as possible, pushed it once more into their small, rapacious brains with so much energy that it made all of them sway back and forth as if about to drop.

GO!

And they were on their way, following an arroyo that would make them impossible to see as they headed up the canyon wall.

Luther was taking the direct route. Not that it was totally

direct. It wove back and forth, a switchback road made for wheeled vehicles. But it afforded cover along the way, folds in the earth, boulders, bushes, and trees. The few places where he might be visible could be traversed with enough speed to make it difficult for her to aim and shoot.

Not that he feared her gunfire. At most, should she hit him, he'd feel a bit of pain but nothing debilitating.

Still, better safe than sorry, he thought as he dashed across a fifty-foot-wide stretch. He heard the *chwhing!* of a bullet bouncing harmlessly off the pavement behind him followed a second later by the sound of the shot from above.

My first shot strikes right where I intended, far enough behind him to miss but close enough to keep him moving up the hill.

My hands are tingling. I hold them up, turn to one direction and then the other. He's not alone in his attack. I'm being surrounded. I'd expected that. But who or what am I being surrounded by?

No time to think too deeply about that. I picture Guy's face in my mind and then Hussein's.

Can you hear me?

If you call this hearing, lass, then that it is.

Guy's voice speaks in my head with just as much wry humor as when it is carried by sound waves.

I hear you, habibi, Hussein answers.

The warmth in his unspoken words touches me more deeply than I'd expected. I have got to ask him just what that word "habibi" means.

But not now.

They're coming.

Ready, lass.

I am ready.

I don't have to send a thought to Tahhr. We feel each other as much as I can feel my fingers holding the gun I'm lifting to fire when my enemy appears in the next place where I expect him to be visible.

Tahhr is ready. I hope I am just as ready as he is.

Once again the round that was fired struck behind him.

Luther almost laughed at that.

Easy thus far. Not his first plan, but one that was going quite well.

That worried him a bit. He doubted that anything unexpected lay in store for him at the top of the ridge. Even if it did, he knew he was prepared for anything. What worried him was that this might prove too easy. He was looking forward to at least a little resistance based on the reputation this Lozen had built for herself. Perhaps the little Apache assassin's image was exaggerated, due more to luck than skill.

He hoped not.

Around another bend at an easy lope, then dive behind that convenient boulder.

Chwinnng!

Excellent. And now time to change his pace.

Luther speeded up, running incredibly faster than any normal human. Even on this steep uphill road he was not breathing hard. His lungs had more than double the capacity of the greatest athletes of the past decades who'd played—and often died—to amuse the elites in the long-gone Intercontinental Games.

But he paused below the last steep ride. If he stood up he should be able to see her no more than fifty yards away. She would not expect him this soon, having judged his pace by the times she saw him and shot so ineffectively.

He looked up and to his left. There, just as planned, one of his red-scaled raptors was waiting, below a ledge that jutted out and hid it from sight. It was twitching its tail, eager to attack. But it was under his control. It would do as he commanded, even though he sensed its deep displeasure at being held back. After they were done dispatching Lozen he would probably have to kill them quickly before they turned on him in resentment.

Alas for them.

Time to make use of them, thus providing an excellent

diversion, though it was likely to lessen their ranks by one or two—providing Lozen's aim at a nearby standing target was better than it had been at a distant one in motion.

Show yourselves! Do not attack!

That nearby raptor turned its head toward him, gaped its mouth open in what he took to be anger and a futile attempt to resist.

Now!

The raptor turned, lifted over the ledge and stood there like a scaly statue.

But only for the briefest of seconds before . . .

Blam!

Headshot, it fell limply back, to go rolling and tumbling down toward the river far below.

Blam!

The second shot, certainly directed toward one of his now deceased allies that had made itself a target in yet another direction, was Luther's signal to leap up and begin his dash toward the distracted Apache girl whose back would now be turned toward him.

Except it wasn't.

And those first two shots fired in rapid succession were being echoed by a volley of blasts that Luther now realized were coming from at least two other directions.

And there it is. A blood-red nightmare creature with long claws and a lizard head lifting itself over the edge of the cliff. Its mouth is open and it's making a sound from deep in its throat that is as jarring as the scraping of nails on a windowpane.

CHIRRRG!

My first enemy to show itself, less than a stone's throw away.

Forget stones.

Blam!

As I fire my rifle, it is the first enemy to fall.

CHIRRG.

This time from behind me. Seemingly a little farther away. I do not turn this time, though. That direction is being covered by Guy, fifty yards downslope and well concealed by one of the two camouflage suits he'd produced from his pack for himself and Hussein.

Blam!

I trust his aim enough to not even be tempted to look that way. Instead I keep my focus on the place my Power is telling me to keep looking. I raise my rifle to my shoulder just in time. As more shots begin to ring out behind me and to my left where Hussein was hidden, the black-haired man, who seems to be even larger than I had expected, leaps up from behind a boulder and charges at me, a knife the size of a small sword in his right hand.

He's moving fast. Too fast, almost a blur. I get off just one shot that strikes him in the chest, but it neither stops or slows him down. I only have time to move to one side, just enough to let his attack go by me, swinging my rifle up to block the swing of the butcher's blade at my throat.

The big knife is deflected, but my hands are numbed by the impact, and my rifle is sent flying. The one known as Four Deaths, Luther Little Wound, plants his foot just short of the edge of the precipice I'd hoped my parry would send him over and regains his balance.

"Nicely done," he says. His voice is deep, incongruously pleasant considering the circumstances. He gestures with his thumb downslope, where the firing has stopped but sounds of battle—chirrging roars and the shouting of men's voices—can still be heard.

"Allies, eh?" he grins, spins his big blade in a lazy circle. "Alas for them. My little red friends are now free to maul and tear as they like, and I doubt your companions will be a match for them."

He lifts his left hand to brush back his thick hair.

"You, though, you are all mine. And I intend to take my time about it. But don't worry about your pretty little face. I'll be leaving that intact so you can be identified when I take your head back to Lady Time."

The fact that he loves to hear himself talk has given me time for the numbness to leave my hands. I unholster my .357, aim it at him.

"Lovely gun," he says, holding the broad-bladed knife in front of his face.

I fire, empty the .357's chambers as I aim at center mass, elevating slightly with each shot.

Blam-blam-blam-blam-blam-blam!

None of those rounds miss. But the ones aimed center mass seem to barely penetrate his body, just make him stagger a step to the side. And the two I meant for his head are deflected by that knife blade, though a piece of one slug does spin back to tear off the top third of his left ear.

"Ah," he says, lifting his left hand to his torn ear, "Didn't expect that. Fine aim."

He lowers his hand and licks the blood from his fingertips, takes a slow step toward me.

"The next blood I'll be tasting is yours."

Still talking. Which gives me the opportunity to holster my gun and pick up the staff that lies at my feet, the staff Guy gave me. I grasp it firmly in both hands, level it so that it is pointed at Luther Little Wound's face.

It makes him laugh out loud.

"A staff," he says, "You challenge me with a staff? Do you know how many masters of every martial art you can name I was trained by? Do you know that I killed every one of them after learning all I needed from them?"

He walks another slow, pace forward, stops when he is no more than eight feet away.

"Go ahead," he says, his deep voice taking on a mocking tone. "Do whatever move you know. I'll have the counter for it. Then I'll take that staff away from you and use it to break your bones, one by one."

I point the staff directly at his right eye.

"Counter this," I say as I twist the staff between my hands and press the hidden trigger.

WHOMP!

The sound of the shotgun slug erupting forth in a burst of flame from the end of the staff is simultaneous with his falling backward as swiftly as someone stepping on a patch of ice. He lands heavily on his back.

Have I killed him? Surely no one could survive a 12-gauge blast to the face.

Except this one. He rolls to his stomach, rises up to his feet again.

One whole side of his face is blackened by the blast. There's a bloody socket where his right eye had been. But he's alive and seems no less strong. Is he really impossible to kill?

"Four Deaths," he growls as if hearing my thought. "I'm Four Deaths. No man can kill me." He coughs, spits blood, laughs. "No woman, either."

He leaps at me, faster than I could have imagined anyone could move. But I get my hands up in time to put the staff between us and as he grasps it I fall backward, my feet in his belly, roll, and throw him over me.

And lose my staff as he continues to hold on to it, ripping it from my hands. I roll over my shoulder onto my feet, turn to see him sending my staff spinning at me. I duck and hear it clatter on the rocks before it flies over the edge of the precipice.

"ARRHH!"

The cry that comes from his throat is so full of hatred and aggression that it almost paralyzes me. But not quite. I've pulled my bowie knife from its sheath and as he lunges at me with his own huge blade, his aim and balance just slightly off because of that missing eye, I parry his leaping thrust as I step to his blind side, use the momentum to swing my own knife up, around, down at his wrist. I put not only all of my physical strength into that blow, I also draw on the power that is pulsing through my hand. And although bullets may bounce off his skin, the sharp edge of a heavy blade seems to be another thing. It cuts cleanly through flesh, tendon and bone, and his hand, still clutching that butcher knife, falls to the ground.

He turns, staggering slightly, blood spurting from the severed artery. With a wound like that unbound, one bleeds out fast. He steps back, to the very edge of the precipice. But then he stops, holds up his arms, stares at his severed wrist. Then, incredibly, as if his body is healing itself as I watch, the bleeding stops. A laugh that is as crazy as it is frightening bursts from his lips.

"HAH! You see. You can't kill me. I am Four Deaths. And now it's time for *your* death!"

He's pulling something from his shirt that looks like a hollow tube, raising it to his mouth.

Should I attack, dive to one side? But before I can do anything, he looks over my shoulder.

"You," he says. And he grins, a grin made macabre by the ruined state of his once-handsome face. "I did for your—"

He never finishes what he was about to say. Tahhr leaps past me, a blur of teeth and claws. Luther Little Wound falls back as my huge guardian, his coat bloodied from his battle with the red lizard monsters, falls on him. He rakes at Luther's body with his claws, opens his mouth to grasp him by the throat and the two of them go rolling, rolling toward the edge of that cliff. I leap forward, grabbing at Tahhr, but I'm too late. The two of them fall locked together. I watch as they strike an outcrop a hundred feet below. It separates them before their two limp bodies plummet the remaining distance to disappear into the brown, violent waters of the flooded stream, and I lose all sight of them.

"Lozen!"

"Lass, are ye all right?"

I look back. Guy and Hussein are approaching from the same direction from which Tahhr appeared second ago. As I lever myself up to my feet I can see that their camouflage suits are torn. Blood is dripping from a gash on Guy's cheek, but aside from that they both seem fine. He jerks his head back downslope, draws his finger across his throat, then nods. And some of the anxiety I'd been feeling in the back of my mind disappears, dispelled even further by glow of Hussein's smile.

He opens his arms toward me, and this time I do not hesitate. I pull him to me, wrap my own arms around him and hug him so hard that I almost crack his ribs. As I bury my head in his chest and feel his breath against my cheek, his lips next to my ear.

"You are all right, habibi?" he says in a soft voice.

"Yes," I whisper back, "I am now." I lean back, holding his forearms. "But Tahhr . . ."

"I know," Hussein says. "We saw them fall." We walk together to the cliff edge and look over. "Ah," Hussein says. "He saved us, you know. Without him those evil things might have killed us."

And would I have been killed by Luther Little Wound? It may be. I still cannot believe how hard my terrifyingly determined enemy was to kill.

Or is he dead? Even after losing an eye and a hand, even after that fall, is Four Deaths really dead?

"It's over, lass," Guy says.

Is it?

"No. We need to find their bodies," I say.

CHAPTER FIFTY-ONE

Peaceful

Two weeks have passed.

We found Tahhr washed up on a sandbar three miles further down where the river made a sudden turn. He was curled up on his side, his eyes closed. Despite their power, the rushing waters had not battered him outwardly. But his breath was gone.

Yet the look on his face was so peaceful that for a moment it seemed as if I saw him alive again, not alone but with a female of his own kind, two little ones wrestling at their feet. The four of them smiled at me and then, as sudden as the disappearance of the sun behind a hill, they were gone.

We buried him, covering his body first with the red and white flowers that were blooming in profusion near the place where we found him.

We never found the body of Luther Little Wound. Search parties combed the riverbanks for miles downstream. Some are still searching. But we found no sign of him, and even when I reached out with my power, I felt no trace of his mind.

"Nothing could have survived that flash flood, lass." That was what Guy said after a week had passed without a trace.

Hussein, though, said nothing. He knew that the lack of any final evidence of my enemy's death left me with a lingering sense of disquiet, like a story with no final end. All that we had to bury was his hand, which we placed in a cairn of rocks on top of that peak, that big right hand's death grip on the huge blade still tight.

Both of us knew it was not over. Even if Luther truly was dead, there were still Ones at Haven who would continue to plot my demise. Sooner or later, unless I wanted their next wave of killers to strike here as they did at our lost valley, we would have to take the fight to them.

Hussein and I are sitting together inside the arbor where I did my fast before the ceremony that returned me to myself. So much myself that I can finally be with him. Really be with him, if you know what I mean.

We're watching some of the others in what I have come to think of as my family. Ana and Luz have the heads together, as usual. I breathed a sigh of relief when Ana first saw Hussein and me arm in arm and she beamed at us rather than looking jealous. She still idolizes Hussein, but the puppy love is gone. That may be because she and Luz are both taking notice of—and being noticed by—some of the teenage boys here. The cool thing is that they seem to be admired as much for their marksmanship with their rifles as their good looks— which keep getting more good looking the more they are looked at.

Victor and his gang of boys are at the very edge of the gathering grounds practicing their archery. They're firing at not just stationary objects, but hoops rolled fast across the level ground and fist-sized balls of rawhide tossed high in the air. Thus far, Victor is the only one who has been able to hit one of those high-lofted rawhide targets, but some of the other boys are coming closer under his expert guidance.

Not everyone is in sight. Mom and Guy are nowhere to be seen. Hmmm. And both Black Star and Striped Horse have wandered off a ways into one of the meadows around White Mountain on business of their own. As for the Dreamer and Lorelei, she has become a regular part of the camp's dispensary, treating minor injuries and ailments as capably as any doctor, while the Dreamer has struck up such a friendship with a few of the older White Mountain and Lakota men who like to read, that he is right now engaged in a discussion with several of them about of one of his beloved books.

Thinking of our Lakota friends, Rose and Phil are heading our way right now. I smile as I look up at Rose, noticing her lower profile has changed some over the past two weeks.

"That's what happens a few months in," she says, one hand on her stomach. "Wait till I am really fat and ugly."

"And beautiful," Phil says, wrapping his arms around her waist.

"Good timing, my brother," Hussein says, raising one eyebrow.

The four of us sit together for a while, no one speaking. It is so peaceful here. I feel as if I could stay here like this forever.

But will that be possible?

I look over at Rose. She shakes her head.

"No," Hussein says, his voice a whisper. "But we will enjoy it while we can, yes?"

"Yes, habibi," I reply.

AUTHOR'S NOTE

Nowat nongoniwi. A loooooong time ago. . .

That is how the traditional stories told by the Wabanaki people who were some of my ancestors often began.

Of course this story—the second novel in a planned trilogy—does not happen long ago. Or does it?

True, it takes place in the future, at a time after the end of the electronic age that we are now in. (An age that may end, according to many concerned scientists, the age of humanity, as thinking machines—and perhaps another kind of humanity— rise to take the place of homo sapiens.) In the future that the readers of my previous novel *Killer of Enemies* and my novella *Rose Eagle* experienced, the world that was once dominated by highly-augmented super humans has vanished with the damping out of all electricity by a silver cloud from outer space. Human beings are struggling in this post-apocalyptic society to survive not just the resultant anarchy and tyranny that has ensued, but also giant genetically modified monsters that seek to destroy them.

So what else is new? Hasn't this all happened before?

That's what our traditional storytellers might say. Especially those who come from the two Native nations who are the forebears of my gritty and quite deadly heroine Lozen. The monsters she encountered in the previous book and those found in *Trail of the Dead* parallel or reflect many of the creatures that were destroyed ages ago by the Hero Twins of Dine (Navaho) and Tinneh (Apache) tales. Those boys, named Killer of Enemies and Child of Water in some of those very ancient stories, are embodied in Lozen. Moreover, after they finished killing those monsters, they began to suffer from "enemy sickness." Killing other living beings, even terrible creatures trying to kill them, knocked them out of balance. They are, you could say, the first recorded case of post-traumatic stress disorder. Only ceremony could restore them to health. So, in more ways than one, Lozen's future is a repetition of their past.

Moreover, my imagined Lozen is not the first Chiricahua warrior woman to bear that name. In the second half of the nineteenth century, the first Lozen was the sister of Victorio, one of the greatest of the Apache resistance fighters. She rode beside him and his ally Geronimo in battle. She was gifted with the power to predict the future and could detect the presence of enemies by holding up her hands and feeling where they were. More than once, her ability saved the lives of her comrades in battle. Thus, in another way, my story is also about the past, since the future Lozen has a similar, but even greater gift. And she both remembers and admires her namesake, as well as the often tragic but also inspiring actual histories of the Chiricahua people.

Which brings me why I've written this book and my previous two ventures into this post-apocalyptic time, and why I have a final book in this series in mind. Yes, it is about what I see as a very possible future. But it is also about the lessons of the past, about parts of Native American history that too few non-Indians have ever heard. Yes, in a way, "the Indians lost," but in many other ways, we never gave up. We are still here. We're still part of this land. Get used to it.

Carrying that into the future, I also want to go beyond the stereotypes that have been imposed on such nations as the Apaches, stereotypes that consistently have depicted them as savage, uncivilized people with no role in the modern world. To be frank, unlike those old episodes of the TV series of *Star Trek* where the non-white junior officer is always the first to die when they land on a hostile planet, I cannot imagine a future without "non-white" people playing a part in it as major players—not just walk-on disposable extras or cardboard cutouts. I want main characters such as Lozen and Rose—and

Hussein (hey, guess what—an Arab!)—to be seen as full human beings with something to offer. People with whom any reader can identify.

Like many other speculative authors I've known, predicting disaster does not mean you want it to happen. Quite the contrary, in fact. Being able to sense danger—like both Lozens— often means being able to avoid it.

That is also, for me, the rationale behind our Native American stories of monsters (including such human ones as several of the odious characters in this book and its predecessors). Monster stories are not just told to frighten. They are told to enlighten. We tell scary tales to remind children—and adults— that life is dangerous. Do the wrong things and you end up injured or dead, or a monster yourself.

Listen to the elders when they share tales of such implacable creatures as Monster Birds, Giant Bears, or such creatures from our Wabanaki traditions as the Chenoo, a cannibal monster who was once human, but became twisted and evil because of his own greed and selfishness. Through following the teachings of such tales, you may learn how to escape danger, or even to overcome it, to live a good life.

One more thing that, I suppose, goes without saying. But I am going to say it anyway. If this novel, and the series of which it is a central part, succeeds it will not be because of those underlying good intentions I've just outlined. Instead, I am attempting in my Lozen stories to do just what our traditional tellers have done since time immemorial. I'm trying to tell a story that will be read because it's a good read, a tale that draws people in, maybe even a page-turner. My first aim is to entertain you.

Here's hoping I've done just that.